Son of the Black Stallion

"The first foal by the Black will be yours, Alec," said Abu Ja'
Kub ben Ishak.

How many dreams, hopes and plans Alec Ramsay had built
on these words of the Arab sheikh! Then, from across the vast
white sands of the Great Central Desert of Arabia and across
the seas, came Satan. When Alec saw him, he felt the colt was
everything he had hoped for.

Little did Alec know what lay ahead of him in the raising of
this wild young horse—a desert-born stallion fearing neither
man nor beast. Could he be tamed and trained? That is the
story—and an exciting one it is!

Books by
WALTER FARLEY

The Black Stallion
The Black Stallion Returns
Son of the Black Stallion
The Island Stallion
The Black Stallion and Satan
The Black Stallion's Blood Bay Colt
The Island Stallion's Fury
The Black Stallion's Filly
The Black Stallion Revolts
The Black Stallion's Sulky Colt
The Island Stallion Races
The Black Stallion's Courage
The Black Stallion Mystery
The Black Stallion and Flame
The Black Stallion Challenged
The Black Stallion's Ghost
The Black Stallion and the Girl
The Horse-Tamer
Man o' War

*All titles available in both paperback
and hardcover editions*

Son of the Black Stallion

By WALTER FARLEY

Random House New York

For Mabel L. Robinson
and all the boys and girls whose
letters of encouragement and suggestions
made possible this book

Library of Congress Cataloging in Publication Data

Farley, Walter
  Son of the black stallion.
  New York, Random House [1947]
  I. Title.   Z10.3.F22So   47–3369
  ISBN: 0–394–80603–4 (trade hardcover)
        0–394–90603–9 (library binding)
        0–394–83612–X (trade paperback)

Contents

Desert Born

1

For days the Bedouin band had ridden across the white sands of the Rub' al Khali, the Great Central Desert of Arabia, and the steady pounding of the horses' hoofs left a rising cloud of sand behind them. The white-robed figures rode in no particular formation, their long guns resting easily across their thighs, their hands lying only lightly upon them. For the danger of a surprise raid by desert bands had passed . . . ahead lay Addis, on the Red Sea, their destination.

There were twenty of them, sitting still and straight in their saddles as their horses moved effortlessly across the sand. Each steed's head was held high, his hot coat shining in the sun, and each pulled slightly on his bit as though impatient to break out of the slow canter to which he had been held for so many days. The men, too, were as impatient as the blacks, bays, and chestnuts they rode. *Ê* . . . yes! It had taken them ten days to cross the Great Desert from the mountain stronghold of their sheikh, Abu Ja' Kub ben Ishak, who led them. Ten days! When other trips had taken them but four! Ten days of constant riding, halting during the day only for prayer, to turn toward Mecca with a reverent *"La ilaha-'llah: Muhammadum rasula-'llah."* And then they would be in the saddle again, their long limbs wrapped about the girths of their mounts.

And as they rode, if their eyes left the sheikh, astride his giant black stallion, Shêtân, it was only to come to rest upon the small black colt who followed doggedly behind the stallion, straining at the lead rope that the sheikh had attached to his own saddle. *Ê* . . . yes! It was the young colt with his spindled, tiring legs who was responsible for this long slow march across the Rub' al Khali. It was he, as much as his great black stallion of a father, who had caused them to ride with heavy hands upon unslung rifles for so many suns. Only for the possession of the mighty Shêtân and his firstborn, worth all the treasures beneath the sun and moon, would other desert tribes dare to challenge the might of the powerful Sheikh Abu Ja' Kub ben Ishak! But now the worst of the trek was over, for ahead was Addis and the ship of the sea which would take the young colt to another land.

Nearing the outskirts of town, the sheikh raised his rifle high in the air, and then slung it over his shoulder; and it came to rest with those of his men.

They were in formation, riding two abreast as they entered Addis and started down the street that would lead them to the sea and the ship that awaited the son of the black stallion.

Two boiler-room men climbed the spiraling iron staircase leading up from the bowels of the tramp steamer, *Queen of India,* as she docked at Addis. Reaching the upper deck, one of them wiped a greasy hand across his perspiring forehead, leaving it streaked with grime. "No better up here, Morgan," he said, as they walked over to the rail and leaned heavily upon it.

Below on the dock, vendors shouted forth their wares to the multitude of onlookers, freight agents and dock hands who laboriously loaded the varied produce of the desert and farms onto the ship. Camels and donkeys, heavily laden with the wares of vendors, milled with the crowd, superbly unbothered by the high-pitched voices of their owners.

"Makes me think of the barkers at Coney Island, Harrity," Morgan said nostalgically.

Harrity didn't answer, for his gaze had left the crowd below and had traveled up the long, narrow, cobble-stoned street that led from the pier. Coming toward them was a group of horsemen. And even from this distance he could see that they weren't like the natives below. Heads moving neither to the right nor left, they rode forward, the hoofs of their horses ringing on the stones. Only for a few seconds did Harrity's gaze rest upon the riders' flowing robes; fascinated, he turned his attention to the magnificent animals they rode. He'd heard tales of such horses as these, owned by the feared and little-known Bedouins, supreme rulers of the desert. But in all his years of traveling up the coast of Arabia, he had never seen even one of them until now.

The horsemen came closer, and Harrity's eyes were drawn to the great black stallion in the lead. Never in the world had he seen a horse like this one, he told himself. This horse towered above the others, his body beautiful to behold. Thunder could roll under those powerful legs, Harrity was sure.

"Look at that band of Arabs comin' down the street," Harrity heard Morgan say.

Without taking his eyes from the mighty black, Harrity replied, "Look at the horses, Morgan. Look at them."

"I'm lookin'. And me who's been to Aqueduct and Belmont, and thought I'd seen the best of 'em."

"Me, too." Harrity paused, then added, "Get a load of that black stallion in the lead, Morgan. If he isn't one of the finest chunks of horseflesh I've ever seen, I'll eat my hat."

"Yeah," Morgan replied. "And he's a wild one, all right. See that small head and those eyes? There's fire in those eyes, Harrity. Look! He half-reared. He doesn't want to come any closer to this mob on the dock. That Arab on his back can ride, all right, but he's no match for that devil and he knows it. See, what'd I tell you, Harrity! They're stoppin' out there. He's goin' to get off."

Suddenly, Harrity realized that the shrill voices of the

vendors and natives had stilled. The dock was unnaturally quiet. Everybody there had seen the Bedouins.

A few of the multitude moved toward the band, but stopped when they were still a good distance away. They had moved as though compelled by the fascination of this wild band, and had stopped in fear of it. They knew this group of horsemen, no doubt about that.

Harrity's eyes were upon the black stallion and the sheikh with the white beard who stood beside him, holding the bridle. The stallion snorted and plunged, and the man let the horse carry him until he had regained control.

"A black devil," Harrity muttered. "A black, untamed devil."

"What'dya say?" Morgan asked.

"That black stallion . . . he's a devil," Harrity repeated.

"Yeah." There was a slight pause, then Morgan said, "And didya notice that little black one just behind him? He's tryin' to work up a lather, too."

Harrity hadn't noticed the young colt, but now he saw him. Standing there on his long legs, the black colt, whom Harrity judged to be about five months old, was being held by one of the Bedouins.

The colt moved restlessly, trying to pull away from the tribesman who held him close. As though imitating the big black in front of him, he snorted and plunged, throwing his thin forelegs out, striking at the Bedouin. The man moved quickly, avoiding the small hoofs, and then closed in upon the savage head and held him still.

"Could be father and son from the way they act." Morgan laughed.

"Yeah," returned Harrity. "Look a lot like each other, too. Coal black they are, except for that small splotch of white on the colt's forehead. Didya notice it, Morgan?"

"Uh," Morgan grunted. "It looks diamond-shaped from here."

A few minutes later they saw the tribesman lead the colt away from the band and in the direction of the *Queen of India.*

"Y'mean that baby is goin' to ship with us?" Morgan said excitedly.

"Mebbe," Harrity replied. "After all, they came into town for some reason, and that's as good as any."

The Bedouin had the black colt part way down the path which the natives and vendors had opened for them when the colt reared again, fighting for his head. The Bedouin let him go up, and when he came down closed in upon his head again. Grabbing the rope halter, the Bedouin moved quickly to the side, avoiding the pawing hoofs.

"That guy is used to handlin' horses," Morgan told Harrity as they watched the scene.

"Yeah. He got around those hoofs all right. Not that a colt like that could hurt him much, though."

"Still, he could put a good dent in the guy," Morgan insisted. "I sure wouldn't want any part of him. If he's like that now, think what he's goin' to be a few months from now, when he gets some beef on him." Morgan paused, and his gaze turned to the black stallion, who was circling nervously around the white-bearded sheikh. "Why, he's apt to be as bad as that devil. Nope, I'll stick to the nice tame ones," he concluded.

They had almost reached the ship when the colt rose again. Once more the Bedouin let him go up, then closed in. But this time, as the colt came down savagely with his teeth bared, he turned upon the man. No cry of pain came from the Bedouin's lips as the colt's teeth sank into his shoulder, but those who were close enough were able to see him grow pale beneath his dark mahogany skin. Moving his hand quickly, the Bedouin brought it hard against the muzzle of the colt, and was free.

The sheikh signaled to one of his men, who ran forward, moved to one side of the colt and grabbed the halter. Then he and the bitten tribesman led the colt past the multitude and up the plank into the hold of the ship.

"And that," muttered Morgan, "is that. Packaged neatly for delivery in New York. Wonder who the lucky person is?" he added sarcastically.

"I'm wonderin', too," Harrity said. "From what I've heard of these Bedouins they prize their horses above life itself. There are few good ones that have ever left Arabia."

"Most likely this one isn't any good," Morgan said. Then he added, thoughtfully, "Still, I'd like to know where these desert Arabs are sendin' that little devil. It's a cinch no one just walked into their front yard and bought a horse. Think I'll go down to the hold and find out. Sam's there, and he'll give me all the info I want."

Shortly after Morgan left, the two Bedouins emerged

from the hold and walked quickly down the plank onto the dock. Without glancing to the right or to the left they hurried to their band, nodded as they passed their sheikh, and mounted.

The group stayed there until the last of the cargo was put aboard the *Queen of India* and the dockhands had thrown off the lines holding the ship to the pier.

Harrity realized that he should be below, working with his men, but the sight of that Bedouin band, sitting still and straight on the magnificent horses, fascinated him.

The *Queen of India* was well away from the pier when Morgan rejoined him. "Sam gave me as much information as he had," he said excitedly. "And guess what, Harrity. That baby we're carryin' isn't goin' to any of those big horse stables in Kentucky. . . . Nope, he's goin' to some guy by the name of Alec Ramsay. And this will kill you. Where does the guy live but in Flushing, New York! Why, that's like goin' to my burg, Brooklyn!"

"Not exactly," Harrity replied. "It's a lot smaller, but maybe there's room for a horse to turn around in."

"Well, it's a suburb of New York, ain't it?"

"Yeah, yeah, you're right. I can't see this horse in either place."

They were walking toward the door leading down to the boiler room when Harrity came to a sudden stop. "Alec Ramsay," he muttered to himself.

"Yeah, that's his name," Morgan said. "What's eatin' you?"

"That name. I know it. I've seen it somewhere," Harrity said, half to himself, half to Morgan. Turning, he went back to the rail of the ship and looked again at the mighty black stallion. The sheikh had mounted him, but the band still hadn't moved. The horse had his head high, his ears pricked, and he too seemed to be watching the departing ship. Then suddenly he raised his head still higher, and there was heard, resounding across the still, hot air, his shrill, piercing whistle. The scream of a wild stallion! Harrity had never heard anything like it and he knew that in all probability few of those on the ship or dock had. It was a long, high-pitched cry that crept to the marrow of one's bones. It was eerie, frightening.

Harrity found Morgan at his side. "Y'mean that came from him?" Without taking his eyes from the stallion, Harrity nodded. And Morgan said, "That was weirder than anything we ever heard in India."

They saw the black horse rear to his utmost height as the sheikh astride him wrapped his long legs like two bars of steel around his girth. Coming down with battering forefeet, the stallion snorted, half-reared, and screamed again. His rider raised a hand in signal to his men, and simultaneously they wheeled their horses.

And as the Bedouin band rode up the street which would lead them back to the desert, Harrity and Morgan heard the muffled scream of the black colt in the hold.

Morgan said, "Guess that's the end of the fireworks, Harrity. We'd better get goin'."

Nodding, Harrity followed, deep in thought. And it wasn't until they were well on their way down the iron stairs that he stopped. "I got it," he half shouted, as his hand grabbed Morgan's arm. "Y'remember that trip the

Queen's boiler went bad on us, and we had to limp back to New York for a repair job?''

"I don't want to remember it," Morgan said, "after the work it caused us."

But Harrity went on. "We hit port just in time to hear all about that big match horse race out in Chicago. Y'couldn't help rememberin' that, Morgan, for everybody was talkin' their fool heads off about it. And it was all over the newspapers, 'n' you couldn't turn on a radio without someone blastin' about it."

Morgan nodded. "Yeah. Sure. I remember that. This match race was cooked up to get those two racers, Sun Raider and Cyclone, together. Boy, those babies sure could run. Broke just about every track record, didn't they?" Morgan didn't wait for Harrity's reply. "And there was lots of talk about what was goin' to happen when those two bolts of lightnin' got together in Chicago. Then there was the big race. . . ." Morgan's brow furrowed and his eyes met Harrity's. "Then . . . then . . ." his words came fast, "I remember now, Harrity. Neither of 'em won! They were both beaten by a mystery horse! A horse someone got into the race the last minute. The name of that horse is right on the tip of my tongue. . . ."

As Morgan hesitated, Harrity said, "He was called the Black, Morgan. Nothin' more, just that. And he was ridden by a kid, a young kid by the name of . . . Alec Ramsay!" Harrity's voice was clipped, excited. "And that black stallion ran all over Sun Raider and Cyclone."

"That's it, Harrity! That's it! Alec Ramsay . . . that was his name, all right. And there was a story, too, about how he got hold of this horse. The papers played it up big.''

"Sure, and we got good reason to remember it,'' Harrity said, lowering his voice. "The kid was comin' back from India on the *Drake* . . .''

"The *Drake* . . .'' Morgan's voice was tense. "She went down off the coast of Portugal with all on board.''

Harrity took it up again. "This black stallion was aboard, picked up at . . . Addis.'' His eyes swept back up the stairs, and he muttered, "That was Addis back there.''

"The horse saved the kid's life, didn't he? Dragged him to one of those islands off the coast. And about a month later, after all hope had been given up, they were picked up and brought to New York.''

"And then to Flushing,'' Harrity added. "Alec Ramsay, Flushing, New York.'' He jerked his head in the direction of the hold. "And that's just where this little devil is goin'.''

Morgan began walking down the steps again, followed by Harrity. "Y'remember hearin' anything more about the Black and this Alec Ramsay?'' Morgan asked without looking back. "After the race, I mean.''

"You know as well as I do how long we were out on that South Africa trip right after,'' Harrity said. "Of course I didn't hear nothin'.''

"I was just thinkin' about that black stallion we just saw,'' Morgan muttered. "He sure looked like what I imagined the Black should look like. From everything I've read about him, anyway.''

Harrity said, thoughtfully, "I was thinkin' about that, too." Shrugging his shoulders, he added, "But he sure can't be in Flushing and Arabia at the same time, that's certain. And I still can't figure out that black baby in the hold. Wonder where he comes in on it?"

"Forget it," Morgan said. "We've got enough to do from here to New York without wastin' our time on puzzles. I'm just glad my name's Morgan instead of Alec Ramsay, and that I live in Brooklyn an' not Flushing. I wouldn't want any part of that horse."

"Yeah," agreed Harrity. "You're right. I'll take my horses just by watchin' 'em from the grandstand at a race track. Nope, I sure don't envy this Alec Ramsay none, either."

The Letter

2

"Alec Ramsay live here, ma'am?" the man asked of the small, plump woman who had made her way down the porch steps of the house in Flushing.

"Why, yes," she replied, slipping a shopping bag lightly over one arm. "Although he isn't in just now," she added.

"I've a special delivery for him," the man explained, extending a large manila envelope.

"I'll sign for it," the woman said.

"You his wife, ma'am?"

"No, his mother." She smiled.

"Excuse me, ma'am." He grinned, holding out his book for her to sign. "But I had to make sure, y'know. No sense losing this thing now, not after it's come all the way

15

from . . ." He stopped and drew the envelope closer to his eyes. "From Arabia," he concluded. "From some guy by the name of Abu Ja' Kub ben Ishak. What a monicker that is!"

The smile left the woman's face at the man's words. And as she took the envelope, he asked, "Anything wrong, ma'am?"

"No," she said, her gaze still on the envelope, ". . . nothing at all." Turning back to the house, she added, "Thank you for bringing it. Thank you very much."

She walked slowly, without looking again at the envelope in her hand. After going up the porch steps, she moved across to the small table beside the hammock and carefully placed the envelope upon it. She stood there quietly for a few moments, then turned and again started to leave the porch.

As she passed the screened front door, a small dog with long, shaggy brown hair peered out. Whimpering, he shoved his nose against the corner of the door and pushed, his short legs rigid.

A slight smile lightened the woman's face as she opened the door for the dog. And as he leapt outside, she said, "All right, Sebastian, you find Alec and tell him it's here. He's been waiting for it a long time."

She watched the dog run down the steps and across the yard, and then set out to do her shopping.

Sebastian traveled fast, his short legs covering the ground with great speed. Crossing the street, he slid to a stop before a high iron-barred fence which kept him from the field on the other side. Then he retracked a few yards, and went to a bar which was bent slightly at the base. His head went through easily, but the bars closed in upon his round body. He stopped for a minute, half in, half out. His soft brown eyes turned in the direction of the old barn a few hundred yards away in the field. Panting, he squirmed his way through. With a short bark, he ran down the graveled driveway and bounded into the barn.

But once there, he came to a dead stop, his ears cocked. The short whinny of a horse came from one of the box stalls, and the dog ran forward, his paws pattering softly upon the wood floor. Reaching the door, he found it ajar, and without hesitating went into the stall.

The old gray horse with the low sway back removed his muzzle from the feed box and, lowering his head, sniffed suspiciously.

Moving across the soft straw, the dog ran between the horse's hind legs and underneath the low-hanging girth as though he were treading on familiar ground. He moved up to the large head and shoved his nose against the horse's muzzle. The old gray whinnied and then drew back to his feed box, munching his oats.

The dog stood there listening quietly for a few seconds. Then he was out of the stall and running past the row of empty stalls toward the rear of the barn. Finally he came to a room and sprang inside, sniffing and with his eyes alert.

A voice came from the end of the room. "It'sa Sebastian. Here, come to Tony."

The dog ran toward the man, who sat on a chair holding

long leather straps across his lap. Sebastian threw his front paws upon the man's knee and let him rub his head.

"Heesa feelin' good, no?" Tony laughed. "Heesa feelin' like the wan young fella he is. *Sì*, Sebastian!" His hands rubbed the back of the dog's ears. "Where sucha small puppy like you get so longa ears, Sebastian? Maybe just a leetle bit of whatya call da bloodhound in you, no?"

The dog barked, his gaze leaving Tony, moving to the far corner of the room, and then back again. With a burst of speed he was out of the room, running past the stalls and through the door.

Outside in the bright sunlight he stopped, as though undecided which way to go. He turned his head, looking across the street at the brown house which he had left. Then he looked in the opposite direction, at the green field adjacent to the barn. His eyes followed the wooden fence that encircled the field until they came to the hollow at the south end. Without further hesitation, he ran to the wooden barred-gate entrance to the field, dashed underneath the lowest crossbar, and went tearing across the long grass toward the hollow.

As he reached the top of the hollow, he barked and his hooked tail wagged furiously. Then he ran down toward the boy who was sitting in the grass, and swarmed all over him.

Alec Ramsay grabbed the dog as he leapt into his lap, and Sebastian's long tongue sought the boy's face. Alec's hands moved underneath the dog's shoulders and he turned him over on his back, holding him between his knees. The dog wriggled at first, but then relaxed as the boy's fingers found his chest. "Hey, Seb," and Alec smiled. "You're not supposed to be out. It's too hot for you. Do you want to get sick again?" But there was no sound from Sebastian as he stretched his head back, allowing Alec to scratch his neck.

They stayed there for some time, the dog content to be in the boy's arms. And as Alec stroked Sebastian, his gaze very often would leave the dog, move across the high, uncropped grass, and come to rest upon the heavy underbrush at the low end of the hollow. There were thistles growing there now, plenty of them. He'd have to fence it off before his horse could graze in the field as the Black had once done. Alec's brow wrinkled. Would he ever see *his* horse running around in this field? Would Abu Ja' Kub ben Ishak keep his promise to send him the first foal of the Black, or Shêtân, as the sheikh called him? Shêtân. It meant *devil* in Arabic. The Black was no devil . . . not to him, anyway.

But it had been many months since Alec had left Arabia and the black stallion, and during that time there had been no word from Abu Ja' Kub ben Ishak. Yet the sheikh had promised, and Alec couldn't believe the Arab chieftain would go back on his word.

The dog stirred as Alec moved his knees. "C'mon, Seb," the boy said. "I guess we'd better get going." He lifted the dog and placed him upon his feet before standing up himself.

What weight Alec Ramsay carried was all in his broad

shoulders, chest, and arms. From there he tapered down to a small waist, slender thighs and legs.

As he walked across the field, Sebastian following closely at his heels, his keen blue eyes sought the barn. He wanted to say hello to Tony, not having seen the huckster for some time, and he knew that very often Tony and his aged horse Napoleon would have completed their neighborhood rounds by this time of day.

The hot August sun overhead caused the perspiration to drop slowly from Alec's forehead and run down the sides of his face and across the high cheekbones. He swept it away with his hand and then brushed an arm across his forehead, pushing his red, tousled hair back from his eyes.

When he reached the barn and went inside, he saw Napoleon. The gray horse shoved his head over the stall door and neighed. Alec stroked the soft muzzle, took several lumps of sugar from the pocket of his corduroy trousers, and gave them to the horse. Suddenly, the quiet of the barn was blasted by Tony's booming voice, and Alec heard him sing, *"To-re-a-dor-e . . .* dada . . . dada . . . DA. *Toreador! Toreador!"*

Alec smiled. Tony was here, all right. With a final pat on Napoleon's nose Alec went to the tack room in the rear, Sebastian padding softly behind him.

"Hi, Tony," he greeted. "Doing some polishing?"

"Allo, Aleec. *Sì,* I maka nice an' clean for my Napoleon. But it'sa all finish now." Tony rose from his chair and hung the harness he had been polishing upon its wooden peg. That done, he turned his bright, black eyes toward the light racing bridle hanging close beside the harness. His hand touched the soft, well-polished leather. "You keepa in good condition, Aleec, no?" he said, without looking at his friend.

"No sense letting it go to rot," Alec replied. "It's a good bridle."

There was a short pause before Tony spoke again. "You heard from thata man . . . what you call heem . . . Ab . . .''

"Abu Ishak?" Alec said.

"*Sì*, that'sa heem," Tony said, nodding his head.

"No," Alec answered. "I haven't heard from him."

"You theenk he will send you da horse like he promise when you leave hees country?"

Alec sat down in Tony's vacated chair and ran his hand over Sebastian before answering. "I think so, Tony," he said quietly.

"If he doesn't, heesa one big liar," Tony said angrily. "You tooka good care of da beeg Black when theèsa man thought he was a drowned, no? Then thees Abu comes along much time later and says to da Black, 'We go,' and offa they go."

"But the Black belonged to him, Tony."

The little huckster rose to his feet, his black eyes upon Alec. "Da beeg Black belonga to you always, Aleec. Hees heart belonga to you. It'sa that that'sa decides, and not papers!"

"Okay, Tony," Alec said resignedly. "He belongs to

me, and I loved him. I guess that's why, even if I could have had him, I'd rather see him in Arabia. It's his home. He's happier there." Alec's eyes met Tony's. "Abu Ishak is a good man, Tony," he said. "He loves the Black as much as I do. And with him he'll bring into the world other fine horses like the Black. I couldn't have done that, Tony. . . . It costs a lot to breed horses." Alec paused a few seconds, and then concluded, "It's better this way . . . I know it is."

There were several minutes of silence before Tony said, "And Abu, he promise you wan of these fine horses after you follow him to hees country and ween big race for him on da Black, no?"

"Yes," Alec admitted, his eyes still on Sebastian. "He said that he would send me the Black's first foal." Then, half to himself, he added, "A colt or a filly . . . I wonder which it will be?"

Tony said, "Did Henree hear heem say this thing?"

"No, but I told him about it on our way back from Arabia." Smiling, Alec added, "No witnesses, Tony, if that's what you're driving at. Besides, there's no way in the world to compel Abu Ishak to give me the first foal. It's up to him . . . his word." Then as though to change the subject Alec said, "Henry and I have been writing to each other. He seems to like his job."

"I'ma glad," Tony returned. "Heesa training race horses again, no?"

"He's working in California for Peter Boldt, who has one of the finest racing stables in the country," Alec told him. "Boldt offered Henry the job soon after we got back from Arabia. It was a swell break!"

"I'ma glad he's happy, Aleec." Laughing, Tony added, "When old men lik'a Henree an' me are happy we can keepa up with you younga fellas." Tony picked up his black battered hat and moved toward the door. "You will be happy, too, Aleec, when the new one arrives. *Sì*, he will come like you say. Now I feel it strong lik'a you."

"Thanks, Tony." Alec smiled at his friend's words of encouragement. Then they left the barn together.

They parted outside the iron gate. Alec watched Tony shuffling up the tree-lined street, and then followed Sebastian as the dog ran toward home. He wished that he was as certain that Abu Ja'Kub ben Ishak would keep his word as he had implied in his conversation with Tony. It was true that he thought of the sheikh as his friend, and had believed him that day in Arabia when the chieftain had said, "The Black's first foal will be yours, Alec, and I shall send him to you." How well he remembered those words of the sheikh! How many dreams, hopes, and plans he had built upon them! They had made his leaving the Black in Arabia much easier, for he had known that before too long there would come to him a horse through whose veins would run the blood of the great black stallion. And this horse would be his, his very own, to love, to raise, and to train for the track. He had raced him a million times in his dreams, had driven him thundering past the turf kings of the day as they stretched for the wire.

And only Henry knew of his dreams and plans. For together they had discussed them on their way back from Arabia and for many months in their letters to each other. And the old trainer's eyes had glowed as bright as his when they talked about this horse to be. But, lately, Henry's letters had arrived less and less frequently. Alec realized that Henry was busy, for Boldt had the largest string of racers in the country and with them had won the top races last year. Yes, Alec decided as he reached the porch steps, Henry had plenty to do besides writing him, even if Henry was "only one of Boldt's four trainers," as he had so often written in his letters. It had been a wonderful opportunity for Henry, getting this job with Boldt. Anyone would have jumped at it. But Alec did miss him.

When he reached the porch Alec flung himself on the hammock, and Sebastian jumped up beside him. Alec knew that his mother was out shopping, and that his father would not be home from work for at least an hour. This would be a good time to think about his horse again, to plan. . . .

Then he saw the envelope propped against the flower vase on the small table. It hadn't been there when he'd left the house. Rising from the hammock, he went over to the table and picked up the envelope. For several seconds the writing upon it seemed to become blurred and then he read again his name and the return address.

Slowly, he walked back to the hammock and sat down. Sebastian moved over to his lap and whimpered. Alec pushed the dog's head to one side and then hastily ripped the envelope open, removing several papers. On top, in Abu Ishak's familiar handwriting, was a short note:

Arabia
July 15th

DEAR ALEC,

As I promised, the firstborn of Shêtân, or your Black, will be shipped to you aboard the steamer Queen of India, *due to leave Addis on the thirtieth of this month, and arriving in New York on the twenty-eighth of August. I'm enclosing all necessary papers, the transfer of ownership, his registration in the Stud Book of Arabia, and papers to claim him upon arrival in New York. Yes, Alec, it is a colt, and he's coal black like his sire except for a small white diamond in the center of his forehead.*

May the great Allah be with you, and may the colt love you as does his sire.

Affectionately,
ABU JA' KUB BEN ISHAK

Alec's eyes were moist as he finished reading the note. And to think that there had been times when he doubted the promise of the sheikh! As he read the other papers enclosed, Sebastian whimpered for attention and Alec automatically patted the dog. Yes, everything was there, just as Abu Ishak had written. Everything that was necessary to claim the colt as *his colt.* Everything, just as he and Henry had planned. This was the beginning!

Alec suddenly jumped from the hammock and shouted

so loudly that Sebastian growled, looking for an intruder. Finding none, the dog leapt to the floor and followed Alec as he ran across the porch.

As Alec flung open the screen door, he turned to the dog and playfully slapped him on the back. "You're going to have a pal, Seb!" he shouted. ". . . A real pal!"

With Sebastian at his heels he ran into the house, climbed the stairs to the second floor, and entered the large front bedroom. Rushing to his desk, Alec seized pen and paper. Before writing, he glanced out the window, and his gaze rested on the old barn and the green flowing field. It wouldn't be long now before *his* colt would be grazing out there, and old Napoleon would again have a neighbor in the stall next to his! Abu Ishak had said the ship would arrive on the twenty-eighth. The twenty-eighth! And today was the twenty-third!

Eagerly Alec turned to the notepaper in front of him and began his letter. "Dear Henry . . ."

Sinister Eyes

3

Alec's mother stood quietly on the porch as her son and husband walked to the small, dark sedan parked by the curb. Her gaze wavered from the car a moment and took in the old barn and green field across the street, then returned as the sedan's motor caught.

She was afraid. Afraid of what this new horse would bring. Twice before a horse, *his* horse, had led Alec to undertakings few men had ever experienced. Undertakings which for him had been adventurous, exciting. But for her and her husband, they had meant months of anguish and concern.

She closed her eyes and made herself think of her husband's words early that morning as they had lain in bed: "His horse is his world, Belle, and we can't drive it out of him. We shouldn't even try." And then she had detected a note of pride in his voice as he had added, "And you remember how that wild black stallion took to him, Belle. Henry told me that he'd never seen anything like it before. And the way Alec could ride him! Why, no tame horse could set foot on the same track with those two! Belle, he just grew up there on his back. . . . He just grew there." Then, when he had turned to her and had seen how worried she was, he had taken her hand and, patting it, had said, "But there's nothing to get disturbed about this time, Belle. It's just a pony he's getting today . . . a little pony whom we'll probably enjoy having around as much as we do Sebastian."

Now her eyes followed the car as it rolled down the street. Yes, she thought, it'll be a pony now, but a full-grown horse before very long. And he'll always have the blood of that wild black stallion running through his veins.

Alec's gaze left his father's long, thin face as the car neared the corner, and his arm went around Sebastian, who sat quietly between them.

"Your mother's a little worried, Alec."

"Yes, I know, Dad. But she really shouldn't be."

"That's exactly what I told her, but you know mothers." Then Mr. Ramsay lowered his voice to that man-to-man tone Alec knew so well and added, "You've had enough excitement in the last few years to last you a lifetime, Alec. So take it easy with the new one, will you?

You'll be able to have a lot of fun with this pony. Then when he's grown up a bit, you can go for nice slow rides through the park. Good bridle trails up there . . . but I guess you know all about them." Sebastian whimpered and Alec's father removed one hand from the steering wheel to pat him. "Yes, Alec, you can make a nice little pal of him, just like Sebby."

Pony . . . nice *slow* rides through the park! Alec wondered what his father would have to say when he told him about Henry and his plans to train the black colt for the track.

"Mind you, Alec," his father was saying, "I'm not trying to run your life. You're old enough now to know what you want, and to do your own thinking. I guess I don't have to tell you that, for you must know that Mother and I are very proud of the way you've been able to handle yourself."

"Yes, Dad," Alec replied quietly.

His father smiled. "Not that I expect this pony to cause any trouble. Not after the way you could handle his sire."

Alec didn't say anything, and they rode for a long time before his father asked, "You're sure the van's going to be at the pier, Alec? You wanted to make all the arrangements, you know."

"Yes, Dad. It'll be there."

"How much is it costing you?"

Reluctantly Alec replied, "Twenty-five . . ."

"Hmmm. Rather steep, wasn't it? Did it take all the money you've saved?"

"No, I still have plenty left. Enough to buy feed and pay Mrs. Dailey."

"Mrs. Dailey?"

Alec smiled. "Dad! Don't tell me you've forgotten. . . . Henry's wife . . . lives in the big house on the corner, and owns the barn and field."

"Oh, yes! I guess I'm getting old, Alec," Mr. Ramsay said, laughing. "Come to think of it, your mother has been charging me with forgetfulness of late." A slight pause, and he added, "I shouldn't have thought Mrs. Dailey would make you pay anything, though, what with Henry having that good job on the coast, and her taking in boarders."

"She didn't want anything," Alec confessed, "but I thought I'd feel better paying her a little." He paused, then continued in a lower tone, "It would be different if Henry was around."

His father turned to him. "Did you write Henry that the pony was arriving?" he asked.

"Yes. The day I got Abu's letter." Alec played with Sebastian's long ears as the dog slept.

"No reply?"

Shaking his head, Alec said with attempted lightness, "I guess he must be pretty busy." Then his gaze turned to the side window, and he watched the heavy New York traffic. It was strange that Henry hadn't answered his letter, he thought. Strange, because the arrival of the colt was what they both had been eagerly awaiting . . . for this was to be the beginning of the long hard grind which they had planned and hoped would lead to the track. And even if Henry was terribly busy, he could have sent a note or telegram. Alec couldn't believe that Henry had forgotten everything they had planned, even though he was working for Boldt and training some of the finest horses in the country.

They were on the Drive running parallel to the East River, and Alec knew that in a few minutes they'd reach the pier.

Sebastian awoke, raised his head, then left Alec's lap. Mr. Ramsay pulled the dog close to him, and Sebastian settled down contentedly again.

Sebastian really was Dad's dog all right, Alec thought, for it was he whom the puppy had followed home one evening. Smiling, Alec remembered the advertisements they had published in the "Lost and Found" column of the local daily paper, his father hoping all the time that no one would claim Sebastian. No one had, and now Sebastian was theirs for keeps.

Slowing down the car, Mr. Ramsay said, "It should be right about here, Alec. Pier Number Six, wasn't it?"

Alec nodded as he watched the numbers on the outside of the long, dirty-white sheds which led back to the East River. Pier Nine . . . Eight . . . Seven . . . *Six.* It was there, just ahead. The car rolled slowly to a stop as Mr. Ramsay pulled over to the curb. Alec had a tight, lumpy feeling in his stomach and his jawbones worked nervously. He was half out the door, with Sebastian at his heels, when he stopped and caught the dog. "Shall we leave him in the car, Dad?"

Shaking his head, Alec's father said, "No, we'd better

not. I can't lock the door . . . broke it yesterday. I'd
rather take him on the leash. I wouldn't want anyone to
steal Sebastian.''

A few minutes later they walked quickly across the
street toward the shed marked Pier Six. Sebastian was
pulling on his leash.

As Alec half ran to keep up with his father's long
strides, he felt in his pants pocket for the folded papers
which would enable him to claim the colt. Upon reaching
the shed, he and his father carefully kept to one side of
the large entrance, avoiding the long line of trucks that
rumbled past them on their way inside to pick up cargo.
"Guess she must be coming in," Alec said excitedly,
quickening his pace until he passed his father, who now
was carrying Sebastian in his arms to keep him out of the
way of traffic.

They had almost reached the far end when Alec saw
the van he'd hired parked in one of the sidings.

"Well, at least your truck's here," his father shouted
above the roar of the motors when Alec pointed to the
van.

They had a good view of the river at the open end of the
shed and saw the *Queen of India* moving slowly toward
the pier. Sebastian barked, and Alec's father put him
down on the ground and held him by the leash. "It'll take
quite a little time for the tugboats to get her alongside the
shed," he told Alec. "Tricky currents out there.''

Alec didn't say anything, and as he watched the small
steamer which lay low in the water, its hold laden with
the produce of the Far East, he had that tight feeling in

his stomach again. In the hold somewhere was his horse, *his* son of the Black!

And then, even above the roar of the trucks and the shouts of the stevedores came a yell, "Hey, Alec!" which spun him around on his heels. Out of the melee behind him, a short, stocky man was running forward, his bowlegs looking as though they were about to give way from carrying the weight of the heavy chest and shoulders.

Alec's face broadened into a wide grin. "Henry!" he shouted at the top of his voice, running to meet him.

Holding the leash taut to keep Sebastian from chasing Alec, Mr. Ramsay watched his son throw his arms around Henry. This was the way Alec wanted it, he thought. The two of them together again. They were so much alike, these two . . . even down to the same bowed legs. And between them there was a bond, perhaps even stronger than blood itself, their intense love for horses and for one horse especially, the Black. Yes, he thought, they were very much like father and son standing there, their arms around each other. Then they were coming toward him, and the tall, slight man let Sebastian pull him forward.

"Henry"—he smiled, as his hand clasped the other's—"I'm sure glad you're here."

"Wouldn't have missed this for the world, Mr. Ramsay," Henry said, grinning back. "I flew in about an hour ago and called the house. Mrs. Ramsay told me you two had taken off for the pier and gave me all the necessary information. So I high-tailed it down." Henry wiped his sun-blackened face with his handkerchief, removed his battered hat and fanned himself. "Hotter here than it is out west," he said; then, bending over, he patted Sebastian, who stood close beside Alec. "He yours, Alec?" he asked.

"Dad's and mine," Alec replied. "He's Sebastian."

"He sure is a cute feller," Henry said, fondling Sebastian's long ears. "He's a cross between a lot of things, ain't he?" He smiled. Then Henry's gaze turned to the *Queen of India* as she moved slowly toward the pier, and his eyes met Alec's. Neither said anything for a few seconds, but each knew what the other was thinking.

"Papers on you?" Henry finally asked. "Got the van?"

Alec nodded. "Everything's set, Henry." He paused, but his eyes never left those of his friend. "And the registration papers are home." For a second or two after he had finished speaking he wondered if Henry would go through with their plans to raise and train the colt for the track. Henry had a big job now; he was making big money. Alec shifted uneasily on his feet.

Then into Henry's steady gray eyes came the look which Alec had hoped to see, and the old man said, "I'm glad it's a colt, Alec. Maybe he'll be like *him*."

"That's asking almost too much." The comment came from Alec's father.

Henry turned to him, then to Alec; and a look born of long association and understanding passed between the trainer and Alec. "I meant, Mr. Ramsay," Henry said, his gaze returning to the tall man who towered above him, "that I hoped the colt would have the perfect conformation of his sire."

"I know exactly what you meant, Henry," Mr. Ramsay replied quietly.

Alec looked at his father. There was a certain tenseness about his face which hadn't been there before, yet his eyes were without the sternness that they showed when his father was angry. Did he have any idea as to what he and Henry intended to do? Alec planned to tell him in time, but not for many months . . . not until he was certain that the son of the Black was ready for the track.

Mr. Ramsay spoke again to Henry. "No, I don't blame you for hoping he's like his sire." His gaze included Alec. "Either one of you," he added. "It's just that I'm hoping he doesn't have that wild, untamable spirit of the Black."

Henry smiled. "No fear of that, Mr. Ramsay. You mustn't forget that the Black was a full-grown stallion when Alec got hold of him. An' he never was clear broke . . . never will be, for that matter. It was just his love for Alec that made him tolerate the rest of us." Henry paused and nodded his head in the direction of the *Queen of India* as she neared the pier. "Now this one ain't goin' to be anything like that, Mr. Ramsay. The schooling and breaking of this colt ain't goin' to be like it was with the Black, or like perhaps you've seen or heard with broncs in the rodeos and the like. Sure, and I've had my share of that in my day, too. Nope, this won't be any fuss at all, Mr. Ramsay." Henry grinned reassuringly and went on, "Y'see, a young colt like this one is brought up knowin' that man is his friend. All y'have to do in most cases is to handle him well with both kindness and firmness, an' he just builds up confidence in people and does most everything you ask him to do. Why, this man Boldt I'm workin' for has a flock of youngsters which we're handlin'. 'Course some of 'em have their quirks and are meaner than others, but they're all comin' along fine, and before they're yearlings they'll all be well under control."

When Henry had finished Mr. Ramsay said, "I see what you mean, Henry, and I suppose you're right. It's just that I can't forget the fire and at times the savageness that was in the Black."

"Fire that was in him while he was runnin' wild in the desert," Henry reminded him.

"But fire that could be passed on to his son, born in the desert."

Henry smiled at Mr. Ramsay's insistence. "Yes, but his son will be brought up knowin' that man is his friend, and never knowin' the freedom of the desert," he concluded.

Alec's eyes had shifted from one to the other during the course of the conversation. There was much truth in all that his father had said. Henry knew it, too; yet the old man had probably figured there was no reason to cause undue concern at this point. The young colt with the blood of the Black running through him could conceivably give them a hard time. But Alec knew that with proper handling and kindness the colt would come around, just as Henry had said.

The blunt prow of the *Queen of India* entered the pier siding, and Alec, together with the others, watched her as she slowly drew alongside the shed. They could see the open door of the hold, and a group of men in blue jeans standing around.

"We'd better get inside the shed," Alec said, his tense voice betraying his emotions. "They'll bring him out that hold door."

With Sebastian straining at his leash, Mr. Ramsay and Henry followed Alec inside. About halfway down the shed Alec left the others and hurried toward a pier official who was standing at the unloading gate.

"It's better to leave him alone now, Henry," Mr. Ramsay said.

Henry nodded, and they walked slowly between two parked trucks to the pier fence. A few yards away the soot-blackened white hull of the tramp steamer pressed heavily against the wooden pier. The door to the hold slid by and then the ship came to a stop as the lines holding her fast to the pier were tied securely by the dockhands.

Henry watched as stevedores ran up the plank leading into the hold and then reappeared a few minutes later, wheeling and carrying cargo. It shouldn't be long now, he thought. Looking along the fence, he saw Alec standing there, his eyes too on the door to the hold.

"He'll be comin' in a minute, Morgan. You'd better hurry if you wanta see it!" a voice shouted from above.

Glancing up toward the deck of the ship, Henry saw a man standing near the rail, his coveralls and face smeared with the black grease of a tramp's boiler room. Another man joined him, and together they leaned far over the rail to get a good view of the hold door just below them.

"Harrity," Henry heard the new arrival say, "from all Sam told me they'll be havin' trouble gettin' anyone to take him off. He's given them nothin' but trouble all the way over. He sure is a lot of horse for a youngster. They shoulda kept him in Arabia, I say!"

Henry's eyes shifted uneasily from the men on the rail to the hold door, then back again. It was probable that they were discussing the colt. He turned to Mr. Ramsay, but either Alec's father hadn't heard what the men said, or if he had, its implication had escaped him. "I think I'll mosey down an' see how Alec is making out," Henry said.

"All right, Henry," Mr. Ramsay replied. "It might be a good idea at that. I'll stay here with Sebastian and meet you at the van."

As soon as Henry had made his way around the parked trucks, his pace quickened. If there was going to be any trouble with the colt he wanted to be around to help Alec. It wouldn't do to have the colt make a bad impression on Mr. Ramsay right at the start. No, that wouldn't do anyone any good.

Then things happened fast, almost too fast for Henry. For he was still making his way through the heavy truck traffic when he saw Alec dart past the official at the gate and run toward the plank. At the same time he heard a short high-pitched scream, an ominous counterpart of the one he knew so well . . . the shrill, challenging whistle of the Black! He jerked his head in the direction of the hold door and saw the black colt half in and half out of the ship. A man in blue coveralls, holding the horse, let the lead rope slide through his fingers as, frightened, he backed down the plank attempting to get away from the young colt's striking hoofs.

"Fool!" muttered Henry. "Why doesn't he close in on him and get his head? A baby like that ain't goin' to hurt him none!"

Henry could see that the young horse was frightened. And as he saw other things, small beads of light flickered in his eyes. The colt was *his* son, all right. Black as the ace of spades, just like his sire except for that white spot in the center of his forehead. It looked like a diamond from here. And he had all the earmarks of a good healthy colt, too. Yep, it was going to be mighty interesting watching this youngster develop.

The man holding the lead rope was standing still now. He was as scared as the colt, and the rope was taut between them. Shaking his head, the colt bared his teeth and struck the air with thrashing forefeet. Then he screamed again, and as the sound of it resounded throughout the pier shed, stevedores and truck drivers stopped their work to watch.

Then Alec was on the plank and moving quickly toward the frightened man. A slight grin flickered on Henry's face as he saw Alec take the lead rope from the man. This was Alec's show, all right, he thought. The kid could do it, too. No doubt about that. Henry's gaze shifted quickly up the pier shed to where Mr. Ramsay was standing. Maybe it was better this way. Maybe Mr. Ramsay had forgotten that if there was anything in this world Alec was meant to be around, it was horses.

Turning back to Alec, Henry saw him standing there, just holding the rope and looking at his horse. To a lot of people, Henry knew, it might have looked as if Alec wasn't going to do much about bringing the colt down the plank, either. But Henry, who was watching the boy, knew better. Alec's lips were moving, and he was talking to the colt in that low voice which Henry had heard him use so many times before when the Black had become panicky.

And it went on that way for all of five minutes, until most of the people who had been watching went back to work. Then Henry saw Alec move forward slowly, still keeping the lead rope taut and his lips moving.

The colt shook his small head savagely, and his ears lay back as Alec approached. And all eyes on the dock turned again to the two of them.

The tight ball in Alec's stomach had gone. He knew what he had to do. And he knew, too, that this was the way he'd wanted his colt to be. Still looking at the blazing eyes, he said softly, "You're fire, boy. You're full of it, just like *him*. You're mine, boy. We're going places together . . . you and I. We're going to use that fire to burn the tracks. We're going to make *him* proud of you.

He'll hear about you, boy. Hear the pounding of your hoofs, even though he's way back in the desert. It's going to be the way *he* wants it, boy."

There was a shrill scream from the colt as he rose on his slim hind legs. Alec, his face suddenly tense, let him rear, the rope sliding between his fingers as the colt went up. Balanced lightly on the balls of his feet and ready, Alec waited until the colt started downward, his hoofs pawing the air. And just before the colt's forelegs struck the wooden gangplank again, Alec sprang forward and came in close to the colt's head until the white lather from the black neck was flung upon him. Quickly he grabbed the halter and closed in hard upon the small head.

Henry chuckled. And when the pier official who stood next to him looked his way, he said, "It's just as easy as that, mister. Just as easy as that."

"He hasn't got him down yet," the man replied.

"Nothin' to it," Henry said, his eyes still on Alec and the colt. No, he could tell Alec wasn't going to have trouble now. Look at him. Just holding that wild baby's head and talking a mile a minute. It didn't matter what Alec was saying, just so long as he kept talking in that smooth, soothing way of his. There! He had the colt's hind legs on the plank and had him moving, too. Henry could see that Alec was holding him well. The colt had to come down; there was no other place to go. "See," Henry said to the pier official as Alec and the colt came down the plank. "See. What'd I tell you?"

"Yep," the man returned, glancing down at the folded

paper in his hand. "Well, it's his horse, ain't it? So I guess he oughta know how to handle him. Alec Ramsay's his name, huh?"

Nodding, Henry kept his eyes upon the colt and Alec as they came toward him. The colt was kicking his hind legs back and making as big a fuss as he could. Occasionally he would throw his forelegs out, but Henry knew that they were no danger to Alec so long as he stuck close to the side of the colt's head.

When they had reached the gate, the pier official said to Alec, "Take him through, kid, and get goin'. Lots of other stuff comin' off that tub."

Winking at Alec, Henry moved over beside him.

"He's it, Henry!" Alec almost shouted. "He's everything we hoped for. I know he is. I can feel it right here in his muzzle even!"

"Y'keep a good hold of it," Henry cautioned. "There's enough noise and commotion around here to drive any horse loco, let alone this one. Keep over here, Alec, away from those trucks."

The colt tried to rear, and dragged Alec a short way; then the boy had him under control again. But the colt's ears still lay back, and his eyes continued to blaze.

And it was his eyes that Henry looked at more and more often as they walked along. They were smaller than his sire's, and the glare from them was fixed and stony. They bothered Henry. For throughout his life the old trainer had prided himself on being able to tell much about a horse from his eyes. And he didn't like what he saw in the black colt's. Too much lurked there . . .

craftiness, cunning, viciousness, yes . . . and something else, too. Something which Henry couldn't figure out. Something which he could only feel . . . and it was sinister. He'd never seen it in the eyes of any horse before, even the Black. And he wondered if, possibly, this colt could be a throwback to his wild forebears . . . horses who had roamed the desert and the little-known lands beyond the Rub' al Khali, arrogant and ruthless, fearing neither man nor beast and harboring a savage, smoldering hatred of both.

Alec was talking half to himself, half to Henry. "Every inch of him is the Black," he muttered. "Every last inch of him. He's going to have the same broad chest and long, slender neck." Turning to Henry, he said excitedly, "Look at the arch on that neck, Henry. And the small head! And he's going to be big! You can tell that by his frame, Henry. Big! Like the Black!"

Henry didn't say anything. Perhaps, he thought, it wasn't going to be so easy after all . . . as easy as he'd told Mr. Ramsay it was going to be. Those eyes did something to the colt.

Tearing his gaze from the black colt, Alec looked at Henry quizzically. His friend's face was sober, thoughtful. It was strange that Henry was so quiet. This is the son of the Black! he almost shouted. His horse! The beginning of everything! Alec found himself wondering again. Had Henry changed, now that he was a big-time trainer again? Had he seen too many of Boldt's fine colts to become excited over any other colt? But this was not just another colt. Certainly Henry knew that!

Alec studied Henry's face as the old man walked beside him, his square jaw shoved out like a toy bulldog's, the furrows in his wrinkled brow deeper than Alec had ever seen them. Something was wrong, Alec knew. Was it that Henry wanted to continue working for Boldt rather than go through with their plans? Did he regret having signed only a year's contract with Boldt, instead of the three-year contract the wealthy race horse owner had offered? Alec knew his present contract would terminate in two months; they'd planned it that way so Henry would be free just in case the horse did arrive. Was that what was bothering Henry? Did he want to renew his contract with Boldt, and make big money instead of going through with the original plans? Plans that could fail if the colt didn't have the speed of his sire?

Alec's face was tense as he turned back to his horse. The colt swerved, attempting to break away, but Alec's grip was firm and he brought him back. If that's what Henry wanted, he thought, he wouldn't stand in his way. But somehow he'd raise and train the colt himself, and the day would come when Boldt, Henry and everyone else would know the speed of his horse.

They neared the van. Alec saw his father standing there, with Sebastian straining at his leash to get to him. His father smiled, but Alec could see that it was forced. The ramp of the van was down, the driver standing alongside. Just lead the colt up the short ramp, and he'd have him inside. Then home, and before long his father would have forgotten all that had happened at the pier.

Henry said, "Want me to help you take him in, Alec?"

"I can manage, Henry. Thanks." Alec's voice was clipped. He moved forward with the colt. Sebastian barked, then whimpered, his tail wagging; he wanted to get to Alec. The black colt swerved again, and Alec knew Sebastian wasn't helping matters any. He was about to ask his father to take Sebastian away from the back of the van when a sudden gust of wind, blowing from the river, swept through the shed. Alec saw his father make a grab at his brown hat as the wind caught it, knocking it from his head. As the hat tumbled down to the ground, his father went after it with both hands, and Sebastian was free. Bounding forward, the puppy ran excitedly to Alec.

Then it all happened very quickly. The colt reared, swerved to the right, then plunged forward, his small hoofs striking out viciously.

And when Alec had him still once more, Sebastian lay inert upon the wooden floor of the shed.

Then his father and Henry were beside him, and his father bent over the dog. Finally he looked up at Alec. "He's still breathing," he said in a strained voice. "I'll get him to a veterinary." Then, carrying Sebastian in his arms, he left them.

Alec stood gazing at his father's back as the older man walked quickly away with Sebastian.

"I don't think the colt hit him square," Alec heard Henry say. "Just glanced him on the side, probably knocking the wind out of him. He'll be okay, I think, Alec. Don't worry."

"I sure hope so, Henry," Alec replied slowly. "I'd hate to have anything happen to Sebastian."

"The colt's excited . . ."

Alec nodded, his eyes on the quivering body of the horse beside him.

"Let's get out of here," Henry said. "It's no place for him."

As they led the colt into the van, Alec said bitterly. "A good start, Henry."

"Yeah," Henry returned, ". . . a good start."

Satan

4

When the van left the pier shed, Alec was sitting between the driver and Henry. Turning his head, Alec could see the black colt through the small window. He was tied securely; everything was all right now.

Henry said, "He'll turn out okay, Alec. Don't worry about him."

Without looking at his friend, Alec said, "I'm not worrying too much, Henry. It's the way I hoped he'd be." Pausing, he added, "I just wish he hadn't kicked Sebastian."

Henry didn't say anything, and after a few minutes Alec glanced at him. The old man's face was still troubled. Alec's gaze left him and returned to the road ahead. For several blocks he was undecided whether or not to bring up the subject which was foremost in his mind. Then he said quietly, "Your job, Henry. How's it going?"

Without hesitation Henry replied, "It's all right, Alec. Boldt's got some fine youngsters this year. He's thinkin' they're the best he's ever had. May be right, too, from the looks of 'em." And then Alec detected a sudden eagerness in Henry's voice as he added, "There's one colt especially that Boldt's staking everything on . . . a gray colt sired by his champion, Shooting Star. That's the horse, you know, that copped all the big stakes a couple years back. Well, Boldt put him in stud and bred him to that great English mare, the Lady, which he bought for fifty thousand dollars. The gray colt's the result, and Boldt wouldn't sell him for any price. He's already named him Boldt's Comet."

Alec remained silent when Henry had finished. It was pretty much as he'd figured, Alec thought. Henry didn't want any part of his black colt. With Boldt, there were horses Henry could get excited about and, at the same time, pull down a good salary each year. With him, there would be no salary, no fine stables, no help, nothing . . . except the son of the Black! And at one time, not so many months ago, the colt had been all that Henry had wanted.

Then the old man said quietly, his eyes still on the road ahead, "But if our colt turns out to be anything like his sire, he'll run Boldt's Comet into the ground, Alec. I'm sure of it."

Our colt! Did that mean . . . *could* it mean . . . ?

Quickly Alec turned to Henry and met his eyes for the first time since they had left the pier. "Our colt," he repeated. "Do you mean it, Henry? You're going to go through with it, just as we planned?"

A confused look swept Henry's face as he studied Alec's tense expression. Then he smiled. "Y'mean, Alec, you didn't think I was?"

Alec's eyes fell, and he heard Henry's deep chuckle. The old man's gnarled hand descended upon Alec's knee as he said, "You'd have to get out the entire New York police force to keep me away, Alec. And then it wouldn't do any good." Chuckling again, he continued. "Sure, I'm going to be there, Alec, and we're goin' to make this black colt into a race horse few will ever forget. Just like the Black," he added reminiscently, ". . . just like the Black."

Alec turned toward Henry, his eyes eager. "We'll do it, Henry!" he half shouted. "Together, you and I . . . just as we planned."

"Just as we planned," Henry repeated.

Alec's face sobered. "But Boldt and your job . . . the big money, Henry . . ."

"Big money. Big business, Alec. And I don't like it." Henry's eyes were again upon the road. Then he went on, his voice serious, giving Alec no reason to doubt what he said. "And when I say big, Alec, I mean just that. No, Boldt's no small-time player, not by a long shot. He calls his horse farm the Mother Lode Ranch, after the gold mine he found back in 'twenty-six when he was pretty near stone-broke. That ranch, some say, is nearly ten thousand acres, an' others say it's closer to twenty thousand." Henry turned and gazed at Alec as he added,

"It must be stocked with over a thousand thoroughbreds. Why, I got a glimpse at Boldt's catalogue once't, and counted fifty stallions and six hundred brood mares alone. . . . Then there are all those youngsters runnin' around. More horses than any man knows what to do with . . . and he's got more trainers, grooms, jockeys and boys workin' for him than Flushing has people." Henry stopped, smiled. "Maybe not quite," he said, looking ahead at the road. "But it's big. Big business to Boldt . . . and a lot more than that, too," he concluded quietly. "I don't want any part of it any more."

The thud of hoofs meeting wood reached Alec's ears as Henry finished. Turning, he looked through the window at the colt. Then, convinced that his horse was all right, he said to Henry, "I'm glad, Henry. Selfishly, I know, but glad." He paused before continuing. "But you've trained horses for big stables before, Henry. Maybe not as large as Boldt's, but big, anyway."

It was a long time before Henry replied. "I know, Alec," he finally said. "Some might say it's because I'm gettin' old. Maybe so. Then again it might be that I found something really worth having when you and I trained the Black practically in our own backyard and then saw him cop the big race in Chicago with you wrapped up in his mane. Yep, things like that really make life worth livin', Alec. An' we aim to do it again, don't we?"

"We sure do, Henry."

"But there's something else, Alec," the old man continued, and now there was a hard, brittle ring to his voice. "Another reason why I'd get out, even if your colt hadn't arrived. It's Boldt . . . Boldt himself.'' Henry paused. "He's half horse, Alec, but not in the same way that mebbe you and I are an' a lot of other people we know. Boldt, with all his horses, wants more horses . . . all he can get, just as long as they're fast. He wants 'em because he fears them, is afraid one of 'em might beat his own. I know from what I've seen, Alec, that it's been his ambition for years to have the fastest horses in the world. With his Shooting Star he came into his own, an' now he has his gray colt and figures there's no stoppin' him.'' Henry turned to Alec. "When I was a kid an' lived in the rangelands, I saw men like Boldt; and my father saw lots more and had rough dealin's with a good many of 'em. They stop at nothin', Alec. Nothin'. Boldt hired me because he knew I'd just come back from Arabia with you and Mr. Volence, and he figured I could tell him a lot about those four Arabian horses Abu Ishak had given Volence. He was afraid of those horses, Alec, and he thought he could get to Volence through me.''

Alec well remembered the horses Abu Ishak had given Mr. Volence, their friend, who had made possible their trip to Arabia in search of the Black. "They were fine horses,'' Alec said quietly, "but they couldn't run on the same track with the Black. Even Volence knew that.''

"Sure,'' grunted Henry, "but by breeding 'em to some of his good stock down in Kentucky, Volence hoped to get something. I suspect the first foals have already come along by this time. But getting back to Boldt, he tried for months to get me to talk about Volence's Arabians 'n' even Abu Ishak. I kept my mouth shut and played dumb 'til there came a time when old Boldt would pass me by without noddin' his head. And that's the way it went. Later I heard he went and tried to buy the horses from Volence, and when Volence wouldn't sell, Boldt swore he'd get even.''

"Nice guy," muttered Alec sarcastically. He thought a minute, then added, "I wonder what Boldt would do if he learned about the Black's colt being here?"

"That's what we've got to keep from him as long as possible, Alec. With his money and pull he could make things uncomfortable some way. The horses Volence brought back are peanuts compared to what your little baby there in back is worth to Boldt. He told me once't that it was his supreme ambition to own a wild desert stallion like the Black. But he can't get to him, an' he knows it. If he learns the Black's son is here . . . well, Alec, we've just got to keep it from him as long as we can. Then when the time comes, we'll figure out what to do."

"Yes," Alec said, "no sense worrying about it now."

They had reached the truck route running parallel to the Parkway leading to Flushing, and in less than half an hour they'd arrive home. Alec wondered if his father had taken Sebastian to Flushing, then decided that it all depended on how seriously Sebastian was hurt. If his father thought the puppy's injuries were critical, he'd find a veterinary in New York instead of making the trip home.

Henry said, "You thought of a name for the colt, Alec?"

"For months I've been thinking about it, Henry."

"Then you've picked one out. What's it to be?"

"Satan," Alec replied, turning to his friend.

"Satan," Henry repeated. "Uh-huh. Satan." He paused, then continued. "Abu called the Black, Shêtân, back in Arabia. Shêtân means devil in Arabic. So his son is to be named Satan. Is that it, Alec?"

Alec's eyes were bright as he nodded. "It's a good name, Henry, isn't it? He's so full of fire."

"Yeah, Alec, I guess it is," Henry replied, his gaze turning back to the road. Those black, sinister eyes of the colt haunted him like the devil himself. He attempted to shrug the feeling off. There might be nothing to it, he told himself. Nothing that couldn't be whipped in time. But he wanted to be around from the very beginning to keep his hand on this colt, for there was no telling what might happen later if he were allowed to get out of control early in the game. It was important, much more important than Alec realized. Finally Henry turned to Alec and said, "I'm flying back to the West Coast early tomorrow morning to quit my job with Boldt. Then I'll be back in a few days."

Alec looked at Henry, studying his wrinkled face with keen eyes. "But your contract, Henry," he said, ". . . it's not up for two months."

"I can talk Boldt into lettin' me go," Henry replied. "I've got ways." Then, grinning, he explained, "Just let me mention that I saw Volence's youngsters when I was east and they looked mighty good to me . . . say, even better than his gray colt . . . that's all I have to do. He'll sack me for that, Alec. I know him and his kind. Boldt can act like a jealous kid when it comes to his horses.''

Alec said thoughtfully, ''You'll lose money on the deal, Henry. Two months' salary, maybe.''

''Mebbe an' mebbe not,'' Henry replied. ''If I do, it's worth it.''

''You're a good friend, Henry.''

''Naw,'' Henry scoffed. ''There isn't a trainer in the country who wouldn't give his right arm to get a crack at the son of the Black. An' don't you forget it, Alec.''

It wasn't until they neared Flushing that Henry spoke again. ''Besides,'' he said, ''another reason for my bein' around is that you're due to go back to that up-state college mighty soon, ain'tcha? Tomorrow is the first of September . . . that means I oughta be back just before you leave,'' he concluded. When Alec didn't reply, he turned and noticed the way Alec avoided his eyes. ''What were you thinkin' of doin', Alec, if I couldn't have gotten back here for another two months? Were you thinkin' of lettin' Tony keep an eye on the colt, or somethin' like that?''

Alec said quietly, ''I was thinking of quitting school, Henry.''

It was several minutes before Henry said anything. ''Have you mentioned this to your father?''

''No . . .''

''But now that I'm goin' to be around, you won't have to quit,'' Henry said.

''I still want to be around, too, Henry.''

''But you'll be back during Christmas vacation an' then there'll be all of next summer.'' Henry's gaze found

Alec's. "Besides," he added lightly, "there's not going to be much to do. Just keepin' watch on him, that's all. And Alec"—he paused—"I know how your folks feel about your goin' to school."

"I know, Henry," Alec replied, almost curtly. "I know, but this is important."

"School's important, too," Henry said slowly. "You once't told me you wanted to know all there was to know about horses . . . what went on inside 'em as well as outside. An' in your letters to me while you were at school y'said the subjects you were takin' were just what you wanted, like animal anatomy and those other things you mentioned."

"*You* never had them," Alec said quietly.

"Sure, and mebbe I'd be a better trainer if I'd had," Henry insisted. Shrugging his shoulders, he added, "It's your life, Alec. Play it the way you want to. I'm jest sayin' that it's goin' to take months and months for the colt to grow up an' our real trainin' won't begin until then."

Alec was silent as the van reached Flushing. There was a lot to what Henry said, he knew. But he had waited a long time for the arrival of his colt, and now that Satan was here he wanted to be with him every day. He wanted to feed him, take care of him, watch him playing in the field, just as he'd done with the Black. And then when the time came, he'd ride him around the field until Henry said the colt was ready to be taken to the track for workouts. It would probably be Belmont, since that track was the nearest to Flushing. And they'd have night workouts, too, so no one would get an inkling of Satan's speed.

Henry said, "You'll get the registration blanks from the Jockey Club?"

Nodding, Alec answered, "Tomorrow, Henry."

"Y'know where it is?"

"Two-fifty Park Avenue."

"Yeah, that's it." Then, thoughtfully, "All you'll need will be the certificate of identification for the veterinary to fill out after he's examined the colt. Then y'send that back together with the colt's pedigree which Abu sent you in his letter. There's a five-dollar fee, too."

"Yes, I know, Henry. I've already checked up on it."

"How about the vet?"

"There's Hancock in Flushing," Alec replied. "He's a friend of ours and won't charge me much."

"It's going to cost money, Alec, training and racing Satan."

"I've saved for it. I'll get more," Alec said.

"And I've got some."

Alec turned to Henry. "You needn't . . ."

"I know I *needn't*," Henry grinned, "but we're partners, ain't we?"

Smiling, Alec said, "Yes, partners." He sat back in his seat, relaxed and content. There were problems ahead, of course, but they weren't insurmountable, and somehow he and Henry would work them out together. "I'll get an application for an owner's license, too, Henry," he said. "Just think . . . *my* horse, *my* colors, and me up there on his back, Henry!" Excitedly, Alec half-turned in his seat; then, as he saw Henry's face, he stopped short.

"*Your* horse," the old man was muttering in a voice so low Alec could barely make out his words, ". . . and *you* riding him." Turning to Alec, he said, "I'm a fool. A blasted old fool. You can't do it, Alec . . . it's no go."

"Can't do what, Henry? What can't I do?"

The old man said sorrowfully, "I should have thought of it. Shoulda thought of it before this." He paused, then said slowly, "Y'can't own and ride Satan both. It's in the rules . . . a jockey can't own a race horse."

"You mean . . . You're sure, Henry? It's in the rules of racing?" Alec's voice was emotionless, dead.

"Yes, Alec, I'm certain." And then as the moments swept by without Alec's saying a word, Henry asked, "You want to ride, don'tcha?" Henry knew what Alec's answer would be even before the boy nodded. "Okay, then, it ain't so bad, Alec, really. There's your dad . . . have him register the horse in his name. There's nothin' in the rules which says a jock can't ride his father's horse. Then it'll still be *your* name on the owner's sheet, and *your* colors, too. I'm sure your father will understand."

Alec smiled grimly. "My dad . . . a race horse owner? Do you think he'd have any part of the colt after today? Are you serious, Henry?"

"Sure, I'm serious. Your father oughta know that what happened today was partly Sebastian's fault. He oughta know that."

"But, Henry, Dad doesn't even like horses. He wouldn't have any part of it, I know."

"I'm not tellin' you you don't know your own father,"
Henry said, "but I've seen his eyes light up at times
when he used to watch the Black. An' I saw it again today
with the colt. Just once't and only for a second," he
admitted, "but that's all that was necessary. He's not
against horses, Alec. Don't you think that."

"But if he won't do it, Henry," Alec's words came
slowly, "will you? Can a trainer own a race horse?"

"Yes," Henry replied quietly, "a trainer can own a
race horse, Alec. And I'll do it, if your dad won't. I guess
there isn't anything I'd like more in the world than to see
the son of the Black runnin' in my name. But that's not
the way it should be. He's *your* horse, Alec, and *your*
name belongs on him . . . with you up on his back, riding
in *your* silks. The two of you are goin' places. I've had my
day, Alec, and now I just wanta sit back an' watch.
Another reason I shouldn't own the colt," he added, his
brow furrowing, "is that the names of all new horses and
owners registered with the Jockey Club are published in
the Racing Calendar . . . that's the official racing maga-
zine. Boldt reads it religiously. He'd see my name and
might get to thinkin' I had something up my sleeve. But I
don't think the name William Ramsay would register with
him. It's better that you speak to your father, Alec."

"Okay, Henry. . . ."

It was almost dark when the van turned down their
block, and behind him Alec heard the colt's hoofs impatiently strike the wooden floor. There was no alternative
now, he thought, but to tell his father of the plans to race

Satan. He couldn't put it off for months as he'd intended to do. And now his father's reaction would be all the more important, because he was to play a part in the racing of the colt. Alec felt the tight, hard ball in his stomach again. Would his father understand how much this meant to him? Would he agree to race Satan in his name . . . *their* name? Was Henry right? . . . Did his father really have a feeling for horses? A feeling that might make him understand? Then Alec remembered his dad's words as they were driving to the pier: *"You've had enough excitement to last a lifetime . . . take it easy . . . go for nice slow rides through the park . . . just make a pal of him."* Alec wondered, and swallowed hard. Then there was school. He had to tell his father that he didn't want to go back. And there was Sebastian, too. If the dog was critically hurt, he'd never forgive himself for letting the colt get away, even if it had been partly Sebastian's fault. "It's the beginning, all right," he muttered to himself. "In fact, it's begun . . ."

"What's that, Alec?" Henry asked.

"Nothing, Henry."

They passed the brown house, and Alec saw a light in the living room. Maybe his father was already there, or maybe it was just his mother, awaiting their return.

The van pulled up in front of the iron gate and stopped while Henry and Alec got out to open it. Then the truck rolled through slowly, and they walked behind it, up the graveled driveway toward the barn. "Napoleon still here?" Henry asked. And after Alec nodded, the old man said, "Good. He'll help quiet down the colt, just like he did the Black." Henry's gaze shifted to the large house on the corner, a few hundred yards from the barn. "You think the missis will be glad to see me, Alec?" he asked, and there was a skeptical look on his wrinkled face.

Alec smiled. "Sure, Henry. You're her husband, aren't you?"

"Makes no difference after you've been married as long as we have, m'boy," Henry replied seriously. "Besides, she never wanted me to get mixed up in big-time trainin' again . . . and I went and done it, over her head like."

"Then tell her you're through with it, Henry," Alec suggested. "Tell her you're quitting Boldt and coming back."

"Good idea, Alec," Henry said, nodding his head. "I'll tell her first thing."

The van backed up to the barn, and the driver sat behind the wheel, waiting for Alec and Henry to rid him of his cargo. They opened the back, put the ramp down, and walked inside.

The black colt stood there in the darkness of the van, his nostrils tingling with a scent that set his blood on fire. And the fire swept through him until his black body was quivering with eagerness and his eyes glowed with hate. His ears lay back, flat against his small head, which moved from side to side defiantly. He pulled at the rope which held him tight, and as the scent grew stronger in his nostrils and the sound of footsteps reached him, he snorted and kicked out his hind legs.

"Careful, Alec," Henry cautioned as the boy moved ahead of him. "He could do some damage if he caught you in the head."

The colt couldn't turn, couldn't see behind him. Alec moved quietly to one side of the van; then, with quickness and agility, he ran forward, closing in upon the fierce head. "No you don't, Satan," he said, as the colt bared his teeth and attempted to bite him. Snorting, the colt tried to pull away from this person who held his head. He heaved upward, frantic for his freedom. But the pressure on his head was still there when he came down.

"Got him, Alec?" It was Henry.

"He's quieting down. Coming out in a minute." Alec untied the lead rope and slowly turned the colt around in the van until he faced the door. Then, still holding him close, Alec led the colt forward, down the ramp, and stopped in front of the barn door. Henry closed the van, signaled to the driver, and the truck left, rolling slowly down the driveway and through the gate.

"I'll see if everything is okay inside," Henry said.

"I got the stall ready this morning," Alec told him. "We'll put Satan in the same one the Black used, right next to Napoleon." As Henry disappeared inside the barn, Alec pressed his head close to the colt's. "Your pop used it," he said softly, ". . . and now it's yours."

Henry reappeared at the door. "Okay," he said. "Bring him in."

Napoleon pitched his gray head over the stall door as

Alec led Satan into the barn. Pricking his long ears forward, Napoleon neighed and watched the black colt eagerly.

Satan stopped in his tracks, refusing to go forward. Tossing his head, he whistled and bared his teeth. As he stood there, tense and rigid, his blazing eyes were fixed upon old Napoleon.

"Guess you might be wrong, Henry," Alec said. "He doesn't seem to be taking to Nap."

"He doesn't seem to be takin' to anybody," Henry growled; then he muttered half to himself, "Those strange, creepy eyes . . ."

Alec tried talking to the colt, but Satan moved restlessly, his eyes still on Napoleon. Suddenly the colt wheeled, staggered as Alec's weight threw his light body off balance, and, recovering, screamed again.

Napoleon's eyes were upon him all the time, soft and wondering.

At last the colt was still. Alec tried to move him forward, but Satan kept his legs rigid. Stroking him, Alec turned to Henry and started to say something. Then, quickly, the colt leapt forward, screaming, carrying Alec with him.

Henry moved fast as Satan, his teeth bared, rushed toward Napoleon. Coming between them, the old man's hand descended heavily upon Satan's muzzle. The blow stunned the colt and as he drew back upon his haunches Henry closed in upon his head.

When it was over, and Alec and Henry both had hold of

the quivering colt, the old man said angrily, "It's goin' to be like raisin' the devil himself. Let's get him down to the end stall, Alec, away from Napoleon."

"Maybe he'll get used to Nap," Alec said hopefully. "Then it'll be like it was."

"Mebbe," Henry muttered. "Mebbe."

They didn't have any trouble moving the colt down the barn, and Alec held him while Henry went into the end stall. Finally he came out and said, "Ready now, Alec. Gave him some hay, too. Mebbe that'll help some."

Alec led Satan into the stall and then stood beside him, his cheek pressed hard against the colt's head. "It's all strange to you, boy. . . . I know it is. You can't help acting the way you do, leaving all you've ever known so far behind you. But it'll be different in a short while, honestly it will. You'll like it here, Satan. . . . Your father did, you know. And you'll get to like Napoleon, too, and he'll understand why you were excited tonight. We all love you, Satan . . . you're *ours* . . . you're what we've been waiting for."

"Comin', Alec?" Henry asked.

Alec's hand trailed along the colt's side as he left the stall.

And as they left the barn, they could hear Satan moving restlessly within, his hoofs occasionally striking the sides of his stall.

They walked in silence until they reached the gate, then Alec said, "I won't see you tomorrow, then."

"It's a five o'clock flight. You'll be sleepin'." Henry

paused, then added, "I'll try to get back inside of ten days, Alec. Don't suspect I'll have any trouble with Boldt . . . not if I handle him right."

"Hope not, Henry."

"You'll speak to your father?"

"Tonight or tomorrow. Maybe tomorrow would be better."

Henry placed his hand on Alec's arm. "Use your own judgment, Alec. It's good, an' you're carrying the ball now."

"Yes," Alec said thoughtfully, his gaze on the house across the street, "it's my ball, all right."

Henry's fingers pressed into Alec's shoulder, and he mumbled something about seeing the missis; then he shuffled up the street toward the big house on the corner. Alec watched him for a moment, and then started across the street.

Bill of Sale

5

Alec watched as his mother rose from her chair and began cleaning off the kitchen table. She had reached the head of the table and her hand was on his dad's empty plate when, hesitating, she turned to Alec. "I believe I'll leave his setting, and keep the food warm," she said. "He may not have eaten."

Alec smiled, trying to relieve the deep concern he saw in his mother's eyes. "He'll be along any minute now, Mom," he said, getting to his feet. And as he helped her carry the dishes to the sink, he added, "He might have had trouble finding a veterinary in New York."

His mother washed the dishes in silence while Alec stood beside her drying them. "Do you think Sebastian might have been seriously hurt?" she finally asked.

"I don't think so, Mom. Henry said the colt's hoof just nicked him."

"You should have kept the colt away from him," his mother said a little sternly as she dried her hands.

"Sebastian . . ." Then Alec stopped. His mother was worried enough now without his going into all the details of the accident. "Yes, Mom," he said quietly. "I know I should have."

The spring lock on the screen door on the porch clicked and then clicked again as the door shut. In another moment Mr. Ramsay was striding into the kitchen, his face white and tired. "Sorry I'm late, Belle," he said, turning to his wife, "but it couldn't be helped." Then his gaze was upon Alec, and the boy felt uneasy until the sternness left his father's eyes. "Seb will be all right in a couple of days, Alec," he said slowly. "Doctor Hancock thinks he was just stunned by the blow, but he's going to keep him around awhile to make sure."

"Sit down, William, while the food is still warm," Alec heard his mother say. "You must be hungry."

Everything was all right now, Alec thought. Sebastian wasn't hurt; his father was eating hungrily; and his mother was moving busily about the kitchen once more. She poured the coffee into her husband's cup and said, "We thought you might have tried to find a veterinary in New York." The tenseness was gone from her voice.

"Decided it would be better taking him to Hancock," Alec heard his father say. "I figured it wouldn't take any longer than looking for a vet in New York."

Excusing himself, Alec left the kitchen, stopped momentarily in the living room, as though undecided where to go, then turned and walked up the stairs, his hand trailing along the well-polished mahogany banister.

He went to his bedroom, and for a moment stood at the window looking at the barn, a dim, uncertain shape in the darkness. It would turn out all right, he told himself again. Things which started out badly had a way of righting themselves. The colt would come around in time. He was certain of that.

He went over to the bed and stretched out upon it, his eyes looking up at the ceiling. He lay there quietly for a few minutes; then his gaze descended to the walls and traveled about the room, dimly lit from the light in the hall. His eyes passed over the Flushing High School banners, stopped at the pictures of the Black, Henry and himself, then went on to the soiled green jockey cap hanging there. Henry's cap, the same one the old man had worn long ago when he had been riding. And the one which Alec had worn when he had ridden the Black in the match race at Chicago. Finally Alec glanced at the empty wall on the other side of his bed. He was saving that wall for the colt, for pictures of him, for his *own* jockey cap . . . his *own* colors. His silks would be black, coal black . . . the color of the great stallion and now his son. Somehow he had known Satan would be black. Alec thought of the white diamond in the center of the colt's forehead. Maybe he'd add a white diamond to his colors, a white diamond on the right side of his shirt.

Alec's gaze left the wall and returned to the ceiling. Perhaps, he thought, he was getting ahead of himself.

Perhaps the colt would never have the speed of the Black. Or they might have trouble with him. Maybe everything wouldn't turn out the way he and Henry thought. Maybe the bad beginning was just an indication of much worse to come. And how well he remembered the words Henry had uttered angrily in the barn, as the colt had attempted to savage old Napoleon: *"It's going to be like trying to raise the devil himself. . . ."* Could it be that Henry actually felt that way about Satan? Alec wondered about it as he lay there. That, and other things. How would his father react when he asked him to register the horse in his name? What would his father say when he told him he didn't want to go back to school? Tomorrow, he decided, would be a better time to talk to him than tonight. Tomorrow, Saturday, when his father didn't have to go to work, and might not have such a vivid recollection of all that had happened today. Tomorrow . . .

Alec didn't know how long he had lain there when he heard the sound of footsteps on the stairs. He recognized them as his father's. They were steady and quick, as compared to his mother's soft, faltering ones.

He heard his father reach the top of the stairs, walk toward his own room, hesitate, go on again, and then stop. It was still enough for Alec to hear the crickets chirping in the field across the street; then he heard the closing of the refrigerator door in the kitchen and the sound of his mother moving about downstairs.

His father's footsteps reached him again; this time they

were coming toward his room! They came to a stop before his half-open door.

"You up, Alec?"

"Yes, Dad." Alec rose to a sitting position on the bed as his father entered the room, switching on the light.

"Just thinking?" his father asked.

Nodding, Alec watched his father's tall frame as the older man walked slowly over to the window and, bending, looked out. Then straightening again, he turned and looked about the room, glancing over the banners, the pictures, and the soiled jockey cap, finally letting his eyes come to rest on Alec. "What are you and Henry up to?" he asked quietly.

It had come much too fast and unexpectedly for Alec. He looked down; but quickly, as though ashamed of his faltering gaze, he looked his father in the eyes again. "We want to race the colt," he replied, ". . . eventually." And the sound of his own voice seemed strange to him.

"Thought it might be something like that," Alec heard his father say slowly.

He wished that he knew his father better . . . wished that he could read his eyes as well as he could Henry's. It would have helped now.

His father walked over to the bed, sat down beside him, and asked, "Do you think he'll have the Black's speed?"

More startled than ever, Alec looked at him. His father's face was still tense, his eyes somber. Yet his voice had been almost casual. "I—I think . . . hope so, Dad," he replied unsteadily.

Bending down, his father picked off a long thread from the legs of his brown trousers. "I read somewhere that most Arabian horses, while long on endurance, were short on speed. And I've heard, too, that they've been very much outbred by the American and English thoroughbred."

"Have you forgotten the Black?"

"No, Alec. I haven't forgotten," he answered in the same tone, his face unchanging. "Strange, too. He was fast and big. Nothing like him in what I've read. They usually mention the *small* Arabian horses."

Alec smiled as he thought of Abu Ishak's hidden stronghold in the land east of the Rub' al Khali. "Abu never thought much of publicity," he said. Then he continued more seriously, "Besides, Dad, the Black wasn't pure Arabian. His dam was pure-blooded, but his sire wasn't."

"What was he then?"

"Abu never told us. But Henry heard that soon after he was weaned he escaped and ran wild in the desert and mountains before Abu's men caught up with him more than a year later. Then a few months after he sired the Black, he escaped again, this time taking the Black with him. It was almost another year before they tracked them down, and then they only managed to catch the young colt, the Black."

"An interesting story," Alec's father said, ". . . very interesting."

Alec looked at him. It was strange to be talking this way to his dad. It was almost like talking to Henry. All his life he had thought of his father as someone to admire, to respect . . . but this was the first time he had looked upon him as a person, a real person who was interested in the same things he was.

"And now you and Henry are going to train the son of the Black for the track. But how about Henry's job out west?"

"He's quitting," Alec told his father. "He's leaving for California tomorrow morning, but he'll be back in ten days, he says."

There was a long silence before his father said, "I'd hoped there wouldn't be any more of this, as I told you this morning." Pausing, he added, "But I guess we knew all the time, Mother and I."

"Dad, it's . . ." Alec began, only to have his father interrupt him.

"I know, Alec. I know exactly how you feel, and that it's your life . . . the life you've chosen." Then he concluded, his voice a little strained, "Your mother and I have talked it over. We won't stand in your way if it's what you really want. And I guess you do."

"It's what I want, Dad," Alec said seriously, "more than anything else in the world. To ride, to train . . . to be around horses all my life."

"Don't know where you get it from, Alec." His father smiled. "It's not from your mother's side, nor mine. City people, all of us."

"People in the city can love horses, Dad."

"Yes, Alec, I suppose so." Mr. Ramsay rose to his feet before adding resignedly, "Well, go to it. You're on your own again." He was near the door when Alec's voice stopped him in his tracks.

"Dad . . . this time would you go into it with me?" Alec heard his own voice fade into the stillness of the room. And he saw his father's back straighten as he came to a stiff halt. "I need your help," he added slowly.

When his father turned to him, Alec saw the bewilderment in his eyes. Then the look disappeared to be replaced by a forced smile. "You're kidding, Alec," he said. "You don't need any help with that colt, and if you do, what help could I, a cost accountant, possibly give you?" He paused. "Or is it money you need?"

Alec's words were slow in coming. "I want to sell my colt to you."

"For one hundred thousand or so?" Then Mr. Ramsay saw the white, drawn look on his son's face and stopped smiling.

"No . . . for a dollar," Alec replied. "Just to make it an official sale."

His father walked across the room and sat down beside him.

"I have to," Alec said quietly. "I can't own him and ride him."

"You can't do both, you mean? Why?"

"It's in the rules of racing. Henry told me."

"Then you want me to own him, so you can ride him. Is that it?"

Nodding, Alec turned eagerly to his father. "Then he'll be running in *our* name, Dad. Running in *our* silks. I want them to be black, all black, except for a white diamond on the shirt, the same diamond the colt has in the center of his forehead. You won't have to do anything, Dad. Just sign the registration papers, which I'm getting tomorrow . . . just register the colt in your name. Will you do it?"

His father was silent a long time, his lined face strained and his eyes somber again. Finally he stood up, walked to the window, and looked out. Then he turned and Alec knew his reply before he uttered a word.

"I'm sorry, Alec, but I can't do it. You say that I'd only have to register the colt in my name and that's all there would be to it. You know better, and I do, too. One thing will lead to another . . . it always has."

Alec watched him without saying anything. He was talking like a father again, and the intimacy and mutual interest Alec had thought they shared for a little while had gone.

"There will be complications all along the way," his father was saying. "There couldn't help but be. The training and racing of a horse is no different from any other business. And I have too much on my mind now, Alec. Too much work at the office." He paused again before going on. "Then there's your mother. It'll be enough that you're mixed up in this without my being in it, too. No, Alec," he concluded, "I can't possibly do it. I'm certain that you and Henry can figure out some other way."

Alec said nothing when his father had finished. He only raised his eyes when the older man sat down beside him again, as though reluctant to leave.

"You'll try to understand, won't you, Alec?"

"Yes, Dad. I understand," Alec replied slowly and with effort.

"You're the horseman of the family." His father grinned sheepishly. "I'm surely not. Wouldn't know how to act as the owner of a race horse."

"But you wouldn't . . ." Alec began, only to be interrupted again by his father.

"I know I truly wouldn't own the horse, Alec. He'd always be yours. Still it would worry me," he said, rising to his feet.

Alec watched his father walk toward the door. He didn't want to argue with him or attempt to talk him into it. No, he didn't want it that way. His dad would have to go into it of his own volition or not at all. He saw his father stop as he came abreast of the textbooks on top of Alec's desk.

"Everything set for school?" his father asked. "Only about ten days left now before you go back." His brow furrowed. "What about the colt?" And then, without waiting for Alec's reply, he said, "Oh, yes, you told me Henry would be back by that time. He'll take care of him, I suppose."

It might as well be now as later, Alec decided. His voice faltered a bit at the beginning, then steadied. "I—I don't want to go back, Dad," he said. "I want to stay here and help Henry."

His father didn't speak for a long time, and when Alec raised his eyes he found him looking out the window again.

"For the past few years your mother and I have

allowed you to make your own decisions, Alec," he said quietly, and his voice, although strained, was without anger. "We did it knowing you had good judgment and figuring, I suppose, you'd be a better man for it. Our confidence in your ability to do the right thing has never been shaken. In fact, we're both mighty proud of you, even though your experiences have caused us great concern and worry at times."

He stopped, and Alec thought he'd finished—until his father turned around and looked at him. "But, Alec, you're going off on the wrong road this time. I know it, and you know it," he added quietly. "You love horses, and I thoroughly understand," he continued. "You want to be a trainer, learning all there is to know about horses. You want to be able to take care of their ailments and a lot of other things. And the courses you're taking in college will enable you to do just that," he concluded.

"Henry never went to college," Alec managed to say defensively.

"Ask him some time if, despite his practical experience, he might not have been able to do a better job if he had gone," his father returned.

Alec's gaze fell. Henry had already answered that question when he'd put it to him earlier in the day. "But it's only right that I be here to help Henry, Dad. Don't you understand?"

"Yes, I understand, Alec. But even *I* know you and Henry can't do much with that colt until he grows up some."

After a few minutes Alec looked up from the floor.

"Perhaps," he said slowly, meeting his father's eyes, "I could transfer to a college here in New York; then I could live at home and be around the colt."

"Yes, you could do that, Alec, *if* I had the money to pay your tuition. But I don't at this time. You're forgetting, aren't you, that you've a two-year scholarship up at school? And that I'll only have enough money to pay your tuition for the last couple of years?"

"Yes, Dad. I'd forgotten."

His father walked slowly across the room, speaking at the same time. "But it's your scholarship, and your decision to make, Alec." He stood there at the door for a long time, and the room was quiet again. Finally he turned and walked back to the bed.

"I'd like you to go back to school, Alec," he said. His eyes narrowed, and the tiny specks of light in them were cold and gray. "I'll make an agreement with you," he continued. "A few minutes ago you wanted me to register the colt in my name . . . to own him, while you rode him." He lowered his voice. "I'll do it, Alec, provided you go back to school this year. Next year, if you and Henry feel the colt is ready for the track and it would be more advantageous to his training to have you around, you can transfer to a New York college and I'll pay the tuition. You'll be living at home and that will save dormitory expenses. What do you say to that, Alec?"

There it was, right in his lap, Alec thought. And his father was standing there, awaiting his reply. Any way you looked at it, the proposition was a fair one. Everything was as he had wanted it . . . except that he would have to leave his colt. And he knew that his father and Henry were right about his going back to school. For in the end he'd probably be a better trainer. And, he reminded himself, it wouldn't be a full year away from Satan. There would be Christmas vacation coming up within a couple of months, and a short time later June would have arrived, and he'd have the whole summer to spend with his colt. And the following fall Satan would be nearly a two-year-old and ready for real training; then he'd transfer to a New York school and be around all the time. "Okay, Dad," he said. "It's a deal."

His father held out his hand and Alec grasped it, saying, "Guess we're in business, Dad."

"Yes," his father replied gravely, "I guess we are." He had started to leave the room after mumbling something about seeing Alec's mother, when Alec stopped him.

"There's just one other thing, Dad." Alec walked quickly over to his desk, sat down, and began writing. Moving over behind him, his father read what Alec wrote:

"To Whom It May Concern:
   I, Alexander William Ramsay, upon this date do sell my black colt, Satan, to William Augustus Ramsay, my father, for the sum of one dollar ($1.00)."

Mr. Ramsay saw his son hesitate as he neared the end of the note, look out the window toward the barn, then turn back to the paper. Quickly Alec signed and dated it before blotting the wet ink.

"I'm dating it tomorrow," Alec said slowly, ". . . we can go downtown tomorrow and have it notarized."

"Pretty official, isn't it?" his father asked, smiling. Then he saw Alec's drawn face and added seriously, "You're sure you want to handle it this way, Alec? He'll always be your horse, you know."

Nodding, Alec answered, "It's the only way, Dad." And handing the note over to his father, he said, "You keep it."

His father read the note again and then placed his hand in his pocket, withdrawing a dollar bill which he gave to Alec. Then he left the room.

And after his father had gone Alec stood looking out the window toward the barn, the dollar bill clenched in his fist.

Satan Runs Free

6

A week had passed since the colt's arrival, and the days had sped by quickly for Alec, too quickly . . . for on the following morning he was to leave for school. He had just finished building the wooden fence extending across the lower end of the hollow to keep Satan from the heavy underbrush and thistles, and now he sat down in the grass and wondered if Henry would arrive before nightfall.

Sebastian, who had been sitting in the shade of the tall oak tree on the rim of the hollow, pulled himself lazily to his feet and trotted slowly down the embankment. When he reached Alec, the dog slumped down in the grass beside him.

Alec stroked the puppy's wet coat. At least Sebastian

was as good as ever, he thought, and that was something to be thankful for. His thoughts turned again to Henry. The old man hadn't written, but perhaps it was better that way. If anything had gone wrong, Alec felt certain that he would have heard from Henry. But what if he didn't show up? What if Boldt made him fulfill his contract, and kept him out there for two more months? What about the colt?

The days Alec had spent around Satan had convinced him that the colt couldn't be left alone, not even with Tony around. For the black-haired huckster disliked Satan because the colt, in turn, hated him and old Napoleon. "In fact," Alec muttered, "Satan seems to hate everyone from the way he acts . . . even me."

He gazed once more at the fence on which he'd spent most of his time during the past week. Everything was ready for Satan to graze in the field now, and maybe that would help matters. Alec knew the colt disliked the lead rope to which he had been held while grazing. Several times during the week he had attempted to break away, and once had even tried to savage him as he had Napoleon that first night. But Alec could handle him now. It was the months to come, when Satan gained in weight and strength, that bothered Alec.

And if Henry didn't get back, couldn't get back for two months, what was he to do? Alec had made an agreement with his father and would be held to it. Neither his father nor his mother would understand why he couldn't leave the colt in Tony's care. Nor did he want to tell them.

His father had gone through with his end of the

bargain, just as he'd said he would. The registration papers had been sent to the Jockey Club after Doctor Hancock had examined the colt and found him sound. Luckily, Satan had kept still under Alec's firm hand that day, and the doctor, who was a good friend of his father, had been impressed. "You've got a good piece of horse-flesh there, Alec," he had said as they left the barn. "A mighty good piece."

It was well that it had turned out that way, Alec thought, for he was sure Hancock had mentioned the same thing to his dad.

The application blanks for an owner's license, which Alec had also picked up at the Jockey Club, had been filled out by his father and mailed. And the bill of sale had been notarized the following day. Yes, Alec admitted, his dad had gone through with it all in his punctual, methodical way. He'd even done a good job, obviously, of breaking the news to Alec's mother, for although her face had borne a strained, gaunt look during the days immediately following the talk between Alec and his father, she had only cautioned Alec to be careful.

Alec rose to his feet and Sebastian looked up, waiting. He had to keep his side of the agreement, too, Alec told himself, for he was more than grateful for everything his father had done. There was no backing out now, even if it meant Tony's taking care of the colt until Henry arrived. But would Tony do it? Alec realized how terribly afraid Tony was of Satan.

Knowing that the huckster would be returning soon from his rounds, Alec picked up his hammer and tool box and made his way from the hollow, Sebastian barking at his heels.

He was still a good distance away from the barn when he saw Napoleon turn into the driveway. Tony was sitting on top of the wagon, holding the long reins. Alec whistled, and Napoleon raised his large, gray head and whinnied.

Tony had Napoleon unharnessed and was leading him toward the barn door when Alec reached them.

"I'ma glad you are here, Aleec," Tony said with great relief. "I no like to go in alone with *heem* there."

"He's in his stall, Tony," Alec reminded him.

"*Sì*, I know," Tony replied, shaking his head. "But he mak'a such a fuss. He no like Napoleon or Tony. We just walka by and he shows da teeth. An' beeg ones he has, Aleec, for such a little fella. Heesa no good, Aleec." Then as he saw Alec's gaze fall, he added quickly in a more patronizing tone, "But he will be, Aleec. Heesa not used to Nappy and Tony yet, but soon everything will be what you call hunkey dokey."

Tony's gaze followed Sebastian as the dog elusively ran between Napoleon's legs. "*Sì!* Looka da Sebastian. Already he forget to be afraid."

"I'd like him to be a little more careful, though," Alec said. "I have to tie him up whenever I take Satan out or he'd be under the colt's legs again. Here, Seb," he called, grabbing the puppy. "I'd better take care of you now."

Alec clipped the leash to the dog's collar, and then tied him to a hook on the side of the barn.

"You take da colt out now?" Tony asked, when Alec returned. And when the boy nodded, Tony said, "We go in first then, heh, Napoleon."

As they entered the barn, Satan raised his small head over the stall door, uttered a short, piercing whistle, then withdrew inside the stall and was still.

Tony heaved a heavy sigh. "I'ma glad he no want to see us," he said. "When he keepsa looking at me it makes me feela funny inside."

Alec didn't reply. He watched Tony as the huckster carried Napoleon's harness down to the tack room, his pace quickening as he passed Satan's stall. As things stood now, Alec decided, he couldn't see Tony taking care of the colt for even a few days, much less two months, if Henry didn't get back. Somehow he'd have to figure out another way—even if it meant talking to his father again about the whole business.

Returning from the tack room, Tony asked, "You heard from Henree?"

"No, but he'll be here any day now," Alec said with a confidence he didn't entirely feel.

Tony had Napoleon halfway into his stall when he stopped, looked quizzically at Alec, and asked, "But if Henree no come before you leave tomorrow, what you do with the colt?"

Shrugging his shoulders, Alec replied, "I really don't know, Tony. I'll have to figure out something." Pausing, he added, "Henry should be here. It's ten days since he left and he said he'd be back by now."

"Dio mio," said Tony to himself, as he finished leading Napoleon into his stall. "It'sa best for all of us that he come."

As Tony emerged from the stall, Alec saw the afternoon paper in the pocket of his denim coveralls. "Mind if I look at your paper, Tony?" he asked.

Tony removed the newspaper and handed it to Alec; then he trudged off toward the tack room again.

Turning the pages quickly, Alec found the sports section. Jim Neville's column was usually filled with authentic race track information, and he had been reading it eagerly for the past week, hoping to find something about Henry and Boldt.

Buried in the middle of the column, Henry's name leapt at Alec from the black type. Excitedly he read: ". . . Henry Dailey is back at the Mother Lode Ranch after a fast trip east. His boss, Peter Boldt, claims that the gray colt, Comet, out of The Lady and by his champion, Shooting Star, will be the fastest horse he's ever owned. Boldt is priming him for the Hopeful, great two-year-old race, two years off . . ."

Alec skimmed through the rest of the column. There was no further mention of Henry or Boldt.

Tony returned, and Alec handed him the paper.

"You take heem out now?" the huckster asked, as Alec moved toward the colt's stall. When Alec nodded, Tony pushed his way into Napoleon's stall, shutting the door behind him.

Satan saw Alec coming and his eyes blazed; then,

snorting his contempt, he moved far back into his stall. Picking up the lead rope, Alec opened the door and walked inside, his face tense and a slight gleam of anger in his eyes. He was discouraged and tired of having Satan act this way after more than a week here. All of them— Tony, Napoleon, Henry, Sebastian, and of course he himself—were the colt's friends. Couldn't he understand that?

Swerving, Satan kicked out his hind legs, coming dangerously close to Alec. Alec muttered and moved forward, keeping close to the side of the stall and avoiding the flying hoofs. He stopped and waited until the anger quelled inside of him. Satan was desert born, he reminded himself. Instinctively the colt was distrustful of every living creature, even those who meant him no harm. It would take time, perhaps a long time, Alec told himself, before the colt learned to trust them. And kindness on their part, more so than anger, would help bring it about sooner. He began talking in a soft tone, and then, when he saw his opportunity, closed in fast and had the colt by the halter. Lunging, Satan tried to bite him, but Alec pushed his head aside. "None of that, boy," he said. "It's bad manners."

As Alec led him from the stall, the colt attempted to push him hard against the side, but Alec turned his shoulders against Satan's light body, and the colt gave ground. "You'll be needing a few more pounds before you can get away with that, Satan," he said.

They moved toward the barn door, and the colt's head

turned toward Napoleon, who was looking out over his stall door. Beside him and a few paces back stood Tony, his eyes fearful.

Alec felt Satan's body quiver with eagerness as the colt came to a standstill and gave way to the fury that possessed him. Throughout the barn rang his challenge, hard and shrill. When silence prevailed once more, he raised his small head still higher. He seemed to be listening intently for some response from Napoleon.

"If you're looking for a fight don't pick on him," Alec said. "C'mon."

At first the colt resisted Alec, then with a disdainful snort he trotted alongside with high head and tail, his light hoofs slapping rhythmically against the wooden floor.

Leading him into the field, Alec allowed the colt to pull away until he had reached the end of the lead rope. Satan continued to pull, but Alec held the rope firmly in his hands, eyes upon his horse. The lush green grass rose above Satan's fetlocks as he stood there quietly, his ears pricked and nostrils quivering. Alec knew that his every faculty was keyed to the utmost, that the colt could and would do almost anything. And he wondered if it would be wise to give him his head, to let him run in the field, as his great sire had done. It was a sight that he longed to see, something to carry back to school with him. The wooden fence encircling the field was too high for the colt to jump over. Perhaps in a year he'd be able to make it, but not now. And the new fence at the south end, built just as high, would keep him out of the heavy underbrush on the far side of the hollow.

Satan's head jerked toward him; then the colt wheeled and slowly ran around Alec, who kept the rope taut. Suddenly Satan stopped, his head cocked again, his short mane swept back by the late afternoon breeze. His nostrils quivered, and his head moved back and forth before he stretched down to graze, his black muzzle buried in the long grass.

Alec left him alone for a long time; eventually he moved quietly up to him and took hold of the halter. The colt's head jerked upward and he turned savagely upon Alec, who kept close to him, avoiding the bared teeth.

Alec's fingers worked quickly as he unsnapped the lead rope from the colt's halter. Then he placed his hand upon Satan's silky neck. "Well, boy, you're free," he said. "Go to it. . . . It's what you've wanted."

The colt moved slowly away from Alec, as though he thought himself still held by the lead rope. Then, upon suddenly realizing that he was free, he bolted with a rush. Down the field he ran, stretching into a gallop. And as Satan ran, Alec felt his heart swell with pride at the beauty of his colt in action. In time Satan would be beautiful, swift and strong, just like the Black. Alec was certain of that. The strides the colt took now were short and unsure, but before many months went by they would be long, steady, and powerful.

Alec drew in his breath sharply as Satan headed for the east fence without slackening speed. Would the colt try to jump, even if it meant destruction? Did he prefer death to the loss of his freedom?

Then, relieved, Alec saw Satan come to a dead stop before the fence, and, wheeling, stand there shaking his head. Then he half-reared and was off again, more slowly this time, running alongside the fence with his head craned as though he were wondering what was on the other side.

"No desert over there, boy," Alec muttered. "You wouldn't like it."

The colt disappeared from sight as he reached the far end of the field and went down into the hollow. Alec left him alone, knowing there was nothing to fear down there as long as the colt wasn't able to get over the fence and into the heavy underbrush.

A few minutes later Satan reappeared, trotting back along the west side of the field. Upon seeing Alec, he stopped halfway up and bolted across the field.

Alec let the colt run until he had covered the field several times, his speed gradually lessening as he ran himself out.

Maybe this was just what Satan needed, Alec thought. Maybe it would make things easier all around.

The sun was hanging low in the west when Alec decided the colt had had enough exercise for one day. Satan was grazing in the middle of the field, and he raised his head as he saw Alec walk toward him. Then, wheeling, he trotted slowly toward the hollow.

"Good a place as any," Alec said, going after him.

He walked quickly, half running at times, for while the

colt had been grazing, Alec had been thinking; and he had decided that tonight he'd have to ask his father to let him stay at home a few more days, awaiting Henry. If his father didn't consent, he'd have to ask Tony to feed the colt until Henry arrived. But Alec didn't like to think about that.

Satan ran into the hollow, and a few minutes later Alec reached the rim. Looking down, he saw the colt grazing. Satan raised his head, snorted, and trotted alongside the fence.

Slowly Alec moved down the hill, attempting to force Satan into the southwest corner of the fence. Alec was talking, moving forward, the colt's wild eyes watching his every move. Alec was only a short distance away from Satan when the colt bolted.

Alec was ready for him. But Satan didn't go up the side of the hollow, as Alec had thought he would. Instead the colt charged straight down upon him, and only Alec's agility, as he threw himself to one side, prevented him from being hurt as Satan swept by.

White and shaken, Alec climbed to his feet. And as the colt disappeared over the top of the hollow, Alec made his way after him.

Satan had traveled fast and was down at the north end of the field, near the barred wooden gate which led to the barn. He was standing there, looking through the cross bars. Sebastian, still tied, was barking furiously at the colt. Alec quickened his pace until he was running.

The gate was a little lower than the fence, and Satan might possibly be able to jump over it. Alec didn't want to think of what might happen to Sebastian if the colt did break out of the field.

Satan was moving back and forth at the gate, his head held high, his eyes upon the barking dog.

Alec was still a good distance away when the colt whirled, trotted back a few yards, and then turned again, facing the gate. Alec ran as hard as he could, for he knew Satan was going to attempt to jump the gate. He was about to yell to attract the colt's attention when Satan moved forward slowly; unsure of himself, Satan was measuring the gate again. And as the colt came to a halt in front of it, his hoofs pawing the dirt, Alec moved quietly toward him.

The wind was blowing from the north, and Alec realized thankfully that his scent was being carried away from the colt . . . and also that Satan's intense hatred of Sebastian was occupying the colt's complete attention at the moment.

Satan was still standing before the gate, his flashing eyes defiantly focused on Sebastian, when Alec slipped up behind him, moved in close, and grabbed the halter, snapping on the lead rope at the same time.

As he felt Alec's hand upon his head Satan reared, carrying Alec with him. Pulling him down, Alec slapped him lightly on the muzzle and began talking. "You're my horse, Satan," he said. "You'll have to get to know me better."

Striking out, Satan attempted to pull away, but Alec's hand was firm, and after several more efforts the colt quieted down. Opening the gate, Alec led him toward the barn.

Sebastian barked incessantly as they neared the door, and there was a loud squeal of fury from the colt.

"Stop it, Seb!" Alec yelled at the dog.

The puppy's barking ceased at the sound of Alec's voice. Then, whimpering, the dog wagged his tail furiously and was still.

"That's it, Sebby boy," Alec said, again turning his attention to the colt.

A few minutes later he had Satan inside the barn and was walking him slowly to his stall. Tony had gone, but as they passed Napoleon the old gray horse raised his head. Satan turned toward him, but Napoleon met his smoldering eyes with only a short neigh.

A short time afterward Alec emerged from the barn and locked the door behind him. Unleashing Sebastian, he moved quickly down the driveway and through the iron gate, wondering what his father would say when he told him he'd like to stick around just a few more days until Henry arrived. A few more days . . . would Henry be back even by then?

He was nearing the porch when he heard the telephone ring inside the house; then his mother's voice reached him as she answered it.

He had the porch door open when he heard his mother say, "Just a minute, he may be coming now. I'll let you talk with him, Henry."

Henry!

Alec was running when he entered the hall foyer. Excitedly he questioned his mother. "Where is he, Mom? He isn't in California, is he?"

Then as his mother handed him the telephone, he heard Henry's voice. "Naw. Naw, Alec. I'm right here . . . at the airport. Just thought I'd call an' tell you I'd arrived, an' everything was okay." Alec heard Henry's deep chuckle as the old man added, "Even thought you might be worryin' about me some."

"Me worrying? Not me, Henry. I knew you'd be here."

"Sure thing." Henry paused. "I got your letter about your going back to school, Alec. I'm glad . . . best thing."

"I'd rather be sticking around, Henry." Alec lowered his voice. "The colt . . . he's still acting up. It's going to be tougher than we thought . . ."

There was a long silence at the other end of the wire.

"Henry . . . y'still there?"

"Sure. Sure, Alec. Now don't get all excited or het up about Satan . . . he'll turn out okay," Henry said reassuringly. Then, "You're leavin' tomorrow?"

"Yes, Henry. Tomorrow morning . . . early."

"Then I'll drop over for a few minutes tonight. After I've checked in with the missis," he added.

"Okay, Henry."

"Oh, Alec."

"Yes, Henry."

"Guess we're off, heh?"

"Right, Henry, and all the way to the wire."

"To the wire," the old man repeated.

"And I'll be back just before Christmas," Alec said. "It's only a few months, that's all it is."

"Sure, Alec. Sure," Henry replied. "An' don't you worry none . . . about the colt, I mean."

His mother was still there when Alec put down the receiver. "Is everything all right, Alec?" she asked with concern.

"Guess so, Mom." Then he saw the anxiety in her eyes and, grinning, placed his arms around her plump waist. "Sure it is," he said. "Sure it is, Mom."

Smoldering Fury

7

As the train neared New York City, Alec fingered the rubber band wrapped around the small package of letters he held in his lap. Then, his face sobering, he turned to the window again. And the snow-covered landscape, with the brightly lit houses and colored Christmas tree lights reflected upon the whiteness, passed by without his consciously seeing it.

It was only when the conductor lumbered down the aisle bellowing, "Gr-rand Ce-entral Station—next. Last stop!" that Alec's gaze returned to the crowded car and the letters in his lap.

That Henry was having trouble with Satan Alec knew, not so much from what the old trainer had written during the past three months while Alec had been away at school, as from what he'd left unsaid. The greater part of Henry's letters had been concerned with incidental information about Tony, Napoleon, and mutual acquaintances in Flushing. When he had mentioned Satan it was only to say that the colt was getting huskier every day, and was going to be a big yearling.

Alec knew Henry too well not to realize that his friend was keeping much about Satan to himself. And then Henry's last letter had arrived, just a few hours before Alec left school for his Christmas vacation at home. If Alec had had any doubts about his ability to read between the lines of Henry's letters, the old man's postscript in his last one had done away with them completely.

The rubber band snapped beneath Alec's fingers as he withdrew the letter from the package. Then he read the postscript again. "P.S. I'm enclosing a snapshot of Satan, Alec," Henry wrote. "You'll notice that the colt has developed a whale of a lot in the past few months. He's going to be a big horse, all right, maybe even bigger than we thought, because he sure is big-boned and thick-bodied. He ain't going to be pretty to look at like the Black—some folks might even call him ugly—but I'm sure from his barrel and haunches that he's going to get places in a hurry. And he's a handful to handle, Alec. It'll take a long time."

Alec picked up the snapshot Henry had enclosed with his letter, and as he looked at the picture of his horse, the heaviness left his freckled face. Satan was becoming burly all right, he mused. And the colt wasn't going to have the beautifully molded form of the Black, as Henry had said. Satan's head was small, but it was wider than the Black's, and his neck was thicker and his ears heavier. But certainly, Alec thought, no one could call him ugly. For his giant body was fired with a volcanic fascination that was beautiful in its smoldering fury. And yet Alec knew that this mighty power had to be checked in some way if Satan was ever to be completely his. Somehow he had to win the love of his colt.

As the train sped into the tunnel which would take them under the city and into Grand Central Station, a tall, angular boy entered the car and, seeing Alec, made his way hastily down the aisle toward him.

"What have you been hiding out for?" he asked as he sat down in the seat next to Alec. "The gang's up in the first car."

"Had some work to do," Alec said, slipping the letters inside the pocket of his jacket.

"Relax," the boy said as he raised a long leg, pushing his knee against the seat in front of him. "It's vacation time."

"Sure, Whiff, I know," Alec replied, smiling. "Merry Christmas."

"Ah," Whiff said happily, "it's going to be a great time. I've got some good parties and dances lined up already. How about you?"

"I'm sitting 'em out and sticking around home," Alec replied.

"You're crazy."

Alec shrugged his shoulders.

Whiff turned to him. "A girl I know is giving a party on January second. Like to come along? It should be good."

"Thanks, Whiff, but I've got a party on myself that night. A birthday party," he concluded.

"I thought you were sticking around home?" Whiff returned.

"I am. It's going to be at home."

"Your birthday?"

"No," Alec said. "My colt's—he'll be a yearling."

"Kinda silly, isn't it? Having a birthday party for a horse?"

"It's all in the way you look at it," Alec replied quietly.

Whiff rose to his feet as the train rolled slowly into the station. "I'd better hop onto my bag," he said. "If you change your mind about sticking around home, give me a ring, Alec."

Alec watched Whiff push his way through the crowded aisle. No, he thought, there wouldn't be any changing his mind, not with Satan at home.

As the train came to a stop, Alec pulled down his bag from the rack above him and joined the line of passengers moving slowly from the car.

Once outside his pace quickened, and when he passed the large clock in the station he saw that it was almost midnight, and that the train had been a half hour late. It would take him about three-quarters of an hour more to get to Flushing, and he wondered if his mother and father would still be up when he arrived home. And Satan—he wanted to see him tonight, too.

When he reached the subway, he ran down the stairs and caught a Flushing train that was just pulling up alongside the platform. He entered the car, sat down, and thought about his horse again.

Henry had mentioned in his last letter that it would take *a long time* with Satan. Exactly how long did Henry mean? Months? Years? Was the colt acting up so much that Henry even doubted their being able to race him as a two-year-old? According to the training schedule they had set for themselves, Alec was to begin riding Satan sometime this coming summer and then they'd go into the track workouts during the fall and winter months, just prior to Satan's second birthday. Then, if all went well, they'd bring him out that year in the Hopeful at Belmont. The Hopeful! It made Alec a little dizzy just thinking about it, for he knew that all of the fastest two-year-old thoroughbreds in the country would be there. Boldt's Comet, the gray colt that the racing world was waiting to see, would be running in it. And along with the others would probably be Mr. Volence's horses.

It had been Alec's suggestion that they enter Satan in the Hopeful, and Henry had finally agreed that they might as well shoot for the big race two years off. Surely, Alec thought, they'd have Satan ready to race by the time the Hopeful was run! Even Henry's admonition that it would take "a long time" couldn't mean almost two years! And in spite of Henry's pessimistic outlook and the apparent savageness of Satan, Alec felt that some way, somehow, he could win the love of his horse—as he had done with the Black.

When the subway train reached Flushing, Alec got off, waited impatiently in the cold night air until the bus came along, and rode to his corner. Then he was striding quickly down the snow-laden street, his eyes on the darkened barn, black against the winter backdrop. To make walking easier, Alec followed the automobile tracks until he was opposite his house. There was a light in the living room, and he knew his mother and father were waiting up for him. Turning, he looked at the barn again and his fingers found the gate keys which were in the pocket of his coat. Momentarily he fumbled them, unde-cided. It would take only a few minutes—just a fast look was all he wanted. His mother and father would under-stand.

Quickly he broke a path through the new snow, trotting to the iron-barred gate. The key turned hard and the gate creaked in the cold as Alec pushed it open enough to slide inside. Then, trotting again, he plowed through the snow, which rose almost to his knees.

Upon reaching the barn, he fumbled with the lock and then swung the door open. Inside he switched on the light. He stopped at Napoleon's stall as he walked through the barn. Lying on his straw bedding, the old gray horse looked up and neighed when he saw Alec.

"Go back to sleep, fella," Alec said. "I'll see you tomorrow."

Alec's pace slackened as he approached Satan's stall and saw the colt standing there, his head raised above the door and the perfectly shaped diamond a startling white against his black forehead. Their gazes met and held for a few seconds; then, snorting, the colt moved back in his stall as Alec approached the door.

"It's me, boy. You're my horse, remember?" And as Alec stood there against the door, talking softly to Satan, his keen eyes moved over every inch of his horse—from the heavy ears, which now lay back almost flat against his head, to the powerful haunches. There was no doubt about it, Alec thought. Satan was going to be big and burly. As big as the Black and, perhaps in time, heavier. Remembering the magnificently sleek body of the Black, Alec wondered if the burly Satan would have the speed of his sire. And he knew that only time would give him his answer.

After a few minutes, Alec opened the stall door and slid inside, keeping close to the wall. He moved slowly, his eyes on the colt and unafraid. The barn light enhanced the ebony sheen of Satan's black body. And as the colt stood there, his deep-set eyes flashing, Alec thought him beautiful, and wondered how Henry or anyone else could think of him as being ugly. And he felt sure that regardless of the bulk and weight which Satan might carry in the years to come, he would have the agility and swiftness of the mighty Black.

Turning his attention to Satan's head once more, Alec felt his heart skip a beat—for more than anything else, the colt's sculptured head reminded him of the Black. That, and the delicate lines of his neck, revealed without a doubt the fine qualities of his blooded forebears.

Satan's body trembled as Alec approached, talking all the while. Then he moved quickly, as the colt's hindquarters turned toward him. And when Satan's hind legs flew back, Alec was close beside his head, a hand already on the colt's halter.

"You've forgotten, Satan," he said softly. "We've gone through all this before. You're my horse, and you must learn that."

He stood there for a long time, stroking the colt's neck, and hoping the fury he could feel inside of Satan would subside. But as the minutes passed and Satan's body still trembled beneath his hand, Alec knew that he had failed, and that further attempts to win the colt's confidence would have to wait until the following day.

"Okay, boy," he finally said, "I'll be seeing you tomorrow."

Still unafraid, but mindful of Satan's rapidly acquired strength, Alec led the colt almost to the door before he released his halter. Quickly he slipped through the stall door—and not a second too soon. For Satan, moving with the quickness of a striking snake, hurled his forelegs at Alec, narrowly missing him, and his hoofs crashed against the wooden door.

Alec's face was white and drawn as he shut the door securely behind him and turned to Satan. The colt's eyes were bright, his teeth were bared, and his body was trembling with the fury that possessed him. Alec's gaze remained on those eyes for a long time. They were deep-set like the Black's, but burning in them was something which hadn't been in the eyes of the colt's sire. It made Alec uneasy, but he finally shook off the feeling. Satan would be his, too, in time.

Snorting, the colt let his hoofs fly again at the stall door, and the heavy sound they made rang through the barn. Alec heard Napoleon's short neigh, then all was quiet again.

Satan would have to be watched closely now. He was getting strong enough to do real damage with those hoofs. Alec wondered how well Henry was getting along with the colt. If Satan acted up constantly the way he had tonight, Henry certainly must have had his hands full just taking care of him from day to day.

The colt had retreated to the back part of the stall, his hoofs pawing the straw until they found the wooden flooring. Alec's gaze left him and turned to the lock on the stall door to make sure he had it fastened securely. And it was then that he saw the long thin iron chain hanging on the adjacent post.

He moved his hand over to it and fingered the iron links thoughtfully. The chain, he knew, hadn't been there before he left for school . . . before Satan had occupied this stall.

Suddenly his fingers tightened about the chain and the muscles in his jaws worked convulsively. He opened his hand and looked again at the short black hairs he had seen on the bottom links. Short black hairs that could have come from Satan's body! Alec shook his head.

Surely Henry couldn't have used this chain upon the colt! He couldn't have struck him with it!

Alec stood there for a long while; then he made his way from the barn. And as he walked through the snow toward home, his face was gaunt with concern.

Throwback!

8

Henry was the first to arrive at the barn the following morning. He stopped when he saw the footsteps in the snow leading from the gate to the barn and back again. He realized then that Alec was home and had visited the barn sometime during the night. The old man stood there for a few minutes without moving, his face grave. Then with heavy feet he went into the barn.

Napoleon whinnied when he saw him, but Henry's eyes turned to Satan's stall. Perhaps, he thought, it was best that Alec had visited Satan beforehand. Now Alec had seen the colt for himself . . . it would be easier telling him.

The colt shook his head, snorting, as Henry walked up to the door. Momentarily the old man's eyes shifted to the long chain hanging on the post, then he unlocked the door and stood there, waiting. The colt moved restlessly, his eyes upon Henry. Finally the old man saw his chance to move in, and with a lightness that belied his heavy frame and age, entered the stall and closed in upon Satan's halter. The colt fought him a moment, then stood still. Cautiously Henry led him from the stall to the cross ties, his eyes never leaving the colt and his senses alert for anything Satan might do. When Henry had finished grooming the colt, he took him back to his stall and locked the door again.

It was more than a half hour later when Alec entered the barn. Henry's face lightened as he lumbered forward to greet the boy. "It's good seeing you, Alec," he said, his arm going around Alec's shoulders.

"It's good seeing you too, Henry," Alec returned, looking at him searchingly.

Their eyes met, and Henry's sobered with Alec's. It was just as he'd figured, he thought. The kid knew, and they might as well come right to the point.

"You were here last night," Henry began.

Nodding, Alec said, "For a little while."

"What do you think of him?"

Looking at Henry quizzically, Alec asked, "What do you mean, Henry? He's going to be burly, as you said. And it'll take time as you also said. He didn't seem to remember me very well last night. But Satan will come around, Henry. I know he will," Alec concluded convincingly.

Henry shot him a rueful glance as he muttered,

"Mebbe, Alec, an' mebbe not. I'm not so sure *now*."

Alec turned to Satan's stall, and his eyes were upon the long chain hanging on the post as he said slowly, "How much trouble are you having with him, Henry?"

"Enough," Henry replied gravely, "an' he's gettin' harder to handle with every pound he puts on."

Alec turned to Henry again, and what he had to say came hard. "You wouldn't be using that chain on him, would you, Henry?"

The color left Henry's face, leaving long heavy lines etched deep against the whiteness of his skin. He suddenly looked very old and tired, and Alec's gaze dropped before the anguish and disappointment in Henry's eyes.

Before answering Alec, the old man looked at the chain. Finally he said slowly, "That was below the belt, Alec."

"I didn't mean it to be, Henry," Alec said sincerely. "It's just that I saw it there last night, and I thought . . ."

"That I was using it on the colt?" Henry interrupted. "You couldn't, Alec! Did you really think I was trying to bring him around by beating him?"

"I didn't know, Henry," Alec replied, trying to explain. "I didn't know what the colt was like, or what you were going through with him."

"You should know me better'n that though, Alec," Henry said. Then, seeing the despair in the boy's face, he placed his hand on Alec's arm. "But I understand how you musta felt, finding the chain like you did," he said. Pausing, he added in a low voice, "Fact is, Alec, I do have it there to use . . . but only providin' I need it."

Alec thought of his visit to the barn the night before and of how narrowly he had escaped the colt's hoofs as he was leaving the stall. "You mean, Henry," he asked slowly, "he's that bad?"

"It's been pretty bad sometimes," Henry replied, "and I'm not gettin' any faster in my old age. The chain is there for my own protection, and I'll admit I'd use it if he got me in a spot where I had to save my own skin."

At the other end of the barn, Satan craned his head over the stall door. When he sighted Alec and Henry he pricked his ears forward, snorted, and withdrew inside.

"I'm sure we'll win him over, Henry," Alec said determinedly. "He just can't live here months on end without finally coming around, learning to trust us."

Henry stood looking at Alec as though undecided whether to go on or not. Finally he said, "Alec, we're both in this together, right up to our necks, so I'm thinkin' I oughta tell you exactly what I think about Satan. An' I'm goin' to let you have it with both barrels, even knowin' how much you love him." Henry paused and led Alec over to a couple of chairs, where they sat down. Then he said, "Alec, I've been around horses all my life, thoroughbreds and broncs, but I'm tellin' you that this is the first time I've ever been really worried about a horse. An' I'm rememberin' the Black. But I'm also rememberin', and you should too, 'cause it's important, that you won the Black's love by findin' some food for him on that desert island when he was starvin'. He loved you, so you could control him . . . an' there wasn't any need of my worryin'. But it's different with Satan. He doesn't love you . . . he doesn't love anybody, even hates old Napoleon. He ain't even capable of lovin', to my way o' thinkin'."

"But," Alec interrupted, "you could have said that of the Black too before we were together on the island."

"Sure, I know, Alec. An' mebbe someday you'll be able to get it out of Satan, too. I hope so, but right now I'm doubtin' it." Henry's voice rose slightly as he continued, "To my way o' thinkin' Satan is a throwback to that wild sire of the Black's whom Abu never could keep in that mountain stronghold of his and who mebbe even today is roamin' wild and free. The Black had that wildness in him all right, and from the looks of Satan it's in him, too, mebbe even worse this time. Take a good look at his eyes, Alec, an' you'll see it there . . . the desert burnin' right in 'em. We can handle him now, but in six months or so, with him puttin' on weight like he is, this barn ain't goin' to hold him. Mark my words."

Alec's hands were clasped upon his lap and he was looking at the floor when Henry finished. "What are you suggesting, Henry?" he asked without looking up.

"I'm not suggestin' anything, Alec. He's your horse, an' I'm only tellin' you what I think and feel about him. He's goin' to be a very dangerous horse, Alec, an' mebbe I'm thinkin' of you climbin' up on his back next summer. An' mebbe, too, I'm thinkin' of your folks."

Alec's eyes met Henry's, and he was silent.

Then Henry said, "They've given you a free hand all along because they figure you'll do the right thing. I wouldn't like to see anything happen.''

"You don't think I'll be able to handle Satan then. Is that it, Henry?''

The old man placed a gnarled hand on Alec's knee. "You can ride with the best of 'em, Alec. An' you know horses, there's no doubt about that. But it's goin' to take more than that to handle Satan. Remember, son, you'll have to do more than just stay up there on his back. You'll have to control him so he'll never give way to the fury that's inside him. It'll be important when you're out there alone, an' even more important when he's with other horses. He'll want to fight, Alec—it's in him, every inch of him.'' Henry lowered his voice as he concluded, "I thought it was goin' to be different this time, but it ain't . . . and as things stand right now I can see it gettin' worse.''

"I'll win his love some way, Henry,'' Alec said determinedly. "Give me next summer to work on him!''

"Our workouts should start then,'' Henry said, "if we want to have him ready for the Hopeful.''

"He'll be ready. I'll get to him, Henry.''

"You still want to enter him in the Hopeful? Even now, after hearin' what I've told you about him?''

Alec nodded.

"It'll cost money, Alec,'' Henry warned. "Lots of money, to start him in that big race.''

"I know, Henry,'' Alec replied. "But I've got a lot saved and I'm saving more by working nights on the local town paper up at school.''

"I'd just hate to see you lose your dough if things don't

work out an' he ain't safe to put in the race," Henry said. "You'll lose every nickel you've shelled out in nominatin' him and keepin' him eligible, y'know."

"I won't lose it," Alec returned slowly. "He'll be in the race, and I'll be up on his back, Henry."

Henry smiled for the first time. "You're a cocky kid, Alec . . . an' mebbe it's better that way. I hope so." Rising to his feet, he walked to the barn door, opened it, and looked out. "It's gettin' warmer," he said.

"About six months until summer," Alec said.

Henry looked at him, then said thoughtfully, "Yeah, six months. He'll be a year and a half old by then . . ."

"And a yearling in a few more days from now," Alec added. "We'll have a party right here in the barn for him, won't we, Henry? We'll ask Tony and my folks . . ."

"You want your folks here?" Henry asked, walking back to Alec.

"Yes," Alec replied quietly. "It'll be better that way. If we didn't ask them they might think something was wrong."

"Not that it is," Henry said slowly.

"No . . . not that it is," Alec repeated.

They were silent for a while; then the sound of Satan's hoof striking the sides of his stall attracted their attention. Alec rose to his feet and, standing beside Henry, asked, "Have you had him outside much?"

"Not this past week," the old trainer returned. "It's been snowin' a lot an' I thought it best to keep him in." Pausing, he met Alec's gaze. "He could use a little exercise this morning, an' the footing ain't so bad out there.''

"He's restless. It might help some to get him out, Henry. Let's do it.''

They walked the length of the barn in silence until they reached Satan's stall. As Alec put his hand on the door Henry asked, "You want to take him?''

Alec nodded and Henry turned over to him the longe line he had picked up on the way. "Careful,'' he cautioned. "He's fast and tricky.''

Well remembering the close call he'd had the previous evening, Alec replied, "I know, Henry.''

Satan turned around restlessly inside the stall, his eyes upon the two figures. Opening the door, Alec began talking to his horse. And behind him he heard Henry say, "Move fast, when you move.''

Watching Alec with a fixed, stony gaze, the colt shook his disheveled head and his black mane fell low about his neck and over his forehead, blanketing the white diamond there.

"You're going to stretch your legs, Satan,'' Alec said softly. "You're going to play. You'll feel better, boy.'' And as he continued talking, he awaited his chance to move in and around the colt's haunches.

After a few minutes Satan's ears pricked forward and his eyes, leaving Alec, turned to Henry. Moving fast, Alec was close beside Satan, his hand slipping quickly to the colt's halter.

"Good boy,'' Henry said, opening the stall door.

Feeling Alec's hand upon his head, Satan uttered a short, shrill whistle and half rose. But Alec held him close and snapped the longe line upon the halter. Coming down, the colt turned upon him with bared teeth, and Alec hit him lightly on his muzzle. "None of that, Satan," he said sharply.

It was a good while before Alec felt the colt quiet down beneath his hand. "I think he's ready now, Henry," the boy called.

Mindful of Satan's cunningness, Alec led him cautiously from the stall and through the barn. As they passed Napoleon's stall, the colt stopped and uttered his piercing challenge once more. Old Napoleon raised his head over the door and neighed back.

Henry grunted. "Guess Satan never will get used to havin' Napoleon around."

As they reached the barn door, the colt's ears pricked forward and his attention was held by the white carpet spread before him. The air was crisp and cold, and Satan's vaporized breath could have been smoke from the smoldering fires that burned within him.

"He's everything a horse should be, Henry," Alec said.

"Beautiful . . . arrogant . . . ruthless," the old man muttered. "He'd be wonderful if we didn't have to control him."

The wind whipped through Satan's mane as Alec led him into the snow. Moving lightly, as though he could have stepped on eggshells without breaking them, the colt pranced beside Alec as they moved away from the barn.

They came to a stop near the gate leading to the field. "The snow ain't so deep here," Henry said. "I'd give him the length of the longe line, but no more. We'd have a tough time catchin' him in this snow if he got away."

Nodding, Alec stroked the neck of his horse and, as Satan pulled away, allowed the line to slide through his fingers. The colt sidestepped away quickly, and only when he had reached the length of the line, a good twenty yards, did Alec draw him up. For a few minutes Satan fought the line that kept him from his freedom, then turned his attention to the snow beneath his feet. He pawed it furiously.

"It's pretty new to him," Henry told Alec. "I only had him out once since we had this snowfall."

"He probably thought it was the desert again until he stepped on it," Alec said, watching his horse.

When the colt turned in their direction again, his heavy ears swept back, then pricked forward. Snorting, he circled the two figures and, longing to be free, pulled on the line.

"Keep a good hold, Alec," Henry warned.

The colt trotted for a long time, sometimes stopping and reversing his tracks on command, his eyes never leaving Alec and Henry. And the two turned with him, their eyes always on the horse.

"I wouldn't trust him any farther than I could throw him," growled Henry, as Satan paused and stood watching them. "Look at those eyes, Alec. You never saw that look even in the Black. It was there when we first got him. It'll always be there."

The colt was again moving around them as Alec said, "We've got to trust him, Henry, if he's ever going to trust us."

"Don't you think that for one minute, Alec," Henry said sternly. "For that's all the time it'll take for something to happen. I've been around him, Alec, an' I know. You let Satan show you he's trustworthy first, before you go trustin' him. I know how much you love him because he's the son of the Black, but don't you go forgettin' that he's not the Black. An' I'm sure no one ever told him that his sire loved you. An' mebbe it wouldn't make no difference with him even if someone had. That baby's sure got a mind of his own," he concluded.

Alec smiled at Henry's last remark, but his face sobered as he realized how serious Henry was.

"You're a horseman, Alec," Henry continued, "so don't you go forgettin' that y'can't let your heart rule your head with Satan. Remember, there's a whale of a lot of difference between bein' afraid of a horse and appreciatin' the power in his body and what he's capable of doin' with it. Keep your head, Alec."

"I will, Henry," Alec promised. After pausing, he added, "But you've sure been painting a black picture."

Jerking his head toward Satan, the old trainer said, "Look for yourself, Alec. His eyes haven't left us for one minute since we've been out here. One of these days it wouldn't surprise me to see him come plungin' at us instead of just tryin' to get away. I've thought of it many times, standin' here just like we're doin' now."

Alec shook his head. "I can't see him doing that, Henry, even though I respect everything you've said about Satan. He'd give anything to be free . . . he still doesn't trust us, and maybe he's even afraid. But he's no killer, Henry. I'm sure of that."

Shrugging his shoulders, Henry said, "Hope you're right, Alec . . . and I'm hopin' even more that durin' the summer, when you can be around all the time, you'll win Satan's love somehow. But it may take longer'n that . . . or it may never come at all. The love of a horse for a human is a strange love, an' I've only seen it come to a very few."

They stood there for a long time, busy with their thoughts, their eyes always upon the black colt who moved constantly about them. Then suddenly a woman's voice called from Henry's house.

"It's the missis," the old trainer muttered. "Guess she must be wantin' me for something." His gaze turned to Satan, then back to Alec. "You want me to help you take him in first?"

"I think I'll keep him out a little while longer, Henry. I won't have any trouble."

"Okay," Henry said, "but watch him, like I said. Mebbe I can get back in a few minutes," he concluded.

Henry was about fifteen yards from Alec when Satan began trotting slowly toward the old man.

"Watch out, Henry," Alec called to his friend.

Henry stopped, as though undecided whether to move on toward the house or to retreat from the snow-packed path the colt had made around them. Satan was still a good distance away from Henry, and Alec knew his friend had enough time to make up his mind. But automatically he shortened the line and moved a few steps closer toward his horse.

Then without warning Satan bolted, and the snow flew from beneath his hoofs as he bore down upon Henry.

Shouting, Alec saw Henry stop in his tracks, his face white. He turned back, retracing his steps.

With savage eagerness, Satan swerved and plunged forward, his eyes red and ears flat against his head.

The line was no longer taut in Alec's hand. He stood there helpless, as the colt moved down upon Henry. Then as the old man stumbled in the snow and fell to the ground, fury replaced the fear within Alec, and he raced forward.

Henry's fall caused Satan to misjudge his distance, and he swept past the inert figure in the snow without touching him. And before he had turned and wheeled back, Alec was beside his friend.

The colt rose above them in all his savageness, his blood on fire and the urge to kill great within him. No longer did his eyes smolder with contempt. Now they were alive and gleaming red with hate. And Satan's black body trembled with eagerness as his savage instinct drove him toward the kill.

But as he came down with thrashing hoofs, destined to blot out forever the hateful man scent tingling in his nostrils, he suddenly pulled up short and his hoofs drove into the snow. Shaking his head, his blazing eyes upon the man and boy, he rose again and fought whatever it was within him that had caused him to stop short with his pounding hoofs.

But he came down again without touching the man or boy, and then stood there, shaking his fiery head.

And Alec, unable to move, unable to leave Henry, was aware of the struggle going on within Satan's black body. Then, as the colt gathered himself to rear again, Alec sprang forward and grabbed his halter.

Once again, Satan moved with all the fury that possessed him as he felt the hand upon his head. Once again, the urge to kill was upon him. He leapt forward, seeking to do away with this boy who desired him to do as he willed. But the hand upon his head was strong and it swung him around. Screaming, he swelled to greater fury and, with gleaming teeth, attempted to turn upon the hand that held him close.

But Alec moved with the colt, avoiding his vicious lunges. And finally Satan stood still, his face flecked with sweat, his flanks heaving.

January 2nd

9

"You're crazy, Alec. I tell you, you are." Henry's voice was short and clipped. "You're lettin' this black devil crawl right inside of you. You've lost all reason. He's vicious and a killer, Alec. You've got to understand that. There ain't no struggle goin' on within his black heart like you say, either. He's all bad, and I'm all for gettin' rid of him. Sell him to Volence when he gets here in a little while. Sell him now, before it's too late. Volence will give you a fancy price for him. Still"—Henry paused, and the lights in his gray eyes flashed—"it would be a dirty trick to pull on a good friend like him. It would be better to put Boldt wise that there's a son of the Black, an' let him suffer with Satan!"

Alec said nothing, and only his eyes betrayed his

agony. For many days, ever since that terrible morning, Henry had been telling him what he was now saying once more. Through all the days that had preceded Christmas and thereafter, they had talked of nothing else. And it was the same today, this day of January 2nd . . . Satan's first birthday. Yes, there was going to be a party, as Alec had planned, but it would be a far cry from the kind of party to which he had looked forward for so many months.

Alec's eyes traveled around the barn, past the green holly and evergreens hanging upon the walls and beams, pausing at Satan's stall; and only the ring of the colt's hoofs striking the floor betrayed his presence. Then Alec's gaze moved on to Napoleon, who extended his long gray neck over the door of his stall, stretching for the holly that hung there. And finally Alec looked again at Henry.

He could read all that was written upon the old man's lined countenance. It was there even when Henry wasn't telling him by his words. But it was neither anger nor bitterness. Nor was it fear, despite his having come so close to death beneath Satan's hoofs. Anxiety and concern alone were written there. Anxiety and fear for him.

"I know how much you loved the Black, Alec," Henry said slowly, and his eyes and voice were sincere. "And I know how much you wanted to love Satan. But it can't work out, Alec . . . not when the one you love has no capacity for love. It never has . . . it never will." Henry paused a long time before continuing. "I love you as a son," he said, looking down at the holly in his hands. "If

I'd ever had a boy, I'd have wanted him to be like you, see. And loving you as a son, I don't want to see what can happen to you around such a killer. I'm an old man, Alec. I'm not afraid of him or anything he might do to me. It's you, with everything ahead of you, that I'm rememberin'. You . . . and your folks, who would feel the same as I, if they knew.''

Alec started to say something, then stopped short. What good would it do to say it all over again, when Henry had only scoffed at what he had said so many times in the past few days? What good would it do to say once more that he had not saved Henry by grabbing the colt in time? That it was something within Satan himself that had, momentarily, overpowered the strong urge to kill, an urge which had been instilled in Satan before he was born by his wild-blooded forebears. Alec was certain that a dreadful but surprising conflict had waged within Satan's black body as he had risen above them. And what had come once could surge more powerfully in the months to come. Alec believed that, and no one, not even Henry, whose experience he respected and whose friendship he cherished, could shake this hope from him.

But what good would it do to tell Henry all over again, to argue once more on this last day before returning to school? Finally he said, "I won't sell him, Henry. I couldn't do it.''

The old man looked at Alec for a long while, then lowered his eyes to the holly in his hands. "All right, Alec . . . if that's the way you want it. He's your horse, and I'll stick. I'll do everything I possibly can for him while you're away." Stopping, he raised his gray eyes and looked at Alec. "But this summer, when you come back, and before you climb up on him, promise me that you'll consider once more everything that I've told you. If he's still vicious, an' I'm thinkin' he will be, promise me you'll not get up on him."

Alec's eyes met Henry's and fell for a few seconds before his friend's unwavering gaze. Then he said slowly, "I'll promise that I won't try to ride him if I don't think I can handle him."

"No more than that?" Henry asked dubiously. "Even if I tell you at the time that he ain't fit to ride? He'll be big then, Alec, remember that. It's going to make what we've gone through seem like a picnic."

"I'll have to be with him, Henry. . . . I can't promise anything more than that now."

Shrugging his shoulders, Henry hung the holly upon the outside wall of the tack room. "You'll see for yourself this summer then, Alec," he muttered. "You'll see for yourself, an' you won't like it."

Dusk had deepened into night when Henry and Alec heard the iron gate creaking in the cold and the sound of voices coming up the driveway.

"Our first party guests," grunted Henry. "I'm still thinkin' it was a mistake to invite anyone. It would've been better to let Satan's first birthday go by unnoticed."

"For months we've been talking about it," Alec reminded him. "My folks would surely think we were having trouble with Satan if we decided not to have the party."

Looking at Alec critically, Henry said, "An' if somethin' goes wrong tonight, they'll surely know we are."

Alec didn't answer, but his face was sober and his heart heavy.

Henry went over to the tack room while Alec moved to the barn door. Opening it, he heard Tony's voice, carried easily to him in the night.

"*Si, si*, I know who you are, Meester Volence. I have heard much talk of you from Aleec and Henree. It'sa good you come to party. *Si*, it'sa good, ver' good."

Then, within the range of light cast from the barn, Alec could see Tony and a tall middle-aged man, not unlike Alec's father in stature, walking toward him. Upon seeing Alec in the doorway, Mr. Volence hastened forward, grabbing the boy's arm. "Alec," he said warmly. "It's been a long time." Then he saw Henry coming toward them, and grasped the old trainer's hand. "And you too, Henry," he added.

Tony had followed Mr. Volence inside the barn and was standing there, holding a small wooden crate in his arms.

"It'sa present for the black one," he told Alec without looking at him. And as he placed the box down on the floor he added, unhappily, "Why I do it, I do not know. He no like Tony or Napoleon, an' we shouldn't like heem."

"It's good of you, Tony," Alec said. Then, turning around, he saw Mr. Volence watching them.

The heavy jowls of the tall man shook as, laughing, he placed a cardboard box on top of Tony's crate. "And my present to the son of the Black as well," he said. "I hope you don't mind my barging in on your party, Alec, but I was in town for the holidays. And when I phoned Henry he told me about it.''

"You know we're glad to have you, Mr. Volence.'' Alec turned to Henry, his gaze thoughtful. The old trainer had said that he hadn't told Mr. Volence anything about Satan, but Alec wondered. Only a few minutes ago Henry had suggested selling Satan to Volence. But it made no difference whether Henry had or hadn't told Volence about the trouble they were having with Satan, Alec decided. For he wasn't going to sell the colt for any price.

Looking up, Alec found that Mr. Volence was gazing searchingly at each of them in turn. The man's jovial face sobered as he said, "You're not a very happy looking lot to be having a birthday party for the colt. Where is he, anyway?'' And as he looked in the direction of the stalls he added, "That's a good name you've picked for him, Alec. Satan . . . I like it. Plenty of fire there.''

With Henry leading the way, they walked slowly down the length of the barn.

"I saw the registration of your colt published in the Racing Calendar a month or so ago,'' Mr. Volence told Alec. "It hit me square in the eyes . . . 'Black colt by Shêtân—Jôhar; William Augustus Ramsay.' I figured,'' Mr. Volence continued, "that he was your father. And then I dropped a line to Henry, knowing you must be away at school, and he confirmed it. Smart of you to register the colt in your father's name so you can ride him.''

They were passing Napoleon's stall when Tony said, "I

stay here with Nappy, if you don'ta mind.''

Only Mr. Volence smiled at Tony's remark, and as he patted the old gray's head he said, "Tony still prefers Napoleon to any other horse you have here, I see.''

Alec nodded, and then they started once more toward Satan's stall.

The colt was far at the back when they reached him, and Mr. Volence, anxious to see the son of the Black, moved quickly to the door before Alec or Henry could stop him.

There was a loud squeal of fury as Satan, his teeth bared, lunged at the hand on the door. Stepping back faster than he had approached the door, Mr. Volence stood there quietly, his eyes upon the colt. Finally he said, "Like father, like son. His head is like the Black's, Alec. Ears are heavier, though. Neck thicker, too. What's his body like? Looks burly from what I can see of it.''

Alec had slipped quietly beside the stall door, and when Mr. Volence concluded, he moved fast and had hold of Satan's halter before the colt saw him. Satan shook his head savagely but quieted down after a few minutes. Opening the stall door, Alec slipped in close beside his horse, as the others, with Mr. Volence in front, stood in the doorway.

Henry's eyes were upon Alec as he held his horse, unafraid. But Mr. Volence's glance swept over the colt. After a time he said, "Satan won't fine down as the Black did. He's going to be bigger, heavier . . . might be too heavy for speed.''

Henry's eyes left Alec. "Look at the hindquarters and legs," he reminded Mr. Volence. "He'll have speed."

The tall man said nothing for a long time, then turned to Henry again. "You planning on running him next year?"

Henry shifted uneasily on his feet, then nodded in Alec's direction "There's the boss," he said quietly.

"We're running him in the Hopeful," Alec replied, his hand upon Satan's neck.

"Shooting for the big one, eh?" Mr. Volence grinned; then he added thoughtfully, looking once more at Satan's heavy body, "He'll have to have speed for that race. Six furlongs and a half," he reminded, "and every top two-year-old sprinter in the country will be in it."

The sound of voices coming up the driveway reached them, and Alec, with a final pat on his horse's neck, slipped quickly out the stall door. Satan shook his head furiously; then with a snort he moved to the back of his stall.

"He's certainly a wild colt, for having been around here for so long," Mr. Volence remarked. "I hope you're not going to have trouble with him."

"Not *going* to . . ." muttered Henry. But then, as Alec caught his eye, the old trainer stopped and turned toward the barn door.

Alec turned with him. His parents and Henry's wife were the only other guests invited to the party, so it must have been their voices he'd heard. When he'd left the house a few hours earlier, his mother and father had said they were coming to the party, but from the way they spoke Alec knew they weren't too keen about it. So far as he knew, neither of them had visited the barn since Satan had arrived, and his mother had never seen the colt. She still referred to him as his *pony*. Pony! It made Alec nervous even to think about it.

The barn door opened and Alec's parents entered, accompanied by Henry's wife, a tall, robust woman. Stomping the snow off their feet, they greeted the others and then proceeded to take off their coats.

Henry hastened forward and was followed by Mr. Volence and Tony, while Alec momentarily stood still, his eyes upon the cake his mother held in her hands. Burning in the center of the chocolate icing was a candle. She began walking toward him, her eyes shining, but only the trace of a smile upon her lips.

"Mom, you shouldn't have done it . . . but you did, and you're wonderful," Alec said, going forward to meet her.

"It's for your pony," she said. "I thought it should be chocolate, because you've often told me how black he was, and it's the closest I could come to it."

They stood there silently for a moment, looking at each other. Then, "Is he down there?" Mrs. Ramsay asked eagerly. "He really should see it, you know. After all, it's his birthday."

Alec hesitated before turning to Satan's stall. "He's in there," he said quietly.

And then his mother moved forward, too quickly for Alec to stop her, and she didn't come to a halt until she was in front of the stall door. "He's in the back, Alec," she said disappointedly. "Have him come forward to see his cake."

Alec stood beside her and saw the colt standing there with only his small head turned in their direction. "He's had so much excitement today, Mom," he said. "Maybe we'd better leave him alone."

"If you think so, Alec," she said quietly. "I surely understand how he must feel with all these people in the barn." She stopped for a moment, peering over the candle, and then said, "He has a small pony's head, doesn't he, Alec? But his body is very large. Why, he's almost as large as your other horse, the Black, and he's only one year old. I really never suspected it, Alec," she concluded.

"He's built that way," Alec said quickly. Taking her arm, he propelled her back toward the others. "Now let's eat Satan's birthday cake. I'm sure everyone wants some."

The party went off better than Alec had dared hope, for no one went near Satan's stall again. His mother, her curiosity temporarily satisfied, concentrated upon Mr. Volence and Mrs. Dailey, while Henry stood quietly beside them, only occasionally joining in the conversation. Alec's father spent a good deal of his time with Tony, and once moved over to Napoleon's stall to pat the old gray's head. Then before he walked back to the small group, he glanced apprehensively in the direction of Satan's stall.

Watching him, Alec had seen his father take a few steps

toward the stall, hesitate, then turn back, rejoining Tony and the others.

They had all insisted that Alec should cut the cake for Satan; and later, each holding a piece, they had faced the colt's stall and Mr. Volence's deep bass voice had led them through a chorus of "Happy Birthday." As they sang, Alec's gaze had moved slowly to each one of them—past the jovial, heavy-jowled face of Mr. Volence; the sheepish, uncomfortable look on the face of his father as he joined the chorus, the look of a man who would rather be some other place; the apprehensive smile of his mother, for she was not yet certain that this pony couldn't do him harm; and then to the hardened face of Henry's wife, the face of a woman who had lived too long around horses without loving them. And, lastly, Alec's eyes had swept swiftly over the strained faces of Henry and Tony, knowing that they, like him, were wondering what the next few months would bring.

Then, after they had finished singing, they had opened Satan's presents. Alec's face had softened when he received them for his colt. There was the crate of apples from Tony. The little huckster had smiled sheepishly as he had said, "From Nappy and me, Aleec. But it'sa better that you feed them to heem." And Mrs. Dailey's face had become less hard when she had said, "Henry and I decided, Alec, that the best we could do would be to give Satan a home. You can forget about the rent for his stall as long as you want him to stay here." And then his father had come forward in his brisk, businesslike way, with only his eyes smiling as he pushed a check into

Alec's hand. "It's something toward his upkeep, Alec, from your mother and me," he said. Coming forward, Mr. Volence had then handed him the long cardboard box. Upon opening it, Alec saw the solid black stable blanket with an inset of white in the shape of a diamond on each side. "Henry told me over the phone that your colors were going to be black except for a small white diamond," Mr. Volence had said. "I thought you could use the blanket."

Alec had thanked them and then had brought forth the light black leather halter which he and Henry had bought for Satan.

A little later everyone had left, leaving Alec alone in the barn with his horse.

As he moved slowly down the barn to see Satan for the last time before returning to school early the following morning, his eyes were moist. Roughly, he brushed away the tears. He had good friends, all of whom loved Satan as he did. And Satan would be worthy of their love. . . . He couldn't, *wouldn't,* let them down.

Killer!

10

The field was a lush green with rolling waves of grass when Alec came home again the following June.

And he found the horse that Henry had predicted he would. For Satan, picking up height and weight through the long winter months, was more vicious than ever, and Henry confessed to Alec that at times he'd had to use the wooden end of his broom to keep the colt away from him.

From the rear of Satan's large box stall in the barn, Henry had built a runway to the field so that the colt could go in and out as he pleased. And the fence encircling the field had been built three feet higher to make certain Satan could not jump over it.

Satan was a big horse now and still growing. He stood close to seventeen hands, and Henry estimated him to be "well over a thousand pounds" . . . heavier than any yearling he'd ever seen.

June passed into July, and July into August, and the time drew near when Alec was to ride Satan, according to the training schedule that had been set so many months ago.

"We ain't in no hurry," Henry said, as Alec brought up the subject once more. "We could wait until next spring," he added, turning to Alec.

"You're putting it off again, Henry."

The old trainer said nothing, and his eyes swept back to the colt grazing in the field.

As Henry and Alec watched Satan, the colt reared, struck out his hoofs, and then raced around the field, his head held high.

"He's playing, Henry. Look at him go!"

"Yeah, playful," Henry muttered, "but with the strength of a devil. An' over a thousand pounds is quite a handful," he concluded.

"I'm ready for him, Henry," Alec said quietly.

There was a long silence before the old man asked, "Remember the night of the party, back in January? Y'promised you'd think about everything I've told you about him, and that you wouldn't get up on him if I didn't think you should." Turning to Alec, Henry added slowly, "Well, now I know you shouldn't, Alec. He's worse than I've dreaded in my worst moments. He'd like nothing better than to catch either one of us off guard . . . an' that would be the end. He's a wild stallion, Alec . . . and mark my words he's goin' to have to be broken like one before it's ever safe to be around him!''

"I promised you, Henry, that I wouldn't climb up on him until I thought I could handle him. . . . That's all I promised,'' Alec reminded him.

"Well?''

Alec's eyes met Henry's. "I think I can, Henry. I want to try *now*.''

Henry heard the determined ring in Alec's voice, but the old man's eyes never wavered from the boy's tense face. And he didn't like what he saw there. Uncertainty was heavy in Alec's eyes. . . . He wasn't nearly as confident as he'd like to have Henry believe. When the old trainer spoke, fury was in his voice. "You fool, Alec. You young fool,'' he said. "With Satan you can't *think* you're ready for him, you just can't *try* to handle him!'' Lowering his voice, he placed a hand upon Alec's shoulder. "Don't you see, Alec, that one chance is all you'll probably get with this animal? An' one chance is all he needs if things go wrong.''

Alec turned to watch Satan as he cantered slowly around the field, his head moving to the right and left, all power, all beauty. Satan was his horse . . . his son of the Black, and he would ride him. For months and months, long before this colt had been born, he had longed to feel the surge of his mighty muscles beneath his legs. Was he to forget all this because of Satan's savage wildness? Qualities which to Alec made the colt what he was, the proud, noble son of a great sire? No, it was not in him to forget, Alec decided, and he would ride Satan in spite of Henry's warnings, in spite of the doubt which he too was beginning to have in his own ability to handle Satan.

Turning to his old friend, he told him, "I've got to ride him, Henry. And what does it matter if it's now or next spring? A few months off won't make it any easier, and if I stay on him we'll be that much ahead."

Without replying Henry turned around and began walking back to the barn. Alec caught up with him a few minutes later, and it was then that the old trainer spoke. His voice was a low, even monotone, and his face had a set expression. "We might as well start then, Alec, seein' you want it that way." He glanced over at the colt. "You chase him into the stall, an' I'll get the bridle ready." Then he walked into the barn, leaving Alec to get Satan.

Alec had walked over to the fence and had the gate open when he saw the broom on the ground. After hesitating a moment, he went over and picked it up, then carried it into the field with him.

Satan saw him coming, and with a snort trotted slowly toward the west fence. Alec let him go and continued to walk down the center of the field, planning to get behind the colt and chase him toward the runway.

Alec moved easily, his muscles loose, his mind clear. A few minutes ago, while talking to Henry, it had been different. . . . Then he had been unsure of himself. But now the contest had begun, and it was as he wanted it.

Now he was behind Satan. He started back up the field, walking a little faster and remaining to the right of his horse, keeping the colt close to the west fence. This procedure of getting Satan into his stall was routine with Alec now, for he had been doing it daily ever since his vacation started. And Satan too knew that he was being driven into his stall once more.

"But this time, Satan, it's going to be different," Alec muttered to himself as he moved behind his horse.

Satan turned as he neared the runway, and his ears pitched forward. Then with a short scream he broke across the field, but Alec, already running, headed him off, and Satan drew back on his haunches again.

Alec was only a short distance from him now. He saw Satan's ears sweep back until they lay flat against his head. Alec tightened his grip on the broom he carried and moved it a little higher in front of him. If it came to that, he was ready, he told himself. But the colt only shook his head until his black forelock fell down and obliterated the white diamond on his forehead. Steadily Alec gazed into Satan's blazing eyes and waited until, finally, the colt twirled and slowly made his way toward the west fence.

Alec walked slowly too, his muscles ready for any move the colt might make. Satan stopped when he came to the northwest corner of the field; the runway was just a few yards to his right. His head turned toward it, then back to Alec. He snorted, half reared, and came down pawing the ground.

Alec moved forward, the broom ready.

When he was less than ten yards away, he could plainly see the anger in the colt's eyes and the fury that possessed his black body. And it was then that Alec felt the uncertainty creep steadily through him again. For everything that Henry had ever warned him about Satan was there for him to see . . . the viciousness, the cunningness, the hate. For a moment, perhaps less, and for the first time in his life, Alec knew what it meant to be afraid of a horse. And he found himself wondering if he shouldn't wait until spring before riding Satan. But the thought passed quickly as a gust of wind swept across the field, catching Satan's mane and tossing it like windswept black flame. Momentarily the colt in front of Alec was the Black, standing there arrogant and ruthless . . . but *his* horse in spite of his savage nature.

Once more all fear of the colt left Alec and he moved forward, talking in his soft, even voice.

Satan's ears pricked forward, then lay back again; he snorted, his teeth gleaming. Suddenly he twirled and trotted slowly down the runway toward the barn. Alec followed, and when the colt entered the stall the boy closed the door behind him. Then he made his way back down the runway toward the front of the barn, wondering what lay ahead of him.

Inside the barn he found Henry waiting. In the old trainer's hands was the bridle they'd used on the Black.

"Let's go," Henry said. "We'll get this on him. He shouldn't mind it much. Not much different than a halter, except for the bit." The old man paused, and his eyes softened for the first time since Alec had told him of his decision to ride Satan. "You're sure, Alec?" he asked. "You want to go through with it?"

"Yes, Henry."

The trainer's body stiffened. "Okay, Alec," he said quietly. "It's in you to try to ride him, I know. Guess it couldn't be any other way. But I'd hoped . . ."

Satan swerved away from them when they entered the stall, but Henry and Alec closed in upon his head, backing him into a corner. Then, while Alec talked to his horse, stroking the black neck, Henry slipped the reins over Satan's head.

"This would be easy with any other horse," Henry growled. "Any other horse, after all these months, would know we weren't goin' to hurt him none."

Satan lunged at the old man when Henry approached him with the bit. "Get a better hold on his head, Alec," Henry said, his eyes never leaving the colt.

Alec moved his hand down on the soft nose, trying to keep Satan still. "It's not going to hurt you, fella," he said softly, "and it's got to be done."

Satan's fiery eyes were upon Henry, and when the old man moved toward him again, he bared his teeth and tried to break away from Alec's grip.

Henry moved in close and, with Alec firmly holding Satan's head, got the bit into the colt's mouth. Then he quickly pulled the bridle over the heavy ears and, fastening it securely, stepped back.

Satan shook his head furiously as he felt the bar of iron in his mouth. Henry stepped in again and helped Alec. Half rearing, Satan struck out savagely, but they brought him down, backing him into the corner. After a while the colt quieted down, and only his champing teeth broke the stillness.

Finally Henry said, "We oughta give him a few days to get used to this." The old trainer's eyes were upon Alec as he added, "And the same thing goes for the saddle

. . . a few days for that, mebbe longer. We'll keep the girth loose for a while, then gradually tighten it. No stirrups, either, for a while. . . . They'd only frighten him an' make it worse. In about a week or more you can be leanin' on the saddle, getting the colt used to your weight on his back. We'll see what happens then."

Alec said nothing. *A week or more,* Henry had just said. And he had thought he would ride Satan today! Why did he stand there, saying nothing? And why, at Henry's words, did this sudden sense of relief sweep over him? Words that meant a delay of days, maybe weeks, before he was to ride Satan. Was he really afraid of Satan? Was that it? Would the weeks of postponement lead to months? And would this fear of the colt eventually grow so strong that he would never have the courage to mount Satan? Alec's heart pounded and the blood rushed to his head at this sudden realization that he was glad to put off his riding of Satan. Hating himself, he turned toward Henry. "Today, Henry," he said slowly, and his own voice was unfamiliar to him. "It's got to be *today.*"

Henry looked searchingly at Alec, and when he saw the determination in the boy's eyes he knew that further appeal would be futile. After a long while he said, "Yes, Alec . . . you're right. It's got to be today."

Henry left the stall and a few minutes later returned with saddle and pad. "Let's get him back a little farther in the corner," he said. "He might try to jump out from under this stuff when we put it on him."

Still champing on his bit, the colt moved restlessly, his eyes upon Henry as the old man closed in on him again.

Alec began talking to his horse, his voice steady once more. And as he concentrated upon Satan, Henry placed the light saddlepad upon the colt's back. Alec felt Satan tremble beneath his hand.

Then the old trainer said, "Get a good hold, Alec . . . saddle next."

Satan bolted as he felt the weight of the saddle, but Alec kept him in the corner, and after a few minutes the colt quieted down with the saddle resting lightly upon his back.

"He's taking it better than I thought he would," Alec said.

Grunting, Henry replied, "He's as cunning as he is vicious, Alec. Mind you, don't trust him for one second."

Reaching underneath Satan's black body, Henry got hold of the cinch and drew it up slowly. "He ain't going to like this much. I'll tighten it just enough to keep the saddle on him, then we'll see what happens."

As the cinch began to tighten about Satan's girth, the colt shook his head furiously and attempted to break Alec's grip on his head. Failing, he kicked back his hind legs and his hoofs crashed into the side of the stall.

Finally Henry stepped back. "It's loose, but the saddle will stay on," he said.

They stood there beside Satan for a while, their eyes upon the colt's fixed, stony glare.

"I wish I knew what he was thinkin' about," Henry muttered.

"He's quiet, Henry, considering everything," Alec said.

"Yeah, but he's waitin' . . . waitin' to strike like a rattlesnake," Henry warned. "I still say we oughta sell him and get outa this while we're both still in one piece."

"There's no turning back now, Henry. . . . We've gone too far," Alec said slowly. His fear of the colt had passed and he wanted to go through with his plan now, regardless of the consequences. He couldn't back down and live with himself, knowing he had been afraid.

At last Henry said, "Let me have his head, Alec, an' you go put some weight on the saddle. Lean on it lightly at first, then gradually put all your weight on him."

Moving beside the colt, Alec did as Henry had told him to do. When he placed his hands upon the dark brown saddle, Satan jumped, but Henry held him down in the corner. And with the colt pressed hard against the wall, Alec gradually applied more weight until his body was resting heavily upon Satan.

As Alec stood in that position for a long time, with Satan quiet except for the shifting, deep-set eyes, Henry said hopefully, "Mebbe it'll work out, Alec. Mebbe he'll take it."

Then Henry turned Satan's head and led him from the stall while Alec walked beside the colt, his right arm and part of his weight still resting on the saddle.

Free of his stall, Satan jumped and Henry and Alec had a hard time with him before they had him under control. As they walked past Napoleon's empty stall, Henry picked up the lead rope and hooked it onto Satan's bridle. "We'll keep him on the rope so in case he bucks you off I'll still have hold of him," Henry said. Then he added,

"An' remember to fall clear, if he does let loose. An' you've got no stirrups, so use your knees good. I know you're not afraid, but you've got to remember what this horse is, an' be ready for anything."

Alec said nothing, but there was a hard look in his eyes and his body was tense.

Outside the barn, the colt moved more restlessly. He tossed his head, trying to rid himself of the iron in his mouth, and his body constantly swerved away from Alec as the boy tried to keep his weight upon the saddle.

They had gone through the gate and were a short distance within the field when Henry brought Satan to a stop. "This is as good a place as any," he said. "Try all your weight on him again and see how he takes it."

Moving closer beside the quivering body of his horse, Alec leaned heavily upon Satan. The colt gave ground, pivoting around Henry, who still kept a firm hand upon his head. Once Satan attempted to jump away from Alec, but the boy moved in hard against him, keeping his weight upon Satan's back.

"He's not buckin', anyway," muttered Henry.

For a long while they remained there with Henry holding the colt's head and watching both Satan and Alec simultaneously. Alec moved with his horse, his body keyed for the test he knew was coming. Occasionally a slight twinge of fear would pass through him when Satan's blazing eyes were turned in his direction, watching him, as though the colt too knew what was coming.

"Okay," Henry finally said. "Get his head, Alec, while

I tighten the cinch some more.''

Nodding, Alec moved forward and watched Henry tighten the cinch. Satan's smoldering eyes seemed to burst into flame when the cinch was drawn about his girth. And as Henry made the straps fast, the colt bolted and Alec had to hang upon his head to hold him. Then Henry was beside Alec, helping him, and within a short time they had Satan quiet again.

"The cinch ain't as tight as it should be, but the saddle won't roll." Henry was breathing heavily from the exertion of the last few minutes, and it was after a long pause that he said, "Guess that's about it, Alec. He's yours now . . . anytime you want to take him." And as Alec moved beside his horse again, Henry said almost under his breath, "Luck, kid."

Alec's face was ashen white and the blood was pounding in his temples when he placed his weight upon the saddle. From the corner of his eye he saw Satan attempt to turn in his direction. Then Henry moved his body and shielded Alec from Satan's blazing eyes. But Alec was certain that the colt knew what was happening and what he was about to do. With no stirrups, he would have to jump upon his horse, throwing his body across the saddle and then, speedily, for he might not have much time, get astride Satan.

Alec stood quietly balanced on his toes, his muscles tense and ready for the spring that would carry him up onto Satan. Moving restlessly, the colt slid away from him. His hands still upon the saddle, Alec moved with him. Then he took two short half-running steps and sprang into the air. His chest hit the saddle and for a fraction of a second his legs dangled over Satan's side. Then quickly, just as the colt bolted, Alec drew up his right leg and threw it over the horse. He had no opportunity to grasp the colt with his knees, for Satan was already bucking, throwing him forward. Alec found himself high upon the colt's neck, his hands desperately clutching the black mane to save himself from a fall.

As Alec recovered his balance, he saw Henry's hand high up on the bridle. Satan fought the old man, temporarily forgetting the weight upon his back. And by the time Henry had the colt under control, Alec was in his seat and his knees were pressed firmly against Satan's withers.

The colt moved restlessly but didn't buck again.

Alec sat there, and gradually his tense body relaxed and he gloried in the feeling of once again being astride a horse like the Black . . . astride the son of the Black . . . *his horse!*

After a few minutes he said, "Henry, you see, he's coming along. He's not bucking. Henry . . . he's going to be everything we wanted. And he can run, Henry, I can feel it all through him. He's charged with fire!"

"Stop it, Alec!" Henry's voice was as cold as ice. "Tend to your business up there. Keep those knees in. Take up the reins. Let go that mane." Henry's commands came short and fast, but his eyes never left the colt for more than a fraction of a second. "It would be better if he did some bucking," he rasped. "Then we'd know what to look out for. He's no bronc, Alec. He's worse . . . he's a killer. Be ready for anything, an' don't you forget it for one second."

Henry said nothing more and Alec, jolted by Henry's sharp words, sat still, his body and mind keyed once more.

Slowly Henry led Satan around in a circle, holding the colt to a walk. And as they went around time and time again, Alec would have relaxed in the saddle but for Henry's constant warnings and stern glances.

As Alec sat there, moving with his horse, he kept talking to him. "I'm not much to carry, Satan," he said. "Nothing at all for a horse like you. And this is what I meant, Satan, when I said we'd do it together . . . you and I. We're going to show them, Satan. We're going to . . ."

Alec stopped short as the colt swerved fast, pulling the bridle out of Henry's hands. Shouting a warning, Henry grabbed hold of the lead rope that was attached to the bridle.

A few feet away from Henry, Satan stopped, his eyes blazing with fire. Then he half reared and Alec's knees dug deep into the black body. Coming down, the colt turned upon Henry, and Alec knew that the old man was too far away to close in upon the horse. Satan moved toward him, then stopped as though suddenly remembering the boy upon his back.

Alec bent far forward close to Satan's neck as the colt

rose again. And this time he reared to his full height. Sliding his hands around Satan's neck, Alec clutched him desperately.

When the colt came down again, Alec saw Henry move toward him but then fall back as Satan's forelegs struck out.

Then the colt rose again, and he didn't stop until he was almost perpendicular to the ground. Only Alec's death-like hold around Satan's neck kept him from sliding off.

As he came down Henry yelled, "Get off him, Alec, and run for it! He'll kill you!"

But before Alec could jump off, Satan was rearing again. And this time, when he reached his utmost height, his eyes were a fiery red.

Alec felt the surge of the giant muscles. He flung himself hard alongside Satan's neck, hoping that his weight would bring the colt down. But Satan rose higher, and his piercing scream shattered the air. Alec heard Henry's shrill warning, "He's taking you over! Jump or he'll crush you!"

The color drained from Alec's face. Then the black head and neck to which he had been clinging fell back upon him as Satan went over backwards. Alec felt himself falling with the giant body coming down on top of him!

Peter Boldt

11

It was a week after the accident when Henry approached Alec's house. As he walked up to the porch, his gaze took in the open windows of the front bedroom, Alec's bedroom. It was good to see the window shades all the way up again, for during the past week, while Alec had been in the hospital, they had been drawn and had only served to make Henry feel more depressed whenever he had passed by.

It was different now, for Alec was home, and the crisp, white curtains gently swayed in the late afternoon breeze.

Sebastian raised himself from the hammock and trotted quickly toward Henry as the old man walked up the porch steps. The puppy was whimpering, and when he reached Henry his front paws began beating a light tattoo on the man's knee. Bending down, Henry ran his hand over Sebastian's brown head. "You're glad to have him back too, aren't you, Seb?" he asked.

The dog whimpered, bending his head backward so Henry could scratch his neck.

Mrs. Ramsay appeared at the screen door and said quietly, "It's nice of you to come, Henry. Alec has been asking for you."

Giving Sebastian a final pat, Henry walked to the door, which Mrs. Ramsay opened for him. Her face was tired and strained, but there was a relieved look about her eyes.

"He's going to be all right," she said, smiling a little. "The doctors were afraid of a back injury, but the X-rays showed nothing. They told us to keep him in bed for a few days, but then let him get up if he wants to. And I'm sure he will," she added, smiling. "Alec never was one to stay very long in bed, you know."

"I'm glad, Mrs. Ramsay," Henry said.

Sebastian slipped between Henry's legs, and with a short bark ran up the stairs.

Mrs. Ramsay let him go. "I've kept him away from Alec all day," she said, "but I guess it's all right now."

When they entered the hall Alec's father joined them, and as he shook Henry's hand, his face was lined with concern and his eyes were somber.

Mrs. Ramsay had already started up the stairs when her husband stopped her. "I'd like to talk to Henry first, Belle," he said deliberately.

She turned to her husband and a long look passed between them; then, nodding, she said, "All right, William."

When Mrs. Ramsay had gone into the kitchen, her husband motioned Henry toward the door and led him out onto the porch again. "I don't want her or Alec to hear what I have to say," he said.

Saying nothing, Henry moved over to the porch railing and sat down on it. He had a feeling something unpleasant was coming and that he might be able to take it better sitting down.

It was a few minutes before Mr. Ramsay spoke, and his words came slowly, as though he were weighing each one before uttering it. "You didn't tell us much about the accident, Henry, when you carried Alec home. There'd been a fall, you said, and he'd struck on the back of his head."

Henry's words came as slowly as had Mr. Ramsay's. "Well, that was about it," he explained. "Satan reared and Alec, with no stirrups, went off." Henry's eyes met Mr. Ramsay's without wavering, for he had decided long ago to tell no one, other than Alec, exactly how he felt about Satan. For Satan was Alec's horse and the boy should decide for himself what to tell his parents about the colt . . . even now.

Mr. Ramsay said quietly, "I know better, Henry. Alec is too good a horseman to fall off, with or without stirrups. You had trouble with the colt."

Henry said nothing, nor did his gaze drop before Mr. Ramsay's intent eyes.

After a few minutes Mr. Ramsay moved over to the railing and sat down beside Henry. "Remember the day at the pier, when we first picked up Satan?" he went on. "You told me that the breaking of the colt wouldn't be any fuss at all." Mr. Ramsay paused, then continued. "I believe those were your exact words, Henry. Furthermore, you said that Satan would have the utmost trust and confidence in you and Alec, so much so that he'd be very easy to control when it came to breaking him. And if I recall correctly it was I who mentioned that it was just possible Satan would have the savageness of the Black and it mightn't be so easy. You scoffed, Henry," he reminded him.

The old trainer shifted uneasily in his seat but still said nothing.

Mr. Ramsay said, "You don't want to talk about Satan, is that it?"

Henry nodded. What good would it do? he asked himself. He had been wrong, and he had known it with his first look at Satan's eyes. There were some things that Henry didn't care to discuss with anyone . . . and a horse with a savage intent to kill was one of them. He'd had to tell Alec, with the boy's life at stake, but he still believed that it was up to Alec to tell his father, if he wanted to.

And as they sat there in silence, Henry wondered how Alec now felt about Satan. Did he still look upon Satan as *his* horse or the killer that he actually was? Never would Henry forget the hideous sight of Satan, in all his fury, intentionally falling over backwards, hoping to pin the boy beneath his giant body. Never had he seen it happen before, with any horse, and he hoped never to see it again. If Alec hadn't kept his wits, if he hadn't been the horseman he was, he wouldn't have thrown himself clear of Satan's back as he'd done, and just in time. The boy had landed a little to the left of the colt as they hit the ground simultaneously, and then Alec's head had struck with a hard thud and he'd been still. And while Satan lay there on his back, his legs thrashing the air and the crushed saddle beneath him, Henry had carried Alec away.

What good would it do to tell Mr. Ramsay all that had happened? Fortunately Alec was alive and recovering. . . . Possibly it could mean the end of Alec's love for Satan and a closed book for both of them.

Mr. Ramsay's gaze was upon Henry again. "I know Satan for what he is, Henry," he said, and now there was a frigidness to his voice that commanded all of Henry's attention. "I went to the barn this morning," Mr. Ramsay continued, "after I'd brought Alec home from the hospital." He paused. "I'd felt something was wrong for a long time, I guess, and I wanted to see for myself. I did, Henry. I couldn't get near him. He's savage, vicious . . . worse than the Black ever was." Mr. Ramsay's words came in short, clipped bursts. "You know it. Alec does, too. And that's exactly what you didn't want to tell me. It was no accident. Whatever happened was done intentionally by that horse. Everything points to it . . . what I've seen for myself, and your silence." He lowered his voice as he concluded. "Alec will never ride him, nor will he have the opportunity to try again. That horse is legally mine, Henry. I'll sell him or give him away . . . and if I can't do either, I'll have him destroyed.''

Henry's eyes were riveted on Mr. Ramsay's white and angry face. He looked at him for a long time before saying, "Satan is *still* Alec's horse. I'd speak to him first.''

"I intend to do that,'' Mr. Ramsay said sharply.

"He may feel different about Satan now,'' Henry suggested.

"I hope so,'' Mr. Ramsay said and, his voice becoming more gentle, he added, "It's his horse, I know, Henry. But he can't feel the same way about him now . . . after this. Could he?''

"He could, Mr. Ramsay,'' Henry replied. "Alec's love for the Black and now for his son is something that most people can't understand . . . could never understand. If that love hasn't died''—Henry paused—"after what's happened, it would kill Alec to lose his horse.''

They sat there in silence for a long time before Mr. Ramsay said in a low, tired voice, "Go up and see him, Henry. He's waiting . . . and that's all I had to say.''

As Henry closed the screen door behind him, he looked again at Mr. Ramsay, still seated on the porch railing, his eyes staring at the floor in front of him. Henry realized what he must be going through.

With heavy feet Henry climbed the stairs. Then as he neared Alec's door, which he found partly open, he stopped for a moment. Before he went forward again, the tenseness had left his face.

He saw Sebastian first, a brown bundle of shaggy fur upon the white bed. And close beside him was Alec, his face as white as the pillow beneath his head. The boy grinned when he saw Henry and pulled himself to a sitting position.

"Should you sit up like that?" Henry asked with concern.

"Sure, there's nothing wrong with me." Alec smiled. "I'm ready to get up, but they won't let me. Not for a couple more days, anyway," he concluded.

"That's good," Henry said, pulling up a chair and sitting down beside him. "But you take it easy for a while. You're a lucky kid, you are, an' you know it."

A slight bit of color rose to Alec's cheeks. "Yes, I know, Henry. He sure knocked me out cold, didn't he?" Alec's gaze left his friend and wandered to the partly open door. "Better shut it, Henry," he said. "I'd like to talk about it."

Henry grunted, but went over to the door and closed it. Maybe it would be better if Alec did talk about it, he thought. Besides, he had to know how the kid felt about Satan . . . for his own good, as well as Mr. Ramsay's.

When Henry returned Alec asked quickly, "How is he, Henry?"

"Y'mean Satan?"

"Sure."

Henry's face sobered. "You know how he is as well as I do. He ain't goin' to change, Alec."

Ignoring Henry's remark, Alec said, "You got him in all right, afterward?"

"Chased him in with a pitchfork," Henry growled, "an' I kept the bridle and saddle on him for days after."

"Maybe he's used to them by now then," Alec said hopefully.

Henry rose to his feet, then sat down again. It was hard to believe, hearing Alec talk this way. He'd expected something different . . . at least, he'd hoped for something different. Alec's burning interest in Satan, after what the colt had done to him, was almost too much. Finally he said, "Alec, you're not goin' on. You can't."

A frown appeared on Alec's face, and he pushed his red hair off his forehead before asking, "I can't, Henry? Why can't I?"

Sputtering, Henry said, "Y-you . . . y-you can't because that horse is a killer, an' you more than anyone else should know it by now. It was no mistake that he went over backwards, Alec. . . . He knew what he was doin' all right."

Alec's face became very serious as he said, almost apologetically, "I'm sorry, Henry, but I think you're wrong. I'm afraid it was my fault, for I pulled him over. I had a good hold on his neck. Remember?"

"You didn't, you crazy kid," Henry blurted, but then he stopped as he realized once and for all that he'd never be able to convince Alec that his horse was bad, a killer. "Have it your way," he said resignedly.

Alec grinned. "And do you know, Henry," he said eagerly, "I honestly feel that the fall did me a lot of good, because it's been a long time since I've had a spill like that. I guess maybe I'd forgotten that there are a lot of things much worse." Lowering his eyes, he added, "I've been afraid of him at times, Henry, I'll confess that. But I'm not afraid any more. That's what the spill did for me." Alec looked back at Henry. "I'll be out of bed in a couple of days, and the doctor said for me to take it easy for two weeks after that. But then he said it would be all right for me to ride again. I asked him, Henry."

Henry shook his head heavily. What could you do with a kid like that? he thought. Nothing! Just hope to high heaven he kept his wits and head while he was around Satan. And, Henry supposed, if Alec lived through it he'd be one of the finest horsemen in the country. And that was what he wanted.

"You didn't tell my folks everything, did you?" Alec asked with deep concern.

"No," Henry replied, "but I think your father is wise to what actually happened."

Alec was silent for a long time, then he said, "It's too bad. I hope he doesn't worry."

Henry looked at Alec, but said nothing. Apparently it had never occurred to the boy that his father might be worried enough to get rid of Satan. No, Alec had complete faith in his father, just as he had in his horse.

They heard the doorbell ring, and then the sound of voices—Alec's mother's and a man's—reached them. A startled look came over Henry's face as the man's voice reached them again. He listened for a few seconds, then quickly rose to his feet. "I'll be back, Alec," he said. Then he was out of the room, closing the door behind him.

Henry walked across to the mahogany banister and

leaned over it. He saw Alec's mother in the hallway below talking to a man whose thin, narrow back was turned toward him. Then the man moved to place his gray hat on the hat rack, and Henry drew a short, sharp breath as he recognized his old boss, Peter Boldt!

Boldt's thin lips drew back in a sickly smile as Mrs. Ramsay told him she'd inform her husband that Boldt was here to see him. And as she disappeared from Henry's view, the old trainer saw Boldt go over to the hall mirror and run his long, slender fingers across the black hair and then down to the steel-gray sideburns, which he brushed lightly with his fingertips.

Henry grimaced and shook his head.

Suddenly Boldt turned and smiled. Mr. Ramsay had entered the hall.

"Mr. Ramsay, I presume?" Henry heard Boldt ask.

When Alec's father nodded, Boldt inquired, "William Augustus Ramsay?"

"Yes. Yes, that's it." And by the tone of his voice, Henry knew that Mr. Ramsay was annoyed. He had enough on his mind today without being interrogated by Boldt.

"I am Peter Boldt."

Henry grinned as Mr. Ramsay only nodded. The name meant nothing to him. Henry saw the smile leave Boldt's face.

"I happened to be reading a back issue of the Racing Calendar," Boldt said slowly, his beady eyes fixed on Mr. Ramsay, "and I noticed that you had registered a colt . . . a black colt by Shêtân out of Jôhar. He was an

Arabian importation, bred by a chieftain by the name of Abu Ja' Kub ben Ishak, I believe."

Henry grunted. Humph! Boldt *believed.* He knew Abu's name full well and he also knew that Shêtân was really the Black! He'd probably tried to get at Abu in any number of ways, and had been so busy doing it that he'd slipped up on the publication of the colt's registration in the Racing Calendar. Henry had known all along that Boldt would find out about Satan sooner or later, but he thought it too bad it had to happen now. For Boldt couldn't have come at a worse time.

A look of surprise came over Mr. Ramsay's face at Boldt's mention of the black colt. "Oh," he said, "you're the race horse owner."

Boldt's lips drew back at Mr. Ramsay's recognition. But suddenly his face froze as Mr. Ramsay asked, "Henry Dailey worked for you, didn't he?"

There was a long pause, then Boldt replied, "Yes, he worked for me. Do you know him?"

Henry shifted uneasily on his feet as he leaned upon the banister. It was too bad Mr. Ramsay had to mention his name to Boldt. Boldt would surely get the tie-up now.

After Mr. Ramsay had told Boldt that Henry Dailey lived on the same block, Boldt was silent for a long time; then, shrugging his shoulders, he said, "It's of no importance. What I've come to see you about, Mr. Ramsay, is the colt. I'd like to buy him, and will give you twenty-five thousand dollars."

Henry saw Mr. Ramsay's body stiffen at Boldt's mention of such a large sum of money. *Twenty-five thousand dollars!* Henry knew that it was more money than Alec's father earned in a year.

It was a few minutes before Mr. Ramsay found his voice, and when he did speak, the words came hard and he stuttered. "T-twenty f-five th-thousand d-dollars?" he repeated incredulously.

Boldt nodded. Mr. Ramsay's eyes looked toward the stairs, and Henry drew back from the banister in fear of being seen. Then the old trainer heard Alec's father commence to say something, hesitate, then add more audibly, "It's a lot of money to me, Mr. Boldt, but . . ."

As Mr. Ramsay hesitated, Henry knew that he was thinking of Alec. And Henry was sure that he wouldn't sell Satan without first talking to Alec. He loved his son too much for that.

But Boldt reasoned that Mr. Ramsay was hesitating because of the sum offered for the colt. He said quickly, "I'll make it thirty-five thousand, Mr. Ramsay, but no more. After all, this colt hasn't been tried. He may be worth nothing to me."

Henry saw Mr. Ramsay gasp at the sum now being offered by Boldt for the black colt! Thirty-five thousand dollars for Satan, the horse he'd sworn that he'd sell, *give away,* or *destroy.* . . . The palms of Henry's hands were wet with perspiration as he watched the tense scene below. What would Mr. Ramsay do? The colt who had almost taken his son's life was legally his . . . sold to him by Alec for *one* dollar!

Mr. Ramsay glanced up the stairway again, and Henry, in his excitement, forgot to slip back from the banister.

The old trainer knew that Mr. Ramsay was wondering how Alec now felt about Satan, wondering if he still loved the colt after his tragic experience of a few days ago.

Henry knew the answer, but Mr. Ramsay didn't.

Mr. Ramsay turned back to Boldt, and when he spoke he had regained full control of his voice. "The sum you have offered for the colt, Mr. Boldt," he said, "is more than fair."

Boldt smiled, and his whole attitude was confident as Mr. Ramsay paused.

Then Henry saw Boldt's body stiffen as Mr. Ramsay added, "But unfortunately the colt belongs to my son, Alec, and I must discuss the matter with him before coming to any decision."

"But you registered him," Boldt said humbly, his calmness momentarily shattered. "You must own him."

Henry was glad that Mr. Ramsay didn't give Boldt any explanation as to why he had registered the colt in his name, or admit that Boldt was actually right in saying that he did own Satan. All that Mr. Ramsay said was, "He belongs to Alec."

Boldt's thin lips were pulled back in a grim, understanding smile, and there was a reptilian light in his beady eyes as he asked, "You will speak to your son, then?"

"He is upstairs . . . sick," Mr. Ramsay replied. "If you will wait in the living room, I will speak to him immediately."

Henry left the banister and walked quickly into Alec's room, shutting the door behind him. Alec looked up at him and Sebastian whimpered as he moved closer to the boy.

"You've got to make up your mind fast, Alec," Henry said, his words terse and clipped. "Boldt's downstairs. . . . He caught up with an old issue of the Racing Calendar, so he knows about the colt. He's offered your dad thirty-five thousand bucks for Satan."

"Thirty-five thousand dollars!" Alec's eyes were bright as he looked at Henry. "Wow! That's a lot of money to Dad! I'm sure he was impressed."

"That's neither here nor there," Henry said quickly. "You've got to make up your mind. Your father's on his way up."

Alec's brow furrowed. "Make up my mind to what, Henry?"

"Thirty-five thousand dollars, Alec! Think what you could do with that money. You could finish school . . . set yourself up in business . . . anything."

When Henry had finished, Alec was looking down at Sebastian. Impatiently Henry said again, "You've got to hurry, Alec. Your dad will be here in a minute!"

"But I've decided, Henry, if that's what you want." Alec's eyes met Henry's again. "I wouldn't sell Satan for thirty-five thousand, one hundred thousand, or any thousand. He's my horse, Henry . . . you know that."

"But, Alec," Henry said, still arguing, "you may never be able to ride him. He may be worth nothing to you."

"I'll ride him," Alec said quietly, ". . . and he'll always be worth more than money to me, Henry."

The old trainer sat down and ran his hands over his face. "Okay, Alec, okay," he finally said. "I shoulda known better than to go into all this again." He paused, then added slowly, "But your father may think differently. It's actually his horse, you know . . . and thirty-five thousand bucks is a lot of dough for him."

Alec smiled and shook his head. "Dad wouldn't do that," was all he said.

A few seconds later Mr. Ramsay entered the room, and as he walked over to the bed Henry got up, gave him his chair, and then moved over to the window.

With his back turned toward them, Henry heard Mr. Ramsay say, "Alec, a Mr. Peter Boldt is downstairs, and he's offered . . ."

"I know, Dad. Henry told me about it."

The old trainer sensed that Mr. Ramsay was looking at him, but he continued to gaze out the window. Then Henry heard Alec say, "Satan means more than money to me, Dad." Alec's words came faster as he continued, "He'll be a great horse, just like the Black . . . and there aren't any other horses like them in the world."

There was a long silence before Mr. Ramsay said, "You still feel this way, Alec, after what he did to you? I know, you see. I was in the barn this morning, and he's . . ."

"Sure, he's fire, Dad," Alec interrupted, and even Henry's body stiffened at the emotion, the blinding love in Alec's voice. "But that's the way he should be. He's no ordinary horse, nor will he ever be. He's like the Black . . . beautiful, savage and noble." Alec's **words** came slower as he concluded, "And soon, Dad, he won't be so savage, for I'll win his confidence and trust."

Once again it was quiet in the room. And Henry knew what Mr. Ramsay's answer would be to Boldt. For Alec's words had been no impassioned plea of a boy for an inanimate thing like a new baseball glove or a car. Nor was it the plea of a boy who was intent upon having his own way. No, Alec's words came from his heart, and they spoke of the strange yet beautiful love this boy had for his horse.

When the old trainer turned back to the bed, he saw that Mr. Ramsay had risen to his feet and was standing beside Alec, looking down at him. Slowly the strained, gaunt look left Mr. Ramsay's face as he attempted to smile. "He's your colt, Alec," he said softly, "and if you don't want to take thirty-five thousand dollars for him, you needn't." Reaching down, he placed his hand on the boy's shoulder, straightened, and then left the room.

As the door closed behind him, Henry fought the impulse to go along, to see Boldt's face when Mr. Ramsay told him of his son's decision. Henry knew that Boldt would be livid with rage. Shrugging his shoulders, the old trainer decided to keep away from Boldt for the time being, for he knew they had not seen the last of him.

The Fight

12

After Henry left Alec, he walked slowly homeward. He knew what he had to do. But it took the next two days before the old trainer had convinced himself that the responsibility was his, and that in spite of Alec's intense love for the colt, he should break Satan himself.

It would not be a pretty sight, for what he intended to do was to purge once and for all the viciousness from Satan's black heart. And it had to be done today, before Alec was up and around.

Henry left the house early in the morning, when the dew was still heavy upon the field and the sky overcast. He walked toward the barn, his face lined, his brow furrowed. As he neared the door he stopped, and opening his clenched fists, gazed intently at the wet palms. It was cool, yet he was perspiring freely, and this bothered him as much as the tense feeling within his chest, a tightness which made his breathing come short and fast. He stood there for a whole minute, telling himself that while he was old and not in the best of condition, he still was capable of doing what had to be done. "I've got to do it," he muttered. "I've got to do it for Alec, or Satan will kill him sure."

Henry's hand was upon the barn door when he heard the rhythmic beat of hoofs, and then he saw Satan travel quickly down the runway and gallop into the field. Scowling, Henry watched him go. He'd hoped to catch Satan in his stall. . . . It would have made things easier. Now he'd have to chase him inside again.

Still scowling, Henry decided it would be best to get the saddle ready before driving Satan back into his stall. He walked into the barn and went to the tack room, ignoring Napoleon's welcoming neigh. Then he picked up a heavy stock saddle and, groaning a little beneath its weight, carried it from the room to the rack just outside of Satan's stall. Finally he went back to the tack room and kneeled down beside a large wooden trunk. Opening it, he rummaged around for a few seconds before withdrawing a leather riding crop, the head of which was a large, solid piece of hard leather. Henry stuck it underneath his arm and was closing the trunk when he saw the coiled lasso. Thoughtfully he picked up the rope and uncoiled it, then recoiled it. It had been a long time since he'd had to use one, but in his younger days he'd been swift and sure. It might be a good thing to have along if he had trouble getting Satan in from the field. He threw the coiled lasso over his shoulder, then picked up another one from the trunk, and uncoiling and recoiling the second lasso, he placed that too over his shoulder. Then he left the barn to get Satan.

Before entering the field, Henry took hold of the end of the riding crop. He'd use it today, if he had to. . . . Both he and Alec had tried kindness with firmness, and they had failed miserably. Now they had to show Satan who was boss. It was regrettable, but necessary. Henry was fully aware of the chance he was taking, and he knew too that he could easily be the loser. If it came to that . . . well, he decided, if Alec learned his lesson that way, it would be worth it. Henry clenched the riding crop between his fists. But Satan would know he'd been in a fight, he'd make sure of that!

A breeze came up and fanned Henry's cheek as he walked into the field, his shoes squishing softly in the wet grass. He knew that Satan had seen him, for the horse had disappeared into the hollow at the far end.

Then as the hot sun broke through the clouds, brightening the field, Satan reappeared and for a moment stood still on the rim of the hollow, his black body silhouetted against the dense gray mist which had begun to rise from the low, damp land behind him.

Henry stopped in his tracks, startled by the almost unreal, weird sight before him. It was as though Satan, the devil himself, had emerged from the smoldering fires of Hell. And now Satan stood there, bold and proud . . . and contemptuous of the man who would attempt to make him do as he willed.

Suddenly Henry felt very old and tired. It was impossible to think that he could conquer Satan. He had no right to be here . . . no right to test his aging mind and body against this wild, untamable horse.

Satan remained there, his head held high, his black mane whipping in the breeze. He was monstrous, and his black body glistened in the sun.

It was a beautiful but unearthly sight, and Henry was afraid.

A long time elapsed before the old trainer moved forward again, his feet heavy. And now shame had replaced the fear within him—the shame of being afraid of a horse for the first time in his life. And then as he walked along his shame was replaced by anger, and he became furious with himself and with this horse who had made him afraid. When he was but a few paces from Satan he stopped, seeking to control himself.

And it was then that the horse bolted away from him, running easily to the east fence.

Henry followed, his hand still clenching the leather crop. But when he neared Satan, the horse tossed his head and swept around him again, running back to the hollow.

It went on that way for half an hour, with Satan contemptuously ignoring Henry's attempts to chase him toward the runway and barn.

Finally Henry, his breath coming heavily, decided to

use the ropes. He removed both lassoes from his shoulder and nervously uncoiled and recoiled each one several times before slowly moving toward the colt again.

Henry judged that it might take him a little time before he was able to get Satan in a position where he could throw the ropes upon him. But he soon discovered he was wrong, for Satan, as though tired of being chased, turned toward him.

Satan's black body was quivering as he pounded the earth. Henry saw the colt's cold, fixed eyes burst into a fiery red, and he knew that the fight would begin now and that he wasn't going to have the opportunity of throwing the heavy stock saddle upon Satan's back and riding him, as he'd planned. For no longer was Satan the hunted and Henry the hunter. . . . Every movement of the horse showed that it would be just the reverse.

"Come on, y'devil," Henry muttered between clenched teeth. "I'm ready for you." He shifted the leather crop to his right hand.

And before Henry's words had died upon the still air, Satan charged toward him. Henry had no time to use his ropes, for Satan was upon him, his mouth open and specked with foam, his teeth gleaming. As Henry brought down the hard leather crop he could see the whites showing in Satan's wild eyes.

Henry struck Satan a crushing blow on the head; then the horse's shoulder hit him heavily, and he spun around before falling to the ground. He lay there dazed for a minute; then, his head clearing, he turned quickly toward Satan.

The horse had withdrawn a short distance but had turned around once more and was facing him. Satan glared furiously, but Henry saw surprise too in his eyes. Then it was gone, and the wild, hideous look was there again.

Henry struggled to his feet as Satan bore down upon him the second time. Once more Henry waited until the horse, livid with rage, was only a few feet away; then he struck Satan another ponderous blow on the muzzle. As the black body knocked him to the ground again, he heard Satan's shattering scream, and it was like a sharp bolt of lightning cracking the heavens. Henry felt the blood rush to his head after he'd hit the ground hard, and he fought desperately to remain conscious. For he knew that if he didn't, he'd never get up again.

The old man struggled to get one knee off the ground, his head turned in the direction of the horse, who had withdrawn and was snorting in rage and pain. Satan charged again, and Henry stumbled to both feet, yelling at the top of his lungs and waving the leather crop wildly in the air. Satan swerved before reaching him and thundered past, his face hideous to see. He pulled up, twirled, and without hesitation came on again.

The lasso was in Henry's hand, and Satan's speed slackened as he caught sight of this new weapon. The horse hesitated before swerving, and Henry saw his chance. Quickly he whirled the rope once above his head. It had to be good . . . he'd never get another chance. Then the lasso went whistling through the air, and for a fraction of a second Henry thought he had overthrown.

But then it settled over Satan's head and fell down upon the high crest, already lathered with sweat. Shouting, Henry fiercely drew back upon the rope, tightening it about Satan's neck. Then, using every bit of strength in his body, he suddenly pulled back, hoping to throw the horse.

Luck was with him, for Satan had started to turn when the rope tightened. Then, with Henry's sudden pull, Satan was thrown off balance. He slipped on the wet grass, stumbled, and with a shriek of terror went down.

Henry bolted forward, the second lasso whirling in his hand. He was beside himself with fury. "I got you, you devil," he yelled savagely, almost incoherently. The times when Satan had come close to killing him were all merged together in his mind, and he was in a blinding passion to overcome this horse. His face was as hideous as the black demon in front of him. For he was no longer a trainer of horses, but a hunter of them . . . and the moment of triumph was near.

Keeping away from the pawing hoofs, Henry let fly the second rope, while he kept the first one taut about Satan's neck. It settled over the horse's nose, and Henry tightened the noose, shutting the gaping mouth. Then he threw himself upon the savage head, shoving it down to the ground with his knees. As Satan screamed in rage, Henry drew the second rope over the colt's ears and around his head, tightening it. Then the old man's hand swept to the pocket of his jacket and furiously he withdrew a long white rag. He pulled it over the wild eyes of the horse, completely blindfolding him.

Henry stayed there for a moment, breathing heavily, and still holding the horse's head down hard on the ground. "You asked for it, Satan," he gasped. "You asked for it, and now you're goin' to learn who's boss."

Finally Henry let go of Satan's head and moved quickly away from the horse until he neared the end of the two lassoes. The fight had only just begun.

Satan got up slowly, his giant body shaking. He tossed his head savagely, trying to rid himself of the blindfold. He shrieked again, and Henry's face turned white at the fury that possessed this horse. Wild and blinded, Satan was apt to do anything. He might even kill or cripple himself as a last resort. For a fraction of a second, Henry thought of Alec, and then Satan's movements commanded all of his attention again.

Cautiously Satan turned, afraid of what he could not see. And just as cautiously, Henry moved around him, carefully carrying the two ropes around the horse's legs. Suddenly Satan snorted and, rearing, rose to his full height.

Henry waited for him to come down, but before the horse's forelegs could strike the ground and Satan regain his balance, the old man jerked hard on the ropes encircled about Satan's hind legs.

His feet pulled out from under him, Satan crashed heavily to the ground. Quickly he was on his feet again, his body trembling, seeking his opponent. He plunged in Henry's direction, but the old trainer had no trouble getting around the blindfolded horse. Once more the ropes encircled Satan's legs, and when they became taut

Henry pulled back. The horse went down hard for the second time.

"It ain't fair, but you've gotta learn," Henry said grimly. He knew it couldn't go on much longer; the colt's spirit or body had to break under those crushing falls.

Satan had gone down heavily several more times, and Henry's body ached from the strain of pulling the colt off his feet. Then, suddenly, Satan changed his tactics. No longer did he run blindly until the ropes pulled him up and Henry threw him to the ground. Instead he tried to figure out where his opponent was by his scent; then he would plunge toward Henry, and only come to a halt when his uncanny sense told him he had run the length of the ropes which bound him. He would turn then and stand still, his nostrils quivering and his feet firmly implanted upon the ground before plunging again in the direction of the hated man scent.

He came close to Henry many times, and only the old man's renewed alertness kept him from being hurt by the flying hoofs. But as the minutes passed and Henry found himself tiring rapidly, he began seriously to doubt that anyone would ever master this horse. The falls Satan had taken had only served to bring out all the vengeance and hate in his giant body, and now he was lunging to kill . . . and Henry knew that if the blinder slipped he wouldn't have a chance.

As Satan plunged past again, narrowly missing Henry, the old man saw that they were nearing the hollow, and his eyes found the tall, lone maple tree which grew on the rim. As a last resort, he could tie the ropes to the tree, thus preventing Satan from getting to him while he left the field. Henry was tired and worn out. He had lost the fight and he knew it. For Satan had more spirit, more viciousness than he had believed possible.

The horse reared and plunged again, and even though he could not see, he was fearful in all his fury. As he swept past Henry, the old man's attention was drawn to the blindfold about Satan's head. Was the rag actually slipping, or had he just imagined it? Then the horse stopped and half turned, and Henry's breath came sharp. The blinder *was* slipping, and in a few minutes Satan would be able to see!

Suddenly the horse bolted, and it was Henry who was caught off balance, for Satan had pulled away from him. The ropes tightened and Henry was thrown to the ground; then he was being pulled along the grass as Satan gathered speed.

Henry was about to let go of the ropes and make a run for it, when he remembered that the blinder would slip from Satan's eyes any second. The old man's skin was burned from his body as Satan's speed increased, and he almost gave in to the agony and complete exhaustion that swept over him. Then suddenly Satan slowed down and stopped on the rim of the hollow. He shook his head savagely and Henry gritted his teeth, for he knew that Satan would rid himself of the blinder this time.

The old trainer cast a desperate glance at the tree, only a few yards away, and with a final effort he rose to his knees; then in a half crouch he stumbled to the tree and sank at its foot. Slowly, too slowly, he wound both ropes around the tree. As he finished tying them, he saw the blinder slip down from Satan's eyes.

Henry didn't try to get away. He was too exhausted to run or to care. He was done, beaten. Alec would find his horse tied to the tree, and Henry only prayed to God that he might learn a lesson from him.

As Satan shook off his blinder, he uttered a shriek and reared. When he came down, his flashing eyes turned in every direction, sweeping past the tree behind which Henry lay. Then, seemingly unmindful of the ropes which dragged behind him, the horse trotted swiftly around the rim until he came to the sharp decline which led to the fence ten feet away. He stood there for a moment as though measuring the jump he would have to make to clear the fence. Then his ears pricked forward and he retracked, coming to a halt not far from the tree.

Henry forced his head up, and through blurred eyes he saw what the horse intended to do. And he knew that Satan was probably making the greatest mistake of his life in assuming that he was free of the ropes which hung so loosely from him. If the impetus of his jump over the fence broke the ropes he would be free, but if they held and became taut with him in mid-air, he would hang himself.

For some reason, Henry found himself trying to stop Satan by attracting attention to himself; but his words were only a whisper as they traveled up his dry, tight throat and reached his swollen lips.

Satan was in a gallop, running like a black phantom toward the fence. Then he gathered himself and with a mighty leap flew through the air.

Henry's narrowed eyes were upon the ropes which he had tied about the tree. He saw the slack taken up quickly, and then the ropes became taut. They held, and the tree swayed. Then the sound of a heavy body crashing down upon the underbrush on the other side of the fence broke the deathlike stillness of the early morning. A few seconds later it was quiet again.

And as Henry sank into unconsciousness, he whispered, "We've both lost, Satan. . . . Both of us."

Lowered Head

13

Alec moved restlessly in his sleep and pitched a little farther toward the edge of his bed. Sebastian, who lay beside him, uttered a low sigh and wiggled closer to the boy's legs. Suddenly the dog cocked his head in the direction of the open window as a high-pitched cry reached him. Then the early morning was still again and the dog's head fell forward upon his front paws once more.

Sebastian was half asleep when Alec rolled over on him. Whimpering, the dog jumped down from the bed and trotted over to the window. He stood looking out for a few minutes, with his front paws on the window sill.

Suddenly the wild cry came again.

Withdrawing his feet from the window sill, Sebastian uttered a sharp bark and ran over to the bed. He stuck his nose into Alec's hand as it hung over the side.

Seconds later Alec opened his eyes. Rubbing the dog's head, he smiled; then Alec saw the bedding half on the floor, and his face sobered. He'd done a lot of dreaming during the night, and it hadn't been good. Satan had given them trouble and his screams had . . .

Then it came again, and it was no dream this time. Alec waited until Satan's piercing whistle had died on the morning air. Then he was out of bed and over by the window. For a moment he thought he saw his horse on the rim of the hollow. But the trees in his front yard partly blocked his vision, and he wasn't sure.

He half stumbled and ran to the closet, his legs weak from the many days he'd spent in bed. Quickly he pulled on his sweatshirt, corduroy pants, and sneakers; then he ran from the room, Sebastian trotting close behind him.

His pace slackened as he reached the stairs and quietly descended. When he got to the front door, he unlocked it and slid out onto the porch, his speed quickening again as he ran down the steps and across the yard.

It wasn't until he had passed through the gate and was halfway up the driveway that he made himself slow down to a walk. After all, he reasoned, probably nothing was wrong, and it wouldn't do him much good to over-exert himself after more than a week in bed. True, he had been due to get up today, but the doctor hadn't said anything about running. It was just that his dreams and Satan's scream on top of them had upset him for a few moments.

Alec looked out over the field as he approached the barn, but Satan was nowhere in sight. A little worried,

Alec went into the barn, only to find the colt's stall empty. When he came out again, his gaze traveled to the hollow, for he knew it was the only place where Satan could be . . . unless he had jumped the fence.

Running again, Alec reached the barred wooden gate, climbed over it, and then sped across the field. He slowed down as he felt the dampness soak through his rubber sneakers. Sebastian streaked by him, and Alec came to a halt. He had forgotten about the dog; having him around wasn't going to help matters.

Alec whistled to the flying dog ahead of him, but Sebastian kept going in the direction of the lone maple tree on the rim of the hollow. Angrily Alec whistled again, but stopped short as he saw the prone figure at the foot of the tree.

Breaking into a sprint, Alec followed the dog. As they neared the tree, he knew that it was Henry who lay there, and his blood ran cold. What had happened? Where was Satan?

When he reached the old man, who lay face downward, Alec dropped to his knees beside him. Hastily his glance took in the torn clothes and bleeding hands; then, slowly, afraid of what he might see, he turned Henry's body slightly sideways. The old man's face was white and ghastly, but at Alec's touch his eyes opened.

"Henry! What's the matter? What happened? Are you hurt badly?" Alec's words came fast and his face was as white as Henry's.

"I had to do it," Henry mumbled. "Had to do it."

"Had to do what, Henry?" Alec said. "What did you

have to do? Where are you hurt?" He helped Henry to a sitting position with his back against the tree.

The old man's burning gaze met Alec's as he muttered, "I ain't hurt. He knocked me out . . . but I killed him. Alec, I *killed* Satan."

Alec's hands were upon the old man's shoulders, his face suddenly distorted with fury. And then he saw the taut ropes about the tree, and his gaze followed them to the point where they disappeared over the fence. His eyes closed and he caught his lower lip between his teeth. When he turned toward Henry again, the anger in his eyes had been replaced by a dead, fixed stare. "He's dead?" he asked incoherently. "Dead, Henry?"

The old man's gaze dropped before the look in Alec's eyes. "He jumped," he said slowly, ". . . with a rope around his neck. I thought I was doin' the right thing, Alec. . . . But I was wrong. . . . I couldn't lick him. . . ."

Without another word, Alec rose to his feet and walked over to the ropes. He stood beside them for a few seconds, as though afraid to touch them. Then suddenly Sebastian's sharp bark broke the stillness and Alec saw his dog standing by the fence.

Alec's eyes became alive again, and with a cry he ran forward. What had possessed him to accept Henry's word that Satan was dead? Why had he stood there doing nothing when, perhaps, his horse was still alive!

His strides shortened as he approached the fence. Then with a leap, his right foot hit the fence above Sebastian's head and his hands found the top rail. For a second his wet sneakers slipped on the wood, then they held, and Alec pulled himself up. When he reached the top, he straddled the fence, and his eyes followed the ropes as they went down sharply to the heavy underbrush below. Then he saw his horse, and the cry which he wanted to utter died in his throat.

Satan lay on his side half covered by the dense brush which grew there. Alec could not see his head and there was no movement of body or legs. As he dropped down from the fence, Alec saw the broken seedlings and brush that Satan must have landed upon after clearing the fence, and a slight spark of hope rose within him. For Satan had completed his jump before the ropes had become taut. The force of his jump had carried him forward until the slack had been taken up, and then he had gone down.

Alec ran forward, unmindful of the brush which tore at his arms and legs, or the thorns which imbedded his skin. He stopped short as he saw the taut ropes entwined about a small seedling, and then the slight slackening of the ropes as they led away from the seedling to Satan's head.

His horse lay there, suffering, but *alive!* His head was pulled backward at a grotesque angle by the ropes about his head and neck. The one about his neck was partly slack, permitting him to breathe with great effort.

As Alec ran forward, he saw white foam specked with blood wheeze from Satan's mouth as he heaved heavily. And he knew that he hadn't arrived a moment too soon. In another few minutes Satan would have strangled to death.

Satan turned glazed eyes upon him when Alec pulled frantically at the noose about his neck. Finally, his fingers fumbling, he loosened it; then he struggled with the second rope about Satan's head until he had it off.

The horse lay still for a moment, his breath coming short and fast.

"It's over, Satan," Alec said soothingly. "Easy, boy. Easy." His hand moved slowly down the long black neck, and even more slowly over the wet, heaving body, his fingers feeling, probing. . . . So far as he could tell, there were no broken bones.

After a long time, Satan's breathing became more normal. Finally he snorted and shook his head, but he still didn't attempt to get up.

Alec removed the loosened noose from about Satan's neck and threw it to one side; then his eyes traveled over the deep burns the ropes had made. He desperately hoped that these alone were the extent of Satan's injuries, and that his back and legs were all right.

Satan turned toward him, and for a moment his eyes were wild and furious again. It was what Alec longed to see . . . for he knew now that his horse was not beaten. His spirit was unbroken.

The boy sat beside the colt for a long time, talking to him and wiping the hardened sweat from his lathered body. And only when Alec's hands approached the burns upon his neck and nose did Satan tremble at his touch.

"I want to help, boy," Alec said softly. "That's all I want to do."

Finally Satan made an effort to get to his feet. Alec

watched him eagerly, hopefully. If only his colt got up, walked!

Pain intermingled with fright and doubt shone brightly in the black colt's eyes as his body lurched forward, then backward. He came to a stop with his unsteady forefeet up, his hindquarters still upon the ground.

"You can do it, Satan." Alec's voice was heavy, pleading. "You've got to do it."

For another moment Satan remained in the same position, his head hanging heavily. Then he seemed to gather himself. His head rose. He drew up his hindquarters, and with a sudden lurch was on his feet.

Alec flung his arms around the colt's neck, and his words were lost in the black mane.

The boy and his horse stood there for a long while, with only the chirping of the birds breaking the early morning stillness. Finally Alec stepped away from the colt. "I'll take care of you, Satan," he said slowly, ". . . and soon you'll be well again. All well."

Satan's body ceased trembling beneath Alec's hand. The colt turned toward him once, his eyes bright with anger again. But as Alec continued talking to him, the fire gradually died, and his head dropped low.

Alec turned him around in the dense brush, his eyes following Satan's every move. His horse moved without limping, and Alec's hopes soared. Satan was all right! He knew it! He could feel it! It wasn't the end. It wasn't at all! And after a few minutes, when he walked him slowly away, he thought that maybe it could be just the beginning!

They went down the path leading around the fence and to the barn, with Alec stopping very often along the way just to touch his horse, to thrill at stroking him without having Satan recoil at his touch as he had done in the past. And Alec found thorns imbedded in Satan's body. When he removed them, his horse flinched, but his eyes were soft and wondering.

"We'll get better together . . . you and I, Satan," Alec told him. "And soon we'll start all over again."

When they neared the barn, the boy's white face was tinged with color, and his colt's head no longer hung so low.

The next two weeks sped by, and as each day passed Alec locked it away forever in his heart. Doctor Hancock, the veterinary, had found Satan sound, with care necessary only for the rope burns. And slowly, but ever so surely, Alec watched the gradual change take place in Satan's disposition toward him. At first, when Satan was regaining his strength, the colt moved about uneasily, his eyes blazing and suspicious again when Alec entered his stall. But when the boy carefully patted the ointment upon Satan's burns, lessening his pain, the colt stood still beneath Alec's touch.

Fascinated, Alec spent the days and, at first, many long hours of the night with his horse, caring for him and watching the savageness and wildness slowly leave his deep-set eyes, to be replaced with a look of recognition and trust.

Henry, his face still gaunt and his body weak from sheer exhaustion after his fight with Satan, watched, but left them alone. He knew that Satan feared and hated him. Every day the horse attempted to kick or bite him, and his sharp, piercing cry would ring through the barn at Henry's approach to his stall. It would always be a fight between the two.

Together, Alec and Satan recovered, and it was as though their respective injuries brought them still closer together. When more than two weeks had passed, Satan whistled at sight of Alec. His deep-set eyes were no longer fixed and stony, but alive and wonderful with a new sense of faith and confidence in the boy.

Each day Henry thrilled at the sight of this new Satan. Alec's gradual dominance of the giant horse fascinated the old trainer more than anything he'd ever seen. And Alec, furious with him at first for attempting to break Satan his way, had forgotten his anger in the display of affection by Satan.

"This might never have come about," Henry had reminded Alec that first week, "if it hadn't been for the fight."

"It would have come, Henry," Alec had returned. "Maybe it came sooner because of it . . . but it would have come anyway. I'm sure of it."

Three weeks later, Alec rode Satan for the first time.

Henry arrived at the barn early one morning, and as he passed Satan's stall, the colt snorted and withdrew his head. Henry walked to the door and Satan moved to the back of the stall, his blazing eyes upon the trainer. Henry's face sobered. He hadn't wanted it this way. But it had to be and he knew Satan would always hate him, yet fear him, too.

Henry stood there a few minutes talking to the horse, but the terrible blazing look never left Satan's eyes. Then Henry noticed the glistening black coat, and knew that Alec had been there before him, currying, combing and rubbing his horse. The straw had been changed, too, and fresh water was in Satan's trough. Henry wondered about it, for it was early, even for Alec.

There was the sound of footsteps on the graveled driveway, and a few seconds later Alec came through the doorway. Taking one look at Alec's eager face and hurried steps, Henry knew that this was the day. Alec was going to ride Satan this morning.

The horse whistled and his ears pitched forward when he saw Alec. He moved toward the door of his stall and stopped, his eyes turning toward Henry.

Alec said, "I'm taking him out, Henry."

"Yeah, I sort of thought you were going to." Henry nodded his head at Satan. "I see you got him ready."

Satan moved to the door as Alec walked over to him, and the boy stroked his head.

Henry stood there in silence, watching them. Satan was a different horse now, and Henry knew he'd never get over the awe of seeing the wildness and savageness disappear from Satan at Alec's touch. There was no love burning in the horse's eyes, but complete trust and confidence were there, and it was all that was necessary for Alec to ride him.

Finally Henry asked, "You're feeling okay?"

"I'm all better, Henry. There's nothing wrong with me now."

"Your folks know?" Henry asked.

Alec shook his head. "No," he said, "I didn't tell them, but they never said I shouldn't ride him."

Shrugging his shoulders, Henry said, "Guess they knew you were going to, anyway."

"This won't be like the last time. You know that as well as I do, Henry. He'll let me ride him now. I've been on his back several times in the stall."

Henry said quietly, "You won't have any trouble, Alec. I know it, too."

It was easy putting the light saddle upon Satan, and Henry drew up the cinch only enough to keep the saddle from sliding. Satan moved uneasily about his stall with Henry there, and Alec had a difficult time quieting him down.

As Henry moved forward with the bridle, Satan lunged at him.

"Better let me put it on, Henry," Alec said, holding Satan's head. "He's probably remembering that rope you had on him."

Alec took the bridle and, talking to his horse, got it on him. Satan champed at the bit but remained still under Alec's hand.

They were outside a few minutes later, with Henry walking slightly behind Alec and Satan. The boy's face was alive with eagerness when he stopped Satan just inside the field and turned to Henry. "Give me a boost," he said quickly.

Alec, with a word to his horse, picked up the reins, moved to Satan's side, and then quickly placed his knee in Henry's clasped palms. Then he was in the saddle fast, his knees pressed close to his horse.

Satan bolted, but Alec was ready for him. Leaning close to Satan's neck, he talked to his horse again while drawing him up. After going about twenty-five yards, Satan came to a halt and stood shaking his head, while Alec stroked him.

Slowly, Alec felt Satan quiet down. The giant body underneath him still trembled slightly, but Alec knew he'd have no trouble with Satan today.

Henry left the field and stood beside the fence. He watched as Alec slowly moved Satan in large figure eights, teaching him to be guided by the reins. The old man grinned, for he'd thought Alec would be so eager to ride his horse around the field that he'd forgo the fundamentals of breaking Satan to his bridle. But the boy was doing everything he'd been told to do.

Henry watched Alec guide Satan through the figure eights for a long time, the horse crabstepping nervously and pulling at the bit, his eagerness to run checked only by the boy's uncanny control over him. It was a sight that made Henry's heart pound with pride. It was ample reward for all the hopelessness, despair and physical agony he had been caused by this horse, whom he had thought untamable and a killer.

Suddenly Satan broke out of his walk into a slow gallop, and Henry realized that Alec had given him his head.

Alec moved forward with the smooth natural gait of his horse. This was the beginning of Satan's long and rigorous training as a race horse! Drawing back on the reins slightly, Alec held Satan to a slow gallop. The horse fought for his head, but Alec talked to him. "Take it easy, boy," he said. "That'll come later. Move nicely now. Move nicely."

And as they swept down the field, Satan's hoofs beating rhythmically upon the ground, Alec thrilled at the power he felt between his knees. He had felt such giant muscles before, but only astride the Black. And he wondered if this big, burly son of the Black would have the tremendous speed of his sleek sire.

As if in answer to Alec's thoughts, Satan's action shifted quickly and he broke from the slow gallop into swift and thunderous strides. For a few seconds Alec let him go, and Satan's mane whipped back, lashing his face. The white fence became a blur; then they neared the hollow, and Alec sought to check Satan's speed. At first there was no response to his sharp pull on the reins; but as Alec called to his horse, he gradually slowed down to an easy gallop. Wiping the tears from his eyes, Alec turned him back up the field. It had been a short run, but Satan had speed to burn. There was no doubt about that.

Henry, his face thoughtful, watched them come back up the field. Satan's action had been beautiful to see, and it looked as though he had speed in spite of his burly size. He had slowed up, too, at Alec's command, which was mighty important with a wild runner like him. "Yet it's too early to tell," Henry warned. "There's too much ahead of us."

"You said it, Henry."

The old trainer turned quickly to find Mr. Ramsay standing beside him, frowning.

"Oh, hello, Mr. Ramsay. Didn't hear you come up. What was that you said?"

"I simply agreed with you, Henry," Mr. Ramsay said quietly. "There is very much ahead of us."

"Yeah," Henry muttered.

"And I meant just that, Henry . . . *us*." Mr. Ramsay's eyes were upon Alec and Satan as he spoke. "It's my son and my horse," he continued. "I'm very much in it. . . . It can't be any other way now."

"Yeah, I guess you are," Henry said slowly, his eyes too turning back to the field.

They stood there in silence until Alec had slowed Satan down to a walk and was approaching the gate.

"Guess he's coming in now," Henry said. "We'd better get out of the way and let Alec handle him."

"And he sure can, Henry."

The old trainer turned at the note of pride in Mr. Ramsay's voice. And when he looked at him he saw that the frown had left his face, and that his eyes were bright and keen. Smiling, Henry muttered, "You said it this time, Mr. Ramsay."

Training Begins

14

It was serious business, this training of Satan, and Henry watched Satan with keen eyes during the weeks that followed. Luckily he had no set rules for the training of race horses, for Henry had learned long ago that horses, like athletes, respond differently to any given training method. It was up to him, he knew, to size up Satan now that Alec was riding him . . . to learn what kind of training the giant black colt needed to bring him along to his finest racing peak.

So, at the beginning, the old trainer talked little to Alec, and when he gave his instructions before the boy took Satan into the field for his daily schooling, his sentences were terse and to the point. Alec would do as he was told, for he too knew that this early training was important if they were to race Satan.

Day after day Alec rode his horse about the field, holding him to a slow jog despite Satan's impatience to break loose and run. The boy knew that Henry's eyes were always upon them, watching their every movement, watching him as well as the horse. And at the end of long miles of jogging, he would bring Satan in at Henry's signal, and the old man would look closely to see if the colt was hot or blowing excessively. Then he would send them out again, to have Alec repeatedly walk his horse slowly up to the fence and, just as slowly, back him away from it.

"It'll help matters a lot when we get to a starting gate," he told Alec the first time he had him do it. "Might as well teach him things like that now," he concluded.

Nor was this early schooling easy on Alec. Satan fought him at times; the boy's hands were raw from holding him in, and his voice was hoarse from talking constantly to Satan, for he knew he could control him as well by his voice as by the reins.

The weeks slid by with Henry insistent upon Satan's learning and relearning his elementary lessons, and Alec grew more and more impatient at the tiring and monotonous work of holding Satan to a jog.

Henry's eyes never left the black colt, and each day, when Alec brought him in, he would run his hands over Satan's legs, searching for heat or puffiness. Finally he told Alec that he thought the colt was ready for slow gallops around the field.

For over a week, Henry made Alec keep Satan down to a half-mile gallop; then, gradually, he had him take him up to two miles, which meant approximately eight times around the field. But the old trainer would not let Alec gallop Satan the entire two miles, much as he knew the boy wanted to let the colt go.

"We've got to build muscle and wind, Alec . . . an' you keep that in mind," Henry told him one day, when Alec had kept Satan in a gallop longer than the old trainer had instructed. "You may think he's ready to be extended, but he ain't . . . not yet. He's still a yearling, Alec, remember that, an' we've got time. Gradual, boy . . . take him up gradually. You've got to have patience . . . even if he ain't."

Alec had nodded in agreement, knowing that Henry was right. It was difficult to be patient with a horse like Satan under him. And it was getting even more difficult to hold him in. For at times Satan was almost uncontrollable, and Alec had all he could do to check his speed.

More weeks went by with Alec taking Satan through the two-mile workout in sections. Henry had him hold the horse to a slow gallop for over a half mile, then walk a quarter, trot a quarter, gallop again for another half mile, before slowing down to a walk for another quarter. And when they came in, Henry would find Satan only slightly hot and breathing well.

"He'll be ready for track workouts soon, Alec," he told the boy.

Eagerly Alec awaited that day. For now, more than ever before, his whole world revolved about Satan. He had transferred to a New York school, and had arranged his classes so he could be home by the middle of each afternoon when they worked Satan. He spent little time with his parents, for at night there were his studies to be done. And any free time he had over week ends was spent in doing odd jobs for local people who would pay him for his work. Alec needed every penny he could lay his hands on. It cost money to feed Satan, and ahead of him too were the fees necessary to run Satan in the Hopeful. There was a fifty-dollar nomination fee to be paid the last of December, only two months away; then, to keep his horse eligible, he would have to pay an additional fifty-dollar fee in March and one hundred dollars in June. And, if things went well and Satan was ready for the big race, it would cost five hundred dollars to start him. Fortunately, Alec had saved his money long before Satan had ever arrived, knowing that he would need it if he was ever to race his horse. And he had just about enough money now to start Satan in the twenty-five-thousand-dollar race. He was willing to risk every penny he had on the horse, for he knew, after the many weeks of riding in the field, that Satan would have the speed when he called upon him.

Through it all, Alec's mother and father watched him with worried eyes, but remained quiet.

Then came the day when Henry told Alec that Satan was ready for the track. "We can't do much more in the field," he said, "an' we oughta get in some good workouts before winter closes in on us."

They sat on the low wooden bench outside the barn, watching Satan graze in the field.

Alec turned to Henry, his face eager. "Where's it going to be, Henry? Belmont?"

"Yeah. It's the closest track, an' I got some friends over there, settin' up winter quarters, who might be of some help to us." He paused, then continued thoughtfully, "I hate to work him nights there like we did the Black, but nothin' else for us to do. He's not ready for other horses yet. You think so, Alec?"

Shrugging his shoulders, Alec replied, "I honestly don't know, Henry. He could be and he couldn't. He's still giving me trouble every once in a while," he concluded frankly.

"Yeah, I know that all right. I'm afraid you always will have trouble controllin' him, Alec. He never will be clear broke . . . not with that wild streak runnin' through him."

"I guess maybe we should keep him away from other horses for a while," Alec said. "He's got to get used to them in time, though," he finished thoughtfully.

"Yeah, I know. He won't be any good to us, even if he can run like a bolt of lightning, if we can't put him in a race for fear of him savagin' some of the other horses. He'd be ruled off the track fast."

"Maybe he'll be all right, Henry," Alec returned hopefully. "He's not too bad with old Napoleon now."

"He's still bad enough with him," grunted Henry. The old trainer was quiet several minutes before he shook his head and said with great concern, "There's more to trainin' a horse, Alec, than just buildin' up wind an' muscle an' speed. You got to teach him how to race . . .

to break from the starting gates . . . to run close to the rail and, at times, away from it, too. There's a lot of stuff like that an' it's easier to teach a horse all of it if he's trainin' with another horse, so you can shift 'em around. It's easiest with four or five horses, but you oughta have at least two horses, if it comes down to that."

After a long silence Alec finally said, "We could take him over to Belmont during the daytime, Henry. Maybe it would be all right."

Shaking his head, Henry replied, "Don't think so, Alec. Not now, anyway. Besides, I don't know any of the trainers over at Belmont well enough to ask 'em to let me work Satan in their string. I was over there yesterday and looked around," he concluded.

"You don't really have to have another horse, do you, Henry?" Alec asked anxiously.

"It would help, Alec . . . help a lot . . . if I could just have another one around to walk or trot through some of these things I have to teach Satan. Just any old nag, who would get along halfway decently with Satan. . . ."

Simultaneously, their gazes turned to the iron gate as it creaked open. There was Tony, leading old Napoleon up the driveway.

Alec looked at Henry. "You said *any* old nag . . . any old nag who might be able to get along with Satan. . . ."

Henry returned his look. "You think . . ." he muttered. "Not that, Alec. I meant any old *race* horse."

"Napoleon would be of some help, wouldn't he?"

"I don't know, Alec. Maybe. Maybe not." Pausing, Henry looked at Tony again as the huckster came up to them. "Besides, Tony would have none of it," he added.

"What you mean 'Tony have none of it'?" Tony asked, bringing Napoleon to a halt. "Tony have none of what you mean?"

Alec said, "We're taking Satan to the track for a workout, and we need another horse to help out. We wondered about Napoleon . . . whether you'd let us take him, I mean." As Alec finished, he saw Henry grimace and shake his head.

"You mean to da race track?" Tony asked, his black eyes upon Alec. And when the boy nodded, Tony clasped his hands. *"Dio mio,"* he exclaimed. "No!"

Henry took a deep breath of relief, but Alec said gravely, "It's too bad Napoleon can't run."

Tony's eyes sharpened, and his hand swept back to old Napoleon's neck. "He no can run, you say, Aleec?" His words tumbled over each other. "My Napoleon was wan fast feller in hees day, and he still go mighty fasta pace down the street. Heesa wan fast chunk of what you call dynamite." Tony rubbed Napoleon's head and talked to him soothingly in Italian. Finally the little huckster turned to Alec, his face set and his eyes burning. "I go for eet, Aleec. I let you run my Nappy against da beeg black, but I go along to watch for him. When we go?"

Smiling, Alec turned toward Henry. "It's your deal now, Henry," he said. "You've got your other horse. When do we go?"

Henry shifted uncomfortably on the bench, his eyes leaving Alec, moving to Tony, and finally coming to rest on the old gray. Then he said, "Maybe he'll do for what I have in mind. Tonight, Alec. We're goin' over tonight around midnight, so no one will bother us. I'm getting hold of a van. . . . It's small, but I guess it'll hold the two of them." Henry paused, then looked at Alec. "You'll have to keep Satan away from Napoleon. You'll have your hands full."

Alec nodded, but his eyes were upon old Napoleon as the horse raised his head at seeing Satan in the field; then the gray whinnied, as though in challenge to the black colt.

It was near midnight when Alec reached the barn. There was no light inside, so he knew that Tony had not yet arrived. Henry had gone for the van, and Alec knew he'd be back within a few minutes.

Opening the door, he switched on the light to be greeted by a soft neigh from old Napoleon. The gray had his head over the stall door, and there was a young, alert look in his large eyes. Alec grinned and went over to him. As he rubbed Napoleon's head he said softly, "You're eager, aren't you, old boy? And you're not afraid of Satan. . . . You never have been, even though he's been pretty nasty to you at times. But you've understood him, Nap, maybe even better than the rest of us."

There was a loud snort from the direction of Satan's stall, and Alec saw the black colt watching them, his eyes blazing. With a final pat upon the old gray's head, Alec walked quickly to Satan. As he went up to him, the colt pressed his muzzle against Alec's sweater while the boy ran his hand through the black mane. "You're first,

Satan, you know that," he said quietly. "You needn't be jealous of Napoleon."

After a few minutes with his horse Alec went to the tack room and, taking off his sneakers, pulled on his riding boots. Next he stood up and drew his corduroy trousers down over the tops of his boots. Walking over to the saddle rack, he lifted the light racing saddle gently, his hands almost caressing the smoothly polished leather. Then, carrying it in one arm, he picked up Satan's bridle and left the room.

Outside, he heard the van coming up the driveway, and he went to the barn door.

The truck rolled slowly to a stop, and Henry and Tony climbed out.

"Everything set?" Henry asked. Then he saw the bridle and saddle in Alec's arms. "Put 'em in the front," he added. "We'll have to get goin' fast, as I've got to have the van back to the garage in a couple of hours."

Tony, his face grave, followed Henry into the barn, muttering to himself in Italian.

"Don't you worry about Nap," Alec told him.

"Me worry, Aleec? I no worry." But the little huckster's voice was heavy with concern.

They put Napoleon in the van first; then, while Henry and Tony moved toward the front of the truck, Alec led Satan from the barn.

The fall night air was cool, and the black colt moved gingerly beside Alec as the boy talked to him soothingly. "Take it easy, Satan," he said. "Just a short ride, then we'll be there."

Satan attempted to pull away from Alec as they approached the ramp leading into the van. Then he saw Napoleon and his shrill whistle shattered the night stillness.

"Keep him quiet, Alec," Henry said. "You'll have my wife and your folks on our necks if he keeps that up."

Finally Satan quieted down beneath Alec's hand, and the boy led him up the ramp. He was almost inside the van when Napoleon turned his head toward them and neighed. Satan came to a stop, snorting, his teeth bared.

"It's Napoleon. He doesn't want to fight," Alec said, stroking his horse.

After a few minutes he was able to move Satan forward again, and they entered the van with Alec between the two horses, keeping the colt far to one side.

"Okay, Henry," he yelled. "Let 'er go!"

As the motor started, Tony turned anxiously to Alec, whom he could see through the small open window. "Keepa heem away from Nappy," he called.

They went down the driveway and turned up the street, with Satan moving restlessly beside Alec, his smoldering eyes on old Napoleon.

A half hour later Henry drove the van into Belmont Park. They passed the long rows of stables, dim uncertain shapes in the moonless night, empty except for the few horses who were quartered there for the winter. A short distance farther, the van rolled slowly past the rear of the long grandstand, and then Henry turned toward the track and pulled up in front of a gap in the fence.

Alec was tense . . . as tense as the black colt beside

him. Napoleon too moved uneasily, as though he knew what was ahead of them.

"It's really starting now," Alec muttered to his horse. "And you'll get used to horses and strange people around you in time. I know you will, Satan."

Henry opened the door and dropped the ramp down. "I'll take Napoleon out first," he said, walking inside.

Fearfully Satan watched Henry as he made his way up to the old gray, and Alec felt the colt's body tremble.

Henry was taking Napoleon out of the van when Satan suddenly snorted and tore the halter out of Alec's hands. Swerving, he crashed heavily into the side of the van before Alec got hold of him again.

Alec was trying to quiet him down when he saw the leather riding crop Henry was holding under his arm. "Your stick, Henry!" Alec said curtly. "Get rid of it!"

Henry threw the crop out of the truck. "Yeah, he remembers and I'd forgotten," he grunted. Then his voice dropped so low that Alec could barely hear him. "I was carryin' it for luck," he said ironically, ". . . it *used* to bring me luck when I carried it."

After Satan had quieted, Alec led him from the van and took him to the gap in the fence. The colt's ears pricked forward and his eyes left Napoleon for the open track that stretched before him. He moved around Alec as Henry threw the saddle on him and tightened the cinch about his girth. His ears lay back and he shook his head, but Alec kept talking to him. Then the saddle and bridle were on and he stood there quietly, his ears pricked forward again and his eyes shifting from the track to Alec.

Alec heard Henry speaking to him, but his eyes never left his horse.

"All set, Alec, an' here's what I want you to do. . . ."

Alec listened intently to Henry's instructions, and when the old trainer had finished, Alec took up the reins and moved to Satan's side. Henry gave him a boost and he was in the saddle, his feet in the stirrups and his knees pressed high on Satan's withers. After taking up the reins, he sat quietly for a moment, and even the black colt was still for the first time.

Tony, a short distance away, held Napoleon by the halter, watching them. Henry stood beside Satan, and when he took hold of the bridle to lead him onto the track, the colt's eyes blazed at him. But Satan stepped along as Henry led him through the gap.

"Okay," Henry said, looking up at Alec. "Do what I told you as well as you can. Hold him in every bit of the way . . . even when you breeze him."

Henry left them, and Alec was alone with his horse. His hand ran down the black neck, and he patted Satan gently while talking to him. Then Alec's eyes turned to the empty grandstand, and from it to the track stretched out before them. It was this that he had been waiting for . . . this, another cycle in Satan's life and his own as well . . . one more step toward the day when the brazen call of a bugle would summon them both to the starting gate, past the crowded stands, the stewards, the jockeys, the strange horses, to await the sharp ring of the bell which would send them flying from the gate. This hardened dirt beneath Satan's hoofs was his testing ground. For on it he must prove that he was a worthy son of the great horse whose blood he carried.

Satan crabstepped lightly down the track as Alec gave him his head a little. Alec knew that the horse was eager to run, but his hands on the reins remained firm. Henry wanted him to work Satan slowly tonight except for the short breeze of a furlong . . . an eighth of a mile to let Satan run! . . . And even then he was to hold him in. "No faster than fifteen seconds, Alec, mind you," Henry had instructed him. "We'll see how he takes to these short furlong breezes before we work him faster or longer. I know it's not goin' to be easy holdin' him down, with him wantin' to run like he does. But you do it, do it the best you can, and it'll pay dividends later on. We've got time, Alec . . . we've got time. Remember that."

Satan shook his head continually and pulled at his bit as Alec took him slowly around the track at a jog. And when they had reached the gap again, Alec's hands and arms were tired from the constant pull over every inch of the way they had traveled.

"Take him up," Henry called, "an' breeze him the furlong, finishing here. Mind you, Alec, hold him in. Keep it fifteen seconds or over, but no faster." Henry flourished a stop watch in his hand.

Turning Satan around, Alec went back past the stands. Satan was getting hot, working himself up again, and Alec knew Henry wasn't going to like it. Stroking his horse, he tried to quiet him.

Finally they neared the furlong pole and Alec guided Satan over to the rail. "Keep him goin' straight an' on the rail," Henry had told him.

He took Satan a short distance past the pole and then turned him around. The colt's body trembled with eagerness as Alec slackened the reins. He held him to a slow gallop until they hit the pole, then gave him more rein.

Gathering himself, Satan bolted forward, gradually picking up speed. Alec held him in, but even so he knew in those few seconds that Satan would never have the fast break of the Black, and that it would take a short distance for the burly horse really to get going.

Like a burr, Alec bent low over the black neck as Satan fought for his head. The white fence went by with ever increasing speed as Satan stretched out. The wind whipped Alec's face scarlet and blurred his eyes so that he could not see. He pulled hard on the reins and repeatedly called upon Satan to slow down. This was to be no fifteen-second furlong breeze. He knew that! Satan was flying, the bit clenched between his teeth.

Desperately Alec fought his horse, but he was no match for the running colt. They swept by the gap in the fence, their speed so great that the white blur seemingly was unbroken.

And it wasn't until they had rounded the first turn that Alec felt any response to the reins or his repeated calls to Satan. Gradually the black colt slowed down, but he still fought for his head. Alec talked to him while holding the reins back, and finally, after they had gone another quarter, brought him to a stop.

When they returned, Alec said, "I couldn't hold him, Henry. I tried . . ."

"I know you couldn't," the old trainer replied, as he ran his hands down Satan's legs. Finally he straightened and watched Satan's breathing for a minute. "Maybe it was for the best. Maybe he got it out of his system for a while. Sometimes a trainer has to realize that it's time to throw all the rules overboard . . . an' I guess this is it."

Napoleon neighed as Tony led him out onto the track. Satan turned toward him and snorted.

"What's next?" Alec asked.

"I want you to jog Satan down the line with Napoleon on the outside. Keep the colt close to the rail. Then we'll alternate by putting Satan on the outside. The idea is to teach Satan to run close to the rail and away from it, when necessary."

Alec sat astride Satan and waited on the track while Henry helped Tony climb up on old Napoleon's back. Tony had no saddle or bridle, and as he settled low into the gray's swayback, Alec smiled. For never, he was sure, had such a pair trod the famous Belmont track.

Tony's face was very serious as he held the rope fastened to Napoleon's halter. The old gray trotted heavily, then broke into a lope of his own accord, his head held high, as he passed in front of the empty stands.

Turning Satan around, Alec waited for them. As they approached, the colt snorted and pawed the ground. But Napoleon, surprisingly calm, never turned his head from the grandstand.

Laboriously, Tony turned Napoleon around and

brought him closer to Satan as he stood beside the rail.

Alec felt Satan's body tremble, and he knew his colt wanted to fight. "You're silly, boy," Alec said softly. "You can't pick on an old guy like Napoleon."

Then Henry was on the track, signaling them to come down.

"Okay, Tony, let's go," Alec said.

Nodding, but saying nothing, Tony urged Napoleon into a trot with Satan running close beside him. They went down the stretch with Alec more concerned about keeping Satan from savaging Napoleon than holding his horse to the rail. But the old gray was completely oblivious of any danger to himself as he loped heavily along, his head held higher than Alec had ever seen it.

They passed Henry and trotted around the track, alternating their positions every furlong, as the old trainer had instructed them to do. And as they went along Tony's face lightened, and occasionally he would grin at Alec and shout something in Italian.

But as they entered the homestretch again, Alec's face was grave, for it was becoming more and more difficult to keep Satan away from the plodding Napoleon. Alec worked on his horse, talked to him, patted him. Satan had to get used to having other horses near him or his speed would be of no use to them whatsoever.

They were nearing Henry once more, when Satan, with a fierce cry, turned upon Napoleon. Alec was ready for the lunge, and struck his horse upon the muzzle as Satan went for old Napoleon's neck. Tony, too, had seen the colt swerve toward them, and with a shout he pulled Napoleon's head away from Satan.

It was over in a minute. Satan bolted at Alec's blow upon his muzzle and he swept hard against the rail; then Henry was there and had him by the bridle. Satan, fearing Henry, stood still, but his eyes were wild and furious. Tony was off Napoleon, and his hands passed gently over the old gray's neck.

"Let's get out of here," Henry said.

Dismounting, Alec took Satan's bridle from Henry. "I'll take him to the van. You'd better calm Tony down. . . . He's plenty excited."

After Henry had left, Alec walked Satan slowly down the track, talking to him. By the time Alec led him into the van, the fire had left Satan's eyes. A few minutes later, Henry brought Napoleon inside.

"He didn't bite him, did he?" Alec asked anxiously.

"No."

"How's Tony taking it?"

"Better'n I thought he would," Henry replied. "He mumbled something about the colt being excited. Strange, coming from him."

"Yes . . . sure is," agreed Alec.

"We've got a job bringing this colt around. You know that, Alec."

"I know."

"You still want to enter him in the Hopeful? Entries close next month."

Nodding, Alec said, "He'll be ready, Henry."

"I hope so, 'cause it's your money, Alec, an' I'd hate to see you lose it," Henry said as he left the van.

Alec turned to Satan to find him gazing at old Napoleon with curious eyes. "You'll have to learn to get along with him, Satan . . . with him and other horses," he said. "You've just got to do it, if you're going to race."

Satan snorted as the van's engine caught, and they moved slowly away in the night.

Fanning Sticks

15

Autumn fell before winter, and winter slid into spring, while Satan's training went on. He was a two-year-old now, larger and burlier than any horse Henry had ever seen in his long career. "But he's got the speed in spite of his bulk," he told Alec.

Yes, after many months of work on the track, Alec knew his horse could run. But neither he nor Henry knew how fast Satan could really run, for the old trainer had insisted upon Alec's holding him in as well as he could, never letting the giant black colt have his head. And Satan wanted to run. Every time Alec took the colt out on the track, he had a fight on his hands. But for some reason which even Alec couldn't explain, the colt never gave way completely to the eagerness which swept his massive body when Alec called upon him to check his speed.

"I've never seen the like," Henry told him. "Satan is the most obstinate, ugliest-tempered horse I've ever seen, yet he's been givin' in to you more times than not."

They had continued to work Satan at night, knowing full well that the colt could not yet be trusted with other horses. But, much to their surprise, Satan's attitude toward Napoleon became more casual, and never again did he attempt to savage the old gray when he worked with him. Tony's attitude, too, surprised both Henry and Alec, for the little huckster, after first vigorously objecting to their using Napoleon again, finally relented; and when one workout followed another and the black colt still ignored Napoleon, Tony relaxed and seemed to enjoy the night sessions as much as his old gray horse did.

With the coming of spring, Satan's workouts were stepped up until he was doing a fast half mile and then galloping out another half under wraps. And as the weeks of fast workouts swept by, Henry watched Satan with keen, eager eyes to make sure he was not asking too much of the black colt. What he saw pleased him, for he knew the two-year-old was fining down well and would be at his best by the end of August when the Hopeful was run. Yes, physically the colt would be ready. But whether Alec would be able to control him when he lined up with strange horses was another story.

It was early June when Henry called an end to Satan's night workouts. "He's ready, Alec," the old trainer said one day as they sat outside the barn, watching Satan in the field. "No sense workin' him any more at night. What we've got to do now is to get him used to havin' other horses around. There's no sense puttin' it off any longer. . . . Only about two months now before Hopeful time."

"I know, Henry," Alec said quietly. Then he added, "He feels less nervous to me, and seems to be doing what I ask of him. Maybe he'll get along."

"He's got to," muttered Henry, ". . . or there's no sense in your puttin' out your good money to keep him eligible. . . . It's cost you a hundred bucks already."

"Another hundred is due the fifteenth of this month, too," Alec reminded him.

"You got it?" And when Alec nodded, Henry asked, "An' how about the five hundred needed to start him in the race. . . . Y'got that too?"

"Just about, Henry . . . but I wouldn't have if you weren't paying the feed bills."

"That's nothin'," Henry grunted. Then he said, "Y'oughta let me help you pay these entry fees. . . . It ain't right for you to be shoulderin' the whole works."

"No, Henry, I want it that way," Alec said decisively. "When Dad sent in Satan's nomination for the Hopeful he wanted to pay, but I wouldn't let him. . . . I wouldn't feel right. I've figured on it for a long time, you know."

Henry was silent for a few minutes, then he said, "All the more reason for us to find out how Satan acts with other horses soon. If he won't run with 'em, we'd better pull out of the Hopeful now before you shell out any more money."

"He'll run," was all Alec said.

They both settled back on the bench, alone with their thoughts. After a few minutes, Alec dug into his watch pocket, withdrawing a folded newspaper clipping. He was reading it when Henry said, "I was talkin' to some of the boys over at Belmont the other afternoon. They'd seen Boldt's Comet cop those two-year-old races down in Florida last winter. He broke the track record first time out, y'know. These friends of mine say he's well-lined an' fast as any sprinter they ever saw, an' they didn't make no exceptions. Boldt's got the best horse he's ever had, they tell me."

"It says so here, too," Alec said, his gaze turning back to the newspaper clipping. "I've been carrying it around for months, thinking it would cool me down when I got too excited over Satan winning the Hopeful. It's Jim Neville's column, and he knows his horses, Henry."

"Yeah, he knows 'em all right. He oughta be trainin' horses instead of writin' about 'em."

Alec read for a moment and then said, "He says here that the Comet was loafing when he broke the record, too." Alec read slowly: "The Comet, a beautiful gray colt which Peter Boldt bred out of his English mare, Lady, and sired by his famed champion, Shooting Star, made his long-awaited debut in the six-furlong fifth dash for two-year-olds at Hialeah Park this afternoon, and broke the race record as he won, eased up, by a half-dozen lengths. Observers immediately proclaimed the flying son of Shooting Star and Lady as a sharp prospect to win the much prized Hopeful next August. . . ." Alec stopped reading and looked up at Henry.

"Then he won his next two races in Florida just as easily," Henry reminded Alec.

"But he hasn't run since, has he, Henry?"

The old trainer shook his head. "No. Boldt knows what he can do now, an' he'll sit back and wait for the Hopeful."

"How about Volence?" Alec asked. "Have you heard anything about his two-year-olds?"

"Yeah. There was some talk about one of his, a chestnut that he's callin' Desert Storm, that he's bringin' along. Volence takes his time, though. He doesn't run 'em early like Boldt does. I heard from one guy that Volence has entered Desert Storm in the Hopeful, too. . . . He also told me that Volence is goin' to run him in an early race durin' the meetin'. I think it was the Union Hotel Stakes. . . . It comes off about a week before the Hopeful."

"Then we'll have a good chance of finding out what he's got," Alec said.

"Yeah," Henry agreed. After a long pause, he said, "We know the Comet has speed . . . that he's a sprinter, Alec. An' remember the Hopeful is only a six-furlong-and-a-half race. . . ."

"A little over three-quarters of a mile," muttered Alec.

"Yeah . . . and Satan hasn't the fastest break I've ever seen."

"But he gathers fast, Henry, once he's going," Alec said.

"Sure, I know . . . an' he oughta be able to catch any

horse runnin'. Even at six furlongs," Henry concluded.

They had sat back in their seats and were quiet again when Henry mumbled, "Well, that's not our immediate problem, anyway. What we got to do is to see if Satan is goin' to run or fight."

"When are we going over, Henry?"

The old trainer rose to his feet, and he turned to look out over the field before replying. "An old pal of mine got in at Belmont a few days ago with a horse he's gettin' ready for the Hopeful. Mike said it would be all right if I worked our horse with his, so I told him maybe tomorrow mornin'. Guess we might as well get right to it, Alec. . . . No sense puttin' it off any longer."

"Yes, Henry," Alec returned quietly. "No sense in doing that."

It was still dark the following morning when Alec met Henry at the barn. The old trainer had the van and was waiting for him.

"Hurry it up, Alec," Henry said. "It'll be light in another half hour, and they'll be working at Belmont."

Running into the barn, Alec reached Satan's stall. The giant black colt neighed when he saw him and shook his tousled head. A few minutes later, Alec had him out of his stall and was leading him toward the barn door. Satan turned his head toward Napoleon as the old gray watched them go by.

"Not this morning, Nap," Alec muttered. "Satan goes without you today."

The sun was up, warming the cool gray of early

morning, when they arrived at the track. Alec found Belmont a far cry from the place they had visited nightly for so many months. There was much activity now as the shouts of men shattered the still air, and already the rhythmic hoofbeats of galloping horses were heard upon the track.

They could smell the fragrant wood smoke burning in the iron stoves as the van neared the long rows of racing stables.

"We've got to go all the way to the end," Henry muttered, turning the van down a graveled road running behind the stables.

They were going slowly now, and Alec's eyes were upon the sleek thoroughbreds as their grooms led them about. Some of them had already finished their morning workouts and were being cooled off beneath colorful blankets, while still others danced nervously as they were being saddled to go out, their exercise boys standing quietly beside them, waiting to be boosted upon their backs. A strong scent of liniment pervaded the air.

Alec looked at Satan through the back window. The colt's ears were pricked and his eyes wide and staring as the strange sounds and the neighing of horses reached him. "He's getting excited," Alec told Henry.

Henry only nodded, slowing the van down as they neared the last row of sheds. He turned the corner and they passed the stalls, most of which were empty. Finally, at the end of the row, Henry brought the van to a stop a few yards away from two grooms who were saddling a good-looking bay colt.

"That's Mike's horse," Henry said. "Mike oughta be around somewhere." Shutting off the engine, he glanced in the direction of the stalls.

Alec listened to the grooms humming to the flighty two-year-old as they saddled him. The bay colt had good lines and looked as though he had speed as well. A stocky little man with a wizened face came around the corner. "Is that Mike?" Alec asked Henry.

The old trainer shook his head. "No," he replied, "that's Mike's jock, Lenny Sansone. He's been ridin' for Mike for years. Len worked in a chemical plant over in Brooklyn when Mike picked him up after Lenny had been spending all his early mornings around the track. He's a great guy, an' you'll like him," Henry added. "There aren't many jocks who can exercise horses as well as race 'em, but Lenny is one of them. He follows Mike's instructions to the letter, an' tells him exactly how his horse reacts to his works. Lots of other jocks, who are good in the afternoon silks, are no good in the morning works, because they want to win races then, too. An' lots of times it's no good for the horses or the trainer's nerves."

Alec saw Lenny Sansone go up to the bay and affectionately place his hand on the colt's head. "What's the bay's name?" Alec asked Henry.

"The Chief," Henry replied. "He has good breedin', but I don't expect he'll be able to match Satan's speed or come close to Boldt's Comet," he added.

A tall, heavy-set man, wearing horn-rimmed glasses

and a battered hat, came around the corner toward them. "Here's Mike," Henry said, opening the door of the van.

Henry introduced Alec to Mike; then the three walked over to the bay colt. "The Chief is coming along fast," Mike told Henry. "I want to blow him out a good stiff quarter this morning. That all right for your horse?"

Henry glanced in Alec's direction, then nodded.

Mike turned to Lenny Sansone, who stood beside him. "If he plays along, when he's out in front, fan your stick at him, Len. He'll move along then."

Lenny nodded, and then his gaze turned to Alec.

Henry said, "Oh, yeah, Len . . . I want you to meet Alec Ramsay. Alec, meet Len."

Alec liked the jockey's eyes and his firm grasp as they shook hands. It was hard to tell Lenny's age, but Alec judged him to be in his thirties.

"I saw you ride the Black in Chicago," Lenny said. "It was good riding on that horse, Alec."

Then Mike said, "Let's get going. It's getting hot fast today. Bring your horse out, Henry."

As Alec led Satan from the van, he felt the eyes of the others upon them, but his gaze never left the black colt. Satan was fretting, working himself up, and Alec talked soothingly to him. Then he heard Mike exclaim, "He's a giant, Henry! Where'd you get him? What's his breeding?"

"He belongs to Alec . . . or rather his father," Alec heard Henry reply.

"And sired by the Black," Lenny Sansone said. "You

don't have to tell me that. . . . He's more burly, but *him*, anyway.''

Mike's voice was excited as he asked, "Does he have the Black's speed, Henry?"

Alec didn't hear Henry's reply, for Satan, his eyes upon the Chief, uttered his piercing challenge.

The bay shot up his ears at Satan's whistle, and moved restlessly beneath Lenny's hand.

Satan made a single effort to jump, which Alec prevented, and then the black colt stood still, his wild eyes shifting from the Chief to Alec, and back again. "He doesn't want to fight, Satan. Take it easy," the boy said.

When Henry came over and saddled Satan, the colt stood quivering beneath his touch.

"It's not as bad as I thought it might be," Henry said, slipping the bridle over Satan's head, ". . . not yet, anyway."

"He's going to be all right, Henry," Alec replied confidently. "I can feel it. He's excited, but he has a right to be. . . . This is all so strange to him. But I'll be able to control him, as long as the Chief doesn't want to fight."

"He won't," Henry muttered. "The bay is a good-tempered colt."

"How about on the track?" Alec asked anxiously.

"With the other horses, y'mean? I guess you'll just have to wait and see how he acts up," Henry answered.

Lenny Sansone was already up on the Chief when Alec mounted Satan. The black colt crabstepped as Henry took him by the bridle, his eyes now upon Henry instead of the Chief. Alec talked to him and, slowly, he felt Satan quiet down beneath his knees.

Mike led his bay colt toward the track, and Henry, leading Satan, followed.

The black colt showed no outward signs of tension as they moved onto the track, but Alec dug his fingernails deep into the palms of his hands to keep them from shaking. He knew how important this workout was. If he could control Satan with strange horses on the track, they would be well on their way to the Hopeful. But if the colt went berserk, giving way to his savage nature to fight other young stallions, he might never race.

Two horses swept by, running hard on the rail, their hoofs pounding over the track. Satan's ears pitched forward and he uttered a short whistle. He was beginning to feel the tension now, and Alec whispered, "Easy, boy. Easy."

Henry, still holding the bridle, looked up at him. "You set, Alec?"

The boy nodded.

"Jog him around the track once along with the Chief," Henry instructed. "Keep away from the rail so the horses that are breezing can get by. Then if everything goes well we'll gallop him easy for a half, an' then blow him out the last quarter with the Chief."

"You mean give him his head?" Alec asked.

Henry nodded and a flicker of a smile was upon his lips. "You've waited a long time, Alec, an' here it is," he said quietly.

Satan moved restlessly, his head craned high, watching the horses on the track. His heavy ears were up, and his black forelock had fallen over the white diamond.

Patting the high crest of his neck, Alec repeated, "Easy, boy."

Henry nodded toward the men who leaned upon the rail in front of the huge, empty grandstand. "They've seen Satan," he said. "Look at them stare. They've never seen a colt as big as this one. An' they'll be watchin' him, Alec, wonderin' if he's got the speed to go with that body."

"They'll see," Alec promised. "They'll see."

Henry stepped back. As Satan jogged away, Alec stood high in his stirrups, holding him back. The colt shook his head, pulling for more rein, but Alec held it tight, talking to him all the while. Reaching out, Satan lengthened his stride, and Alec knew he wanted to catch up to the Chief, who jogged a short distance ahead.

"Easy, Satan. Easy," Alec whispered. "It's early yet."

Three horses breezed quickly past them, and Satan's muscles rippled as he bolted after them. Still standing in his stirrups, Alec kept a tight rein. "Easy, boy. Lots of time for that. Easy, Satan," he whispered.

One ear cocked back as the colt listened; then he slowed to a jog again.

Alec stroked Satan's neck. "You're ready, boy. I knew you'd be. You're not going to fight. You're going to run . . . and you'll run with the best of them. You're a champ, Satan, but you'll go easy today. For one quarter I'll let you run, but that's all. You'll go light today, boy, but soon it'll be all the way."

Alec gave the colt a little more rein, and he loped easily along as other horses swept past them. Finally they neared the Chief as they entered the backstretch halfway around the track.

Lenny Sansone, also poised high in his stirrups, holding the Chief in, turned in his saddle as Alec came up. "He's a mighty nice horse, Alec. . . . Haven't seen anything like him since the day I saw the Black run," he said admiringly. "How does he ride?"

"Like the Black," said Alec with a grin.

"You're serious?" Lenny asked. "You think he has his speed? He's pretty big. . . . Looks as if he has the endurance, but he's big for a sprinter."

"He can move," Alec said.

Satan snorted and swerved alongside the Chief; for a moment his teeth were bared.

"He could be nasty," Lenny said as Alec pulled Satan away.

They finished their jog in front of Mike and Henry, and when the old trainer came up to him, Alec said, "He did it, Henry!"

"Yeah," Henry replied, "not bad. Now jog around to the three-quarter pole. Then gallop a half an' blow him out for a quarter like I told you. Mike's having Len do the same with the Chief. You'll be finishing right here."

As Alec turned Satan around, he heard Mike say to

Lenny, "Turn it on that last quarter, Len. An' remember, if he starts to lag, fan your whip alongside him. He'll move then."

The sun was well up in the sky, and all the other horses had left the track. Alec noticed, though, that their trainers, exercise boys, and grooms still lined the rail in front of the grandstand. They wanted to watch the big black colt run.

Lenny moved up alongside Alec as they rounded the first turn. "We'll see what both of 'em have now," he shouted. "The Chief here has the speed, but sometimes he just plays along when I get him out in front, so I have to show him this." He pointed to the whip stuck in his boot.

As they neared the three-quarter pole they let up on their reins, and the horses swept by at a slow gallop.

Satan fought for his head as he gained momentum, his long black tail streaming behind him.

The Chief surged to the front, Lenny keeping him close to the rail. Alec made no attempt to catch up. Still half-poised in his stirrups, he was holding Satan back. Henry had said a slow gallop for the first half; Alec intended to do just that and not let Satan out until they hit the last quarter pole.

Satan was furious as Alec held him in and the Chief lengthened his lead. "Easy, Satan. Easy," Alec said. "This is just to get the feel of it."

The colt's ears cocked back, then pricked forward again as he reached out, fighting the bit.

The white rail of the track whipped by as they thundered down the backstretch and approached the last turn, with the Chief running easily a good four lengths ahead.

"Easy, Satan. Easy," Alec called to his horse. "Just a little farther now."

Satan wanted to run, and having the bay colt in front of him made him furious. Alec's arms felt like weights from the constant strain of holding his horse in check. The rail swept by at ever increasing speed, and Alec knew that he wouldn't be able to hold Satan back much longer. Then, through blurred eyes, he saw the final quarter pole flash by. In front of him, the Chief leapt forward as Lenny gave him his head.

With a cry of relief, Alec loosened the reins and bent low over Satan's neck.

The sudden blinding speed momentarily swept his breath away, and for a few seconds Alec clung desperately to Satan's black mane. Then the wind was whipping his face scarlet, and almost hysterically he heard himself yelling, "Now, Satan, now!"

But the giant colt needed no urging. Free, he ran like fire before the wind. He came down the homestretch with thunderous strides, engulfing the ground between him and the hard-running bay colt.

With about three hundred yards to go, Alec saw that this would be no race, for Satan would pass the Chief like a bullet. Disclosing amazing speed, the giant black bore down upon the bay, and Alec drew up the reins to bring Satan up on the outside. They were near now. . . . Another stride and they'd be flying past.

Suddenly Lenny reached for his whip and fanned it alongside the Chief to get more speed out of him. From the corner of his eye Alec saw it sweep by.

Satan saw it, too. He threw back his head, pulled up, swerved far across the track, and crashed hard against the outside rail.

The Sanford

16

They stood in the middle of the field, Alec keeping a firm hold on the lead rope attached to Satan's halter, and Henry standing close beside him.

"You don't think that leg will get worse when we put him on the track again?" Alec asked anxiously without moving his eyes from the colt. "You're sure?"

"I tell you again, no, Alec," Henry replied. "For the last couple of weeks, ever since he went through the fence, you've been askin' me that, and I've been tellin' you that in another few days or so his leg will be as good as it ever was . . . just as long as we keep him from playin' around too much, as we've been doin'. We've got to have patience for just a short time longer. Those muscles have got to be strengthened slowly, Alec. . . .

It's got to be like we were moldin' glass."

Satan stopped grazing and shook his head, pulling hard on the lead rope.

"He wants to run, Henry."

"Yeah, I know. He's got the feel of the track now and is anxious to get back to it." Henry paused, then added, "It's best to play it safe, though, Alec. We'll keep him on the lead rope for a few more days, then put him out in the field by himself before takin' him to the track."

"You think he'll be ready to go in the Hopeful then, Henry?" Alec asked eagerly. "It's less than two months off now."

"Plenty of time," Henry muttered; then his face sobered as he added, "The leg won't give him any trouble. . . . It's his fear of the whip that worries me, as I've been tellin' you all along."

"I know, Henry," Alec answered thoughtfully. "We've got to lick it some way."

"He'll never forget my usin' the whip on him, Alec." Henry's face was grim and his brow furrowed as he recalled the morning he had tried to break Satan so many months ago. "I've got to figure out some way to overcome that or he'll never finish a race."

"Maybe using blinkers, as you said, Henry," Alec suggested. "He'll only be able to see straight ahead then."

"Maybe," Henry repeated. "Maybe . . . if you can get him out in front before the other jocks start usin' their sticks."

"He runs like the wind, Henry. He'll be out in front."

"The Comet ain't no mild breeze, either, Alec," Henry cautioned. "An' there'll be Volence's Desert Storm. . . . The fastest two-year-olds in the country will all be there. Nope," he went on. "You can't be too cocksure about that race, Alec. The slightest swerve on Satan's part, an' he's licked runnin' against such horses."

They were silent for a long while, as Satan circled slowly about them, his head craned and heavy ears pricked forward.

Finally Henry said, "If you're out in front comin' down the homestretch, it'll be all right, Alec. But what's worryin' me as much as anything is the start. . . . You know as well as I do that they'll all be using their sticks then, too."

"I've been thinking about that, Henry," Alec replied thoughtfully.

"You'll have trouble keepin' him on the track if he acts the same way he did with the Chief," Henry grunted. "You can't run too wide an' lose ground with those fast horses in the Hopeful, Alec. It's too short a race. An' remember, they're runnin' the Hopeful over the Widener Course this year an' that's a straightaway for the whole six an' a half furlongs."

"I know, Henry," Alec replied quietly. "And maybe a straightaway is best for Satan. If I draw an outside position, I can bring him straight down the track, keeping him away from the other horses."

"Mebbe," Henry agreed thoughtfully. "An' the blinkers will help in that case. But we've got to do more than that, Alec. Between now and the Hopeful, we've got to try to undo all the harm I'm responsible for.'' Henry paused, then continued, ''I'm goin' to get some sticks an' we're goin' to put 'em all about Satan's stall, so he can get used to seein' 'em around. Then I want you to start carryin' a stick when you're ridin' him in the field an' over at the track. We've got to get him used to seein' sticks around, Alec. . . . We've got to,'' Henry concluded.

A few minutes later Alec led Satan into his stall; and as he stood beside his horse, he said, ''You won't let us down, will you, fellow?'' While Satan nuzzled his shirt, Alec rubbed him between the eyes.

''He's right as rain,'' Henry said.

''He's ready to go,'' Alec said. ''Or he will be in a few more weeks.''

When they were outside again, Henry drew Alec over to the wooden bench. ''I've got something on my mind,'' he said, sitting down.

''Don't you think we've got enough already?'' Alec replied half jokingly, as he sat down beside his friend. Then he saw the tense look on Henry's face and his own sobered. ''What is it?'' he asked.

''I want you to do me a favor,'' Henry said without looking at him.

''Sure.''

''About two weeks before the Hopeful, there's a seventy-five-hundred-dollar race for two-year-olds at Belmont called the Sanford,'' Henry said slowly. ''I'd like to see Satan in it . . . an' I want to pay the entry fee.''

Alec started to object, but Henry interrupted him. "I've got the dough, Alec. It only costs a hundred an' twenty-five bucks to start him, an' entries don't close until next week.''

Alec looked at him for a long while before saying, "You mean you want to see how he goes. . . . That's it, isn't it, Henry?''

"You might call it that. It's good preparation for the big race. It's run over the Widener Course like the Hopeful will be.''

"And if he doesn't go well . . . if he swerves and gets licked . . .''

Henry's eyes fell. "If that happens I'd say save the five hundred bucks it would cost you to start him in the Hopeful an' forget the whole thing. We could then work on him and maybe race him next year.''

Alec didn't say anything.

Henry continued. "You've already shelled out two hundred keepin' him eligible for the Hopeful during the past year. . . . You'd lose that, but save yourself the five hundred.''

Alec looked at him, his eyes flashing. Finally he said, "He'll win the Sanford . . . and the Hopeful.''

Henry's eyes flashed back as he said, "Then you'll let me enter him?''

"You're sure you can spare the money?''

"I've got it," Henry said. "I want to do it, because if I

hadn't used the whip on Satan we wouldn't be havin' this trouble. An' maybe," he went on thoughtfully, "his runnin' in the Sanford will help matters some. At least we'll know where we stand."

"How about Boldt's Comet and Desert Storm? Do you think they'll be in the Sanford?" Alec asked.

"No," Henry returned. "Boldt is waitin' for the Hopeful, an' Volence is runnin' Desert Storm in the Grand Union Hotel Stakes a few days after the Sanford, so he won't be in it either. It'll be a walkaway for Satan, if he doesn't give you any trouble," he concluded.

"We'll work on him, Henry."

"An' I'll get the blinkers and the whips when I go to New York this afternoon."

They were walking down the driveway when Mr. Ramsay came toward them carrying a long cardboard box.

Alec greeted his father with curiosity in his eyes, for it was very seldom that he came home for lunch.

"I wanted to give you this before I went into the house," Mr. Ramsay explained, handing the box to Alec. "Keep it in the barn," he said hastily, his gaze turning in the direction of the brown house across the street.

Alec's intent eyes traveled from the box in his hands to his father, then back again. "You want me to keep it for you?" he asked in bewilderment. He looked at Henry, and he saw that the old trainer was as amazed by his father's strange actions as he was.

"No . . . it's yours, Alec," Mr. Ramsay replied.

"They're your riding silks . . . black except for the white diamond on the sleeves. That's the way you wanted it, wasn't it?"

Alec met his father's eyes. "Dad," he said, ". . . you really did it . . . you went out and ordered them yourself . . ."

"It was nothing, Alec. Nothing at all," Mr. Ramsay said quickly. "I thought that since I registered the colors with the Jockey Club, the least I could do was to buy the silks for you." Abruptly, Mr. Ramsay turned to Henry. "What's the status regarding Alec's jockey license, Henry? He must have one to ride, mustn't he?"

Henry smiled. For Mr. Ramsay's precise manner couldn't conceal his keen interest in the race which was so close at hand. Henry shook his head. "No, Mr. Ramsay," he replied. "Alec doesn't need a license. . . . In fact, he can't get one until he has ridden in two races. What we're goin' to do is to get permission from the stewards the day before the race. We won't have any trouble. . . . It's a formality every new rider has to go through."

"You're sure now, Henry?" Mr. Ramsay asked, concerned. "It wouldn't do to have anything go wrong before the Hopeful."

"I'm sure," Henry returned. Then he added, "Oh, yes . . . we've decided to enter Satan in a race at Belmont two weeks before the Hopeful."

"Good. Good," Mr. Ramsay said. "Then he'll have won a race before running in the Hopeful."

Henry didn't say anything, but Alec said, "Yes . . . that's right, Dad."

"We'll send in his nomination for this race tonight, then, Henry," Mr. Ramsay said. Turning to Alec, he added, "Don't mention my buying these riding silks to your mother, Alec." Pausing, he said confidingly, "She wouldn't understand."

Nodding, Alec smiled. "Yes, Dad, I know . . . she wouldn't understand."

Satan was nominated for the Sanford, and the month of July sped by with weeks of exacting, relentless work on the part of Henry and Alec. For a while the giant black colt was kept upon the lead rope; then, when they both saw that his leg had fully recovered, he was turned loose to spend long days in the field, grazing, dozing, and very often galloping thunderously about, his sharp whistle ringing in the air.

Day and night they watched him, their eyes as keen and eager as Satan's.

"He's galloping as free as he ever did," Henry said.

"He's ready to go . . . and he wants to reach out," Alec said. "It's time, Henry . . . only about three weeks to go now before the Sanford."

During the days that followed, Henry had Alec ride Satan in the field, and the boy carried a whip in his hand, swinging it lightly alongside the colt. Satan swerved hard at the beginning, but as the days sped by it seemed to Alec that the colt's fear of the stick became less intense and, more often than not, when he swung it alongside him, Satan would continue running without paying any attention to it.

"He's getting used to it," Alec told the old trainer. "I know he is!"

"Don't be too sure, Alec," Henry returned. "It might be different in a race when he gets a glimpse of those jocks actually *hittin'* their horses with their sticks. But," he added, "there's no doubt he's gettin' used to seein' those sticks hangin' up in his stall and you carryin' one without usin' it on him. Maybe, Alec, maybe . . ."

"And the blinkers should help in the race too," Alec said optimistically, as he tapped Satan between the eyes.

Two weeks before the running of the Sanford, they again worked the giant black colt in the early mornings at Belmont. And as Alec breezed Satan down the track, the new black hood covering his small head, even Henry grew optimistic as the colt ran without swerving when Alec swung his whip alongside.

"You get him out in front, and we've got it," he told Alec.

"It's the start I'm still worried about," Alec returned. "With all those jocks using their sticks, there's no telling what might happen."

"Yeah," Henry muttered. "We've got to wait for that."

The day of the Sanford broke cool and gray, the August sun hidden behind heavy clouds. It was a little after dawn when Alec arrived at the barn to find Henry already there, the old trainer's lips as tightly drawn as his own.

Alec said, "Hope it doesn't rain."

"It won't," Henry reassured him. "It'll be a dry, fast track." Shrugging his shoulders, he added, "Makes no difference, though . . . he can plow through mud as well as anything."

Napoleon neighed as they walked past, but they had eyes only for the black colt this morning.

He stood up to his fetlocks in the straw bedding, watching their approach. He shook himself as Alec entered the stall, and shoved his head against him.

"Today's the day," Alec whispered, rubbing the heavy ears.

Henry entered the stall, carrying a pail of oats. Satan moved restlessly as Henry poured the oats into his feed box.

Alec pulled the colt's head down toward him and said, "Just oats today, Satan . . . no hay. . . . It's race day." Satan shook his head as though he sensed what was ahead of him. His head came up and his eyes were bright and burning. Alec led him over to the feed box and then left the stall with Henry.

As Satan crunched his feed, Henry scrutinized the giant muscles rippling beneath the glistening black body. "He's right, Alec," he muttered. "As ready to go as he ever will be."

Alec didn't say anything.

After a few minutes Henry spoke again. "Soon as he's finished eating, we'll take him over to the track. . . . We'll blow him out this morning to get the kinks outa his legs an' then sit back an' wait for the race."

"You got a stall over there?" Alec asked.

"Everything is set," Henry replied slowly. "It's up to him now."

Clad in his new black silks, Alec sat still and tense on Satan's back as he followed the line of thoroughbreds onto the track for the running of the Sanford. The colt crabstepped restlessly, and Alec loosened the reins a little.

"This is it, boy," he whispered. "Easy now . . . I'm with you."

They were alone, on their own. Behind them, back in the paddock, was Henry. He hadn't said much when he had boosted Alec up. He didn't have to. Alec knew what he was expected to do. "Luck, Alec," was all Henry had said.

The large grandstand was packed with a milling crowd awaiting the running of the Sanford; and people were decked deeply along the rail as well, waiting. Their shouts reached a mighty crescendo as the horses appeared on the track.

Satan's eyes blazed and he half reared. Pulling him down, Alec forgot everything but his horse. "Easy, Satan," he said. "Easy does it. Take this one in your stride, fella. . . . The big one is coming up in a couple of weeks. This is just a prep, boy. . . . You've no competition here, none at all."

Alec followed the other horses with his eyes as they paraded past the grandstand. He talked soothingly to Satan, but his gaze swept over the other thoroughbreds in the race. They were all good two-year-olds, as Henry had said, but they weren't in the same class with Boldt's Comet, who had whipped most of them soundly during the winter racing in Florida.

Satan shook his black-hooded head and whistled shrilly as they neared the end of the stands. The other thoroughbreds moved nervously at Satan's challenge, but none of them showed fight. The voices of the crowd were stilled for a few seconds, and Alec knew that thousands of eyes were upon him and his horse. Somewhere in that packed throng were a few who would watch Satan run with more than casual eyes. . . . Alec knew his father was up there, and Henry would be at the rail by now. Nine chances out of ten Boldt was there too, and Volence as well. They alone knew the breeding of his black colt. They alone knew that he was the son of the mighty Black!

Fortunately Alec had drawn an outside position, which he had wanted for this race. As Satan loped around the track toward the starting stalls near the backstretch, Alec kept him close to the far rail.

When he arrived at the starting gate, he saw that the other horses were already walking into their stalls. The starter was ready, waiting for him. Talking to his horse, Alec moved Satan up.

They were at the head of the Widener Course, a long straightaway leading diagonally across the infield. Far down the stretch, opposite the packed stands, was the finish line. Six furlongs, Alec thought . . . three-quarters of a mile. It was a short race, even shorter than the Hopeful. As Henry had said, Satan couldn't afford to lose too much ground at the start. He would have to be brought out fast. Alec's gaze shifted to the other jockeys. They had their whips in their hands, and apparently were going to use them hard at the break. He didn't like it.

Alec saw to it that Satan was facing straight ahead as he moved into the starting stall. The boy's face was tense; the gate doors would open any second. There was only one horse on his right. It was as he had wanted it. He'd bring Satan straight down as far away from the other horses as possible.

A horse backed out of his stall. The starter waited for him to be brought in again. Satan was working himself up, and he tried to turn his hooded head toward the other horses. Already the reins had beat the perspiration on his neck into a white lather. Alec was as tense as his colt, waiting . . . waiting.

The gate doors flew open, and a mighty shout from the stands swept across the infield: "They're off!" Then the roar of the crowd died beneath the rolling thunder of pounding hoofs.

They broke fast and with a mighty surge swept away from the gate like a giant wave hurtling itself shoreward with ever increasing momentum.

"Move, Satan! Move!" Alec shouted as his colt bolted forward with the others.

For a few seconds there was just a blur of pounding hoofs and flashing silks. Then out of the melee several horses on the rail burst forward, their jockeys cutting away with their sticks.

Alec felt Satan hesitate as he saw the swinging whips on his left; then the colt swerved hard to the right. Alec let him move over, his voice alone urging him on. The horse on the outside came up fast as Satan fell back and Alec's face went white when he saw the jockey using his whip. Satan checked his speed again when the horse came up on his right, and swerved back toward the inside rail only to see more thrashing sticks.

Calling to Satan, Alec pulled him to the outside of the horse which had swept forward on their right. Then, with a clear track ahead of him, he sat down to ride.

With thunderous strides, Satan bore down upon the other horses as they pounded down the straightaway. Alec gave him his head, and as he called repeatedly to him Satan extended himself, his feet barely touching the ground.

Far on the outside of the track, Satan passed the lagging horses in the race and moved up to the leaders. Through wind-blurred eyes, Alec saw the hindquarters of the horses in front rise and fall.

Satan was closing in upon them fast, but Alec wondered if his horse would be able to overtake them before reaching the wire. . . . He had lost much ground at the break.

Satan pounded the dirt with great strides. Alec saw that there were only three horses in front of them. The leaders were running hard, but Alec knew that their jockeys were saving something for the final drive that would come in the last few seconds. Then they'd go for their sticks again.

Alec's hand fell to his horse's wet neck, and he called to him. As Satan responded, one of the horses in front was driven a little to the right by his jockey. Alec kept Satan going straight ahead, knowing that he couldn't afford to lose ground again by turning Satan away from the hard-running horse in front. He had to take a chance. He had to drive Satan straight through to the wire.

Alec felt Satan surge forward with blinding speed as he called upon him. The giant black colt hurtled past the third-place horse before the jockey had gone for his stick. The ground swept by in waves beneath Satan's flying hoofs, and he drew up quickly alongside the second-place horse, running a half-length behind the leader. The white rail flashed by; the mass of humanity in the stands rose to its feet, screaming; and just ahead loomed the wire.

Alec saw the jockey in front go for his stick. He felt Satan hesitate and swerve slightly toward the outside again. Alec's hands fell upon the black neck and he shouted to Satan as the hard-running horse in front surged forward. With a hundred yards to go, Satan's ears swept back when Alec called to him; then he leveled out again.

The giant colt came down to the wire like a black thunderbolt. There was no stopping him now. Never had he run so fast. Alec's breath came short at Satan's speed. With blinding fury, Satan passed the horse in front and swept under the wire, winner by two lengths!

It was more than an hour later when the track security police got the curious spectators away from Satan's stall and Alec was alone with the men closest to him . . . his father, Henry, and Mr. Volence. Tired and worn, he listened to them.

His father said, a little cautiously, "I just don't think, Alec, that you should have held him back quite so long. Why, you gave them such a lead that I was really worried."

Alec smiled wanly, while Henry said, "It couldn't be helped, Mr. Ramsay."

"It was good riding, Alec," Mr. Volence said quietly, as he stood in the background. "Henry told me what you're up against. You'll have to work on him some more, though."

"Yes, we have to, if we're to do anything in the Hopeful," Henry said.

"We can do it in two weeks," Alec said confidently. "He gave me trouble at the start, but he came through coming down."

"Yeah," Henry agreed, "he did that all right. And the seventy-five hundred dollars he won can buy a lot of hay."

Mr. Volence said, "He has blinding speed, Alec. He's a worthy son of his sire." After pausing, he added, "But remember, the Hopeful is only six furlongs and a half. Satan can't possibly give Boldt's Comet or my Desert Storm much of a lead and still win. I say that as a friend and not as the owner of a horse who is out to beat yours."

A few minutes later Mr. Volence left, accompanied by Alec's father. When they had gone, Henry turned to the boy. "He's right, you know, Alec."

"Yes," Alec returned, "I know."

Alec was ready to leave when Peter Boldt suddenly appeared at the barn. Henry, who had been in Satan's stall, came out, closing the door behind him. "What do you want?" he asked Boldt.

Boldt's thin lips drew back in a smile; then, ignoring Henry, he turned to Alec. "Will you take fifty thousand dollars for him now?" he asked.

Alec shook his head without speaking.

Boldt moved over to the stall door, but Henry blocked his way.

"I'm asking you nicely to get out of here," Henry said. "*Nicely* . . . for the last time."

"You're growing out of your breeches, aren't you, Dailey?" Boldt asked sarcastically.

Alec saw Henry clench his fists. "You'd better go," the boy said. "I'm not selling Satan for any price."

Turning to him again, Boldt said, "You can't win with him in a fast race. I saw what happened today."

"I'm not selling," Alec said firmly.

The color rose in Boldt's cheeks as Henry moved toward him. Slowly he backed away to the door, his face bitter. "You won't even race him again," he rasped. "I'll see to that. There'll be no Hopeful for your horse." Then, turning, he moved hastily away from the stall without a backward glance.

"Wonder what he meant by that last crack?" asked Alec, concerned. " 'There'll be no Hopeful for your horse,' " he said, repeating Boldt's words.

"No good, you can bet your last penny on that," Henry grunted.

Alec was silent for a few minutes, then he said, "It's one thing on top of another."

"Yeah."

Alec went over to Satan and rubbed his head. "But you did it today, boy. . . . You came through, just as I knew you would," he whispered. "And you'll be running in the Hopeful . . . and winning it, too."

Accused!

17

After the running of the Sanford, it could no longer be kept a secret that there existed a son of the Black. Jim Neville probed into the breeding of Satan, winner of the Sanford. The noted sportswriter talked to Boldt, Volence, Henry and Alec, and when he had finished he sat down and wrote his story. The news traveled fast. Neville's column was picked up by the wire services and carried throughout the world.

"It's out now all right," grunted Henry the next day, as he read the newspaper with Alec standing close beside him.

"Maybe it's for the best," the boy replied quietly. "We couldn't have kept it to ourselves much longer."

Bending over Henry's shoulder, Alec read with him:

Henry Dailey, that old Montana magician of the trainers, pulled another trick out of his bag yesterday when he uncovered Satan, the strapping son of the Black, who won the six-furlong Sanford with a bristling drive to the wire.

It will be recalled that the Black is the horse which won fame overnight three years ago, when he astounded the track world and carved a large niche for himself in turf history by administering a sound licking to the two turf giants of that year, Cyclone and Sun Raider, in the unforgettable match race in Chicago. Soon after that race the Black was returned to Arabia, where he is owned by the Sheikh Abu Ja' Kub ben Ishak.

Satan, more burly than his famed sire, showed tremendous speed once he got under way, and it is likely that the giant black colt, owned by William Augustus Ramsay, will be capable of matching strides with Peter Boldt's unbeaten and highly regarded Comet when they meet in the Hopeful two weeks hence.

Piloted by Alec Ramsay, son of the owner and the kid who rode the Black in the Chicago match race, Satan broke alertly, but dropped back suddenly to last place as Cue, Skytracer and Whang, in that order, shot to the fore and opened up daylight over the field. After a couple of furlongs, Ramsay brought his giant colt up fast on the outside. Satan came down to the wire with terrific speed. He pulled up when Hine and Lauritzen, riding Cue and Skytracer, began fanning their mounts with their sticks, but then came on to win by two lengths.

When Henry had finished reading, he turned to Alec. "Like Volence said," he muttered, "we can't have any pulling up in the Hopeful."

Nodding, Alec walked into the barn. He made his way quickly to Satan's stall and moved in beside his colt. Satan nuzzled him, and Alec rubbed the horse between the eyes. Finally he said, "No more pulling up, Satan. You have nothing to be afraid of. . . . No one is going to use a stick on you." Reaching up on the side of the stall, Alec grabbed one of the whips which Henry had put there. "Look, boy," he said, holding the whip up to Satan, "you don't have to be afraid of this."

Satan drew back at sight of the whip in Alec's hand, but the boy held him, talking all the while, and finally the fear left the colt's eyes. Alec moved the stick up beside his muzzle and gently rubbed it against the soft skin. "You won't be hit with it again, Satan. . . . I promise you that," he said. "You'll see a lot of this in the next two weeks, boy . . . more than you ever did before . . . and you'll get used to it. . . . So, when you run the Hopeful, there'll be no pulling up, Satan . . . no pulling up. . . ."

And Alec meant what he told Satan. The days that passed were more exacting for the boy than ever before. He spent long hours with Satan, and the stick was always a part of him. Alec carried it when he rode; he held it in his hand whenever he entered Satan's stall; and very often he would rub the stick gently across the giant body. "Easy, boy. Easy," he would say, "there's nothing to be afraid of."

And while it was exacting work for Alec, it was nerve-racking business for Henry. With intent but sober eyes he watched Alec attempt to undo the harm for which he alone had been responsible. "I taught it to him," he would growl constantly. "It's my fault, Alec. It'll take months. . . . You can't do it. . . ."

But Henry's pessimistic outlook only served to drive Alec to working harder with his horse. He spent more time in the stable than he did at home. His mother became really alarmed as Alec grew quieter than ever before, his young face heavy with concern. His father told him, "It's just a horse race, Alec. Don't let it get you so."

But he was wrong, for it was more than just a horse race to Alec.

No longer did Alec ride unseen in the field. Curious throngs gathered outside the high iron-barred fence, their faces pressed hard against the bars hoping to see the horse which had received so much publicity since winning the Sanford.

Unmindful of them, Alec continued to work his horse, fanning the stick alongside as he rode, noting the slightest swerve on Satan's part. Over a week passed in this manner, and as the day of the Hopeful drew near, Alec told Henry, "He'll do it. . . . He's not swerving or pulling up any more. He's ready, Henry."

"I hope you're right," Henry replied slowly. "I hope you're right, Alec," he repeated. His keen eyes swept over the horse, then he added, "You know him better'n anyone else . . . but good behavior now doesn't absolutely mean that it'll be the same under silks.''

"I know, Henry . . . but he'll do it for me. I'm sure he will.''

As they left Satan's stall Henry said, "Only three days to go now.''

"Yes . . . three days,'' Alec repeated quietly.

Outside they sat down on the bench and relaxed under the rays of a hot noonday sun. Finally Henry pulled a newspaper from his pocket and said, "You knew Volence's Desert Storm copped the Grand Union Hotel Stakes yesterday, didn't you?''

"Yes, I'd heard,'' Alec returned.

"He beat a good field. . . . Only Boldt's Comet was missing. He broke the track record too,'' Henry continued thoughtfully. Then, picking up the newspaper, he added, "Here's what Jim Neville writes: 'A six-furlong track record which had stood the test of twelve long years and the efforts of tons of high-class horseflesh was exploded at Belmont Park yesterday when Charles T. Volence's Desert Storm made his debut to win the Grand Union Hotel Stakes in 1:10^4/s.' ''

His eyes looking toward the ground, Alec listened while Henry continued to read. Then when the old trainer neared the end of the column, Alec looked up as Henry said, "Get this, Alec. . . . Neville says here, 'This great exhibition turned in by Volence's small chestnut colt definitely established him as a top threat to Peter Boldt's Comet in next Saturday's running of the Hopeful. The Comet will have to be at his peak to win over Desert Storm, if yesterday's race is any indication of the way

Volence's colt will run for the pot of gold on Saturday. Boldt's gray favorite was a ball of fire during last winter's racing in Florida, copping the four races he ran there and setting two track records. The Comet has been away from the races since then, but from all reports Boldt has him at his peak in anticipation of winning the Hopeful. Recognized also as a threat to both the Comet and Desert Storm is William Ramsay's giant black colt, Satan, who won the Sanford two weeks ago.' ''

Alec said nothing until Henry had folded the newspaper and placed it in his pocket. Then, rising to his feet, Alec said, "Sounds like a good race, Henry."

"Yeah, mighty good," the old trainer agreed, getting up from the bench.

They were walking down the graveled driveway when Alec saw his father's black sedan coming down the street. It stopped in front of the gate and Mr. Ramsay got out.

"Something's up," Alec said. "He's home in the middle of the day again."

"Couldn't be another set of silks, could it?" Henry smiled.

Mr. Ramsay called to them from the car, and as they approached, Alec saw that his father's face was grave.

"I've been summoned to appear before the stewards over at Belmont," he told Alec. "You're to go along, too."

"Y'mean they've called you up?" Henry asked, his brow furrowing. "What do they want?"

"I was called at the office. The person on the telephone simply said that it was important that Alec and I appear at a two o'clock meeting," Mr. Ramsay explained. "You know as much about it as I do," he concluded.

"Are we going now?" Alec asked, concerned.

"Yes, get in the car, Alec."

"I'd better be going along, too," Henry grunted. "If there's any trouble I want to be in on it."

As they climbed into the car, Alec turned to Henry. "You said trouble, Henry. What trouble could there be?"

"I dunno," the old trainer replied, as the car moved down the street. "But there has to be some trouble or you and your father wouldn't be goin' before the stewards."

Henry was right. Alec knew that as soon as they walked into the stewards' office at the track. Three men sat behind a long rectangular table, awaiting them. And seated in a deep red-leather chair to one side of the stewards was Peter Boldt, his thin lips drawn back in a sickly smile.

It was then that Boldt's parting words of a few weeks before came sharply to Alec's mind. "There'll be no Hopeful for your horse," he had said. "You won't even race him again."

Henry, his face white with anger at sight of Boldt, had come to a stop a few feet in front of Alec. Mr. Ramsay hesitantly walked forward toward the stewards' table. Alec saw that his father was groping for words. He didn't belong here; his every movement disclosed it.

One of the stewards stood up. "Mr. William Augustus Ramsay?" he asked.

Peter Boldt smirked when he became aware of Mr. Ramsay's feeling of strangeness and discomfort. Obviously Mr. Ramsay didn't like being called on the carpet. Then Boldt's gaze caught Henry's movement as his old employee moved toward him. The smirk left Boldt's lips and he slid his chair closer to the stewards' table.

Alec was listening attentively to the gray-haired man behind the table who was speaking to his father. "Mr. Ramsay," the man said slowly, "we regret to tell you that a charge has been made against you by Mr. Boldt."

Alec saw his father look quickly at Boldt, then back again at the man behind the table. He noticed too that his father was regaining his composure. There was a sharp ring to his voice as he asked, "What is the charge?"

"Mr. Boldt has charged you with false registry of the black colt, Satan. He claims that your son Alec is the owner, and that you falsely registered the horse in your name so your son could ride him." Pausing, the man riffled through some papers before him. "We have your original application for registry of the black colt sired by Shêtân out of Jôhar and bred by Abu Ja' Kub ben Ishak of Arabia. We also have the colt's pedigree as recorded in the Stud Book of Arabia. However, Mr. Boldt charges that the colt was sold to Alec Ramsay, your son, by Abu Ja' Kub ben Ishak." The gray-haired man glanced at Peter Boldt before continuing. "Mr. Boldt, as a licensed owner, has the right under the rules to raise an objection to any horse racing at this meeting. We, in turn, have the power to call for proof that a horse is neither itself disqualified in any respect, nor nominated by, nor the property, wholly or in part, of a disqualified person. In default of such proof being given to our satisfaction we can declare a horse disqualified.''

As the man paused, Alec's gaze turned to Peter Boldt. There was nothing to fear now, Alec thought. They had proof that he had sold Satan to his father, and Satan would run in the Hopeful! Henry's eyes met Alec's and he nodded his head approvingly.

The gray-haired man was talking again. ''Mr. Boldt has provided us with true copies of the transfer of ownership of the black colt referred to from Abu Ja' Kub ben Ishak to Alec Ramsay. Mr. Ramsay, we would like to see evidence that the colt Satan was your property at date of registry, and proof that he does not belong to your son Alec as Mr. Boldt charges.''

Alec saw his father's unwavering eyes leave the man behind the desk and come to rest upon Boldt. Slowly he said, ''The evidence is at my home. I have a bill of sale to prove that the colt rightfully belongs to me and that I did not falsify the registration.'' Mr. Ramsay turned back to the steward. ''When shall I bring the evidence?''

''Tomorrow morning at eleven o'clock,'' the man said. ''If you can produce proof of ownership at that time the charges will be dismissed. If not, I'm afraid that we must bar the colt from racing again at this meeting.''

''I'll have the evidence here at eleven,'' Mr. Ramsay promised.

After they had left the room Henry said, ''I'd like to stay here and wait for Boldt.''

''You'd better come along with us, Henry,'' Alec

returned. "It won't do any good to beat him up."

"It would do me a lot of good," Henry grunted. "He picked up all this nonsense about you not owning Satan when he walked into your house that day and tried to buy Satan from your father, who told him he wouldn't sell before talkin' to you 'cause Satan was *your* horse."

"Let Satan lick his horse in the Hopeful . . . that'll be worse than anything you can do with your hands, Henry," Alec said.

They were at the head of the stairs, with Henry still insistent upon waiting for Boldt, when Mr. Ramsay said soberly, "I'd rather have you come along and help me look for the bill of sale, Henry."

As one, they turned to him with anxious eyes.

"Dad," Alec said quickly. "You mean you don't know exactly where it is?"

Mr. Ramsay avoided their eyes. "I had it in the safe deposit box until a few weeks ago, when Satan won the Sanford," he explained slowly. "Then I took it out to show it to some of the boys at the office. They didn't think I owned him, you see," he added with attempted lightness. "I remember putting it in my pocket afterward and going home, so I must have it somewhere in the house. I can't remember just where, though. . . . I was looking for it last evening."

"And you didn't find it . . ." Henry said.

"Dad," Alec asked pleadingly, "did you ask Mom? . . . She always knows where things are."

Mr. Ramsay shook his head. "No," he said. "I haven't

had a chance to yet.'' Pausing, he added, ''Yes, Alec, I'm
sure you're right. . . . She'll know where it is.''

''Somebody better know where it is,'' Henry said,
as he led the way down the stairs. ''Somebody's got to
know where it is by eleven o'clock tomorrow morning.''

It was after three o'clock in the afternoon when they
arrived home. Alec and Henry were out of the car before
Mr. Ramsay had brought it completely to a stop. As they
reached the porch Alec stopped and, turning in his
tracks, yelled to his father, ''Which suit were you
wearing, Dad?''

''The blue one,'' Mr. Ramsay shouted back as he
stepped from the car. ''The blue serge . . . but it isn't
there, Alec. I've looked. It must be somewhere else.''

''Somewhere else.'' Henry grunted as he ran up the
porch steps behind Alec. ''A house with six rooms an' an
attic, an' it's *somewhere else.*''

Alec and Henry had gone through the blue serge suit
and were cleaning out the pockets of Mr. Ramsay's other
suits, when Alec's mother entered the bedroom.

''Alec! What on earth are you doing?'' she asked
anxiously.

''The *paper,* Mom. Dad's lost it.'' Then, as Alec saw the
bewilderment in her eyes, he explained, ''The bill of sale
I gave Dad, when I sold him the colt.''

''Oh, I know where it is,'' she said, smiling.

Alec and Henry turned toward her, their faces brightening.

Then she said, ''He keeps it in his safe deposit vault,

Alec. He told me it was very valuable and he didn't want to lose it. You know how he misplaces everything," she concluded.

Heaviness enshrouded their faces again. "Yes, Mom, I know," Alec said slowly. "That's just it. . . . He's lost it. He took it out of the box."

There was a short bark and a pattering of feet. Sebastian entered the room and went to Alec. The boy rubbed the dog's head, but his eyes were still upon his mother.

Henry said, "Now, Mrs. Ramsay, if he brought it home and put it down, where do you think he'd put it?"

Mrs. Ramsay shook her head as she answered, "Henry, if you'd ever lived with him, you wouldn't ask that. He'd be apt to put it down anywhere in the house."

" 'Anywhere in the house,' " Henry repeated, grimacing. "Well, let's go, because we've got to find it."

As Henry went back to the job of searching the closet, Alec told his mother, "We've got to find it, Mom, or Satan won't be able to run in the Hopeful."

"You mean," his mother said slowly, "that you won't be able to race if you don't find the paper?"

Alec nodded, then turned to help Henry.

The afternoon passed as they meticulously searched every room without finding any trace of the paper. Tony had been called in as he was passing by, and the huckster had eagerly joined in the search.

"We need every pair of eyes we can get," Henry told Tony. "Good or bad."

"I'ma good man with the eyes," Tony returned seriously.

"Take the attic then," Henry said. "We ain't looked up there yet."

"I never go in the attic," Mr. Ramsay interrupted soberly.

"Better look anyway," Henry told Tony. "C'mon, Alec, let's go through the bureaus again. It's after seven now."

"I'll pull up the chair seats again," Mr. Ramsay said, wiping the perspiration from his forehead. "It just may have slid out of my pocket."

As Alec and Henry climbed the stairs, Mrs. Ramsay called to them. "Don't you want dinner? You must be hungry."

"I couldn't eat, Mom," Alec replied.

Henry said, "You might do me a favor, Mrs. Ramsay, by callin' the missis and tellin' her I won't be home until late."

"I'll be glad to, Henry," Mrs. Ramsay answered. "How late shall I tell her you'll be?"

"Not until eleven o'clock tomorrow morning, if we don't find that paper," Henry said, following Alec up the stairs.

The search went on as the hands in the hall clock climbed to midnight and then began descending. Mr. Ramsay insisted upon his wife's going to bed at two o'clock; then, an hour later, he and Tony fell asleep sitting on the living-room couch.

It was after four o'clock and the sky was tinged with the gray light of dawn when Alec and Henry walked heavily out onto the porch and sat down on the steps.

"Just a few minutes' rest . . . then we'll go at it again," Henry said.

"Do you think it's any use?" Alec asked. "We've been over the house at least fifty times."

"What else is there to do?" Henry asked.

"He might never have brought it home. He might have lost it."

"We could try the newspapers," Henry suggested.

"No," Alec said. "It's too late to make the morning papers." He looked at his wrist watch. "We have only six hours to go, Henry."

Henry was silent for a few minutes. Then he said, "We might ask him about the boys in his office . . . the ones he showed it to. Maybe they've got it, not knowin' how important it is."

"He said he's sure he had it with him when he left the office," Alec returned.

"I wish he was sure he knew what he did with it," Henry mumbled, discouragement in his voice.

Alec allowed his head to fall back against the porch post. He shut his eyes for a few seconds, then struggled to open them again. Slowly he turned toward Henry. His friend's head was resting heavily upon his knees. Alec closed his eyes again. Just a few minutes' sleep was all he wanted . . . just a few minutes. . . . Then they'd have to look for the paper again. . . . They had to find it before eleven. . . . That paper . . . that silly little paper couldn't keep Satan out of the Hopeful . . . a paper that had only cost his father a dollar . . . just one dollar . . . and ahead of them, two days off, was a twenty-five-thousand-dollar race. . . . But the money wasn't important . . . ahead of them was Boldt's Comet. . . . Satan had to pass him, had to beat the gray.

Alec's head fell, and he was asleep.

Mrs. Ramsay

18

Mrs. Ramsay had been in bed for a long time, but she hadn't slept. She lay there, still and quiet, her eyes open. In the darkness, she could see nothing, but her ears were alert to every sound. She heard the men's footsteps on the attic floor above, the sound of their voices as they searched the house again and again from attic to cellar. The hours passed . . . from two, to three, to four . . . and still they searched. Their footsteps lagged now . . . and there were fewer of them than earlier.

She ran her hand over her husband's empty pillow. Poor Bill, she thought. Why did he have to get mixed up in all this? He had no business in it. And now the fault was his; for he alone had been responsible for the safekeeping of the paper which they said was so important. She did not regret that it was lost. She admitted that. And more. She was glad . . . no, perhaps that wasn't the right word. Relieved, rather. It was a relief to know that Alec was not to ride Satan in the race that was to be run the day after tomorrow. There would be no need now to worry about his safety in such a race . . . for without the paper, Satan could not run. And it was as she had wanted it.

Still staring into the darkness, she thought of Alec. To her, he was still a boy and not the man he claimed to be. Perhaps, she admitted, it was because he was her only child. She had tried hard not to disclose her anxiety, her concern and deep love for Alec. She wanted him to be the man she'd always hoped he'd be. And yet, it was difficult to forget the years that had gone by, and to realize that he needed her guiding hand no longer. She was clutching desperately at something that was slowly going beyond her reach. It had to come, she realized that. And at times she had thought herself reconciled to it.

But tonight she was clutching Alec's hand once more . . . and she was very much aware of it as she lay there. Only half-heartedly had she helped search for the paper. She hadn't wanted to find it. She didn't want to spend next Saturday afternoon waiting at home, thinking of her son riding Satan in that big race. It would be dangerous, and she was afraid for him.

The sound of footsteps ceased, and the house was quiet. Her head turned toward the window, and she saw the gray lightening of the sky. Soon it would be morning, and the night had passed without their finding the paper.

She lay still for many minutes; then, without knowing

why, she got out of bed and left the room. The lights were still on in the hall below, and she walked slowly down the stairs. Entering the living room, she saw her husband and Tony sitting on the couch, sleeping. She stood looking at them, puzzled. Tony, with his mouth wide open, was snoring. He had had a hard day, she knew, and in another few hours would be on his way again . . . yet he had spent most of the night looking for the paper. And her husband . . . his thin, gaunt face propped hard against his hand was more haggard than she had ever seen it. He was taking the loss of the paper very hard. And she thought again that he had had no right to get mixed up with this horse. Yet how could he have helped it? Wasn't she herself now a part of it? And hadn't she been ever since the day the young colt arrived?

She walked slowly over to the door and slipped outside. She saw Henry first, his large head dropped low upon his chest. And she wondered how he could sleep in such an awkward position. Then she saw her son, sitting against the post. She was startled at first glance. There was nothing boyish about his face as it lay there pressed hard against the wooden post. It was the face of a man in the making . . . hard, strong, yet heavy now with anguish and disappointment.

Had she been foolish enough to believe that, if Satan did not run next Saturday because they had not found the paper, there would not be another race? She realized now that next Saturday would not be the end. For Alec knew what he wanted, and that was to race his horse. Time after time he had told her that. And she had always thought it would only be a short while before he would change. But looking at her son, she knew better now.

Quietly she turned and went back into the house. She stopped by the banister in the hall, and for a moment stood still, thinking. Her gaze turned to the clock as it began striking five. She knew what she had to do, and there was still time . . . six hours.

She moved softly from room to room, not overlooking a single place in her search for the paper. When she reached the attic door she stopped. Her husband never went up there, so it would be a waste of time to look in the attic. According to him, the paper had been on his person the day after the running of the race. That had been on a Tuesday, and she had been doing her laundry. She had been in the cellar, she remembered, when he came home from the office. Suddenly there was a flicker of light in her eyes. *Cellar. Laundry.* She had heard him come into the house. She had called to him to help her with the heavy laundry basket. He had come down to the cellar and carried the basket upstairs for her. She remembered that he had stumbled on the stairs while carrying it, and almost fallen. The paper might have slipped from his pocket and fallen underneath the cellar stairs!

Moving quickly, she went down to the first floor and then into the cellar. She went beneath the stairs and searched the floor for a long time. Then, disappointedly, she moved away from the stairs and looked around the cellar. The cement floor had been swept clean, and there was no other place where the paper could have fallen.

She was starting upstairs when she saw the large

wicker laundry basket in the corner. She went up another step, then stopped, her gaze returning to the basket. It couldn't be there, she told herself. She had used it twice since the day her husband had helped her, and there had been no paper in with the clothes. Or, if it had been there, it must have blown away when she hung the wet wash up in the yard to dry.

Yet without knowing why, she went back down the stairs and walked over to the basket. It was empty, as she had known it would be, and there was no paper to be seen. Still, she pulled it down from the bench and placed it under the cellar light to make sure nothing was stuck between the wicker staves. She looked at it for a long time, as though unwilling to call an end to the search which she had started.

The clock in the hall was striking six. An hour had passed since her search had begun, and time was growing short. Reluctantly she placed the basket back upon the bench. And as her hand left the edge, she felt something softer than wood beneath her fingers. Quickly she turned the basket on its side, and there, wedged deep beneath the handle on the inside of the wicker staves, was the corner of a paper.

She forced herself to wait a moment, not wanting to tear the paper in her anxiety to get it out. In her heart she prayed that it would prove to be what she sought. Ever so slowly, and with trembling fingers, she moved it from side to side, slowly prying it loose. It could be it, she told herself. It could have slipped from her husband's pocket and fallen into the basket, to be wedged in later by the wash.

It came out easier now; and finally she held the folded piece of paper in her hands. Her heart pumped heavily, for she knew it must be Alec's paper. She unfolded it, and his writing leapt up at her. . . . *"I, Alexander William Ramsay, upon this date do sell my black colt, Satan, to William Augustus Ramsay, my father, for the sum of one dollar. . . ."*

She read no more. Turning quickly, she ran up the cellar stairs with the quick, light steps of a woman many years younger.

Race Day

19

Three-quarters of an hour before the running of the Hopeful, Alec walked about the jockeys' locker room. It was noisy, and crowded with tough, wiry men; the air was heavy with the pungent smell of liniment mixed with the stench of wet silks belonging to riders whose races were over for the day. And above all the voices rose the hissing clatter of the showers.

Wrinkled, hardened faces turned curiously toward Alec as he made his way to an empty locker. The jockeys riding in the Hopeful pulled on their clean silks, and close beside them stood their valets ready to help them with their boots and tack. Hastily Alec glanced around the room. He recognized many of the jockeys from photographs which he had seen in the newspapers, but he knew none of them. He was hoping to find Lenny Sansone, who he knew was riding the Chief in the Hopeful, but the black-haired jockey wasn't around. Alec sat down on the bench and began taking off his clothes.

The hissing of the showers suddenly stopped as the last of the jockeys who were finished for the day came out of the shower room, their wooden clogs ringing loudly on the floor as they walked to the lockers. The faces of some were as young and pudgy as a child's. Many of them stopped to talk in eager voices to the men who were riding in the big race.

Alec pulled on his black silks. Not much longer to go now, he thought. His body was tense and his throat dry. He was nervous, and he knew it. Relax, he told himself. You're not doing yourself or Satan any good. If he was tense, his horse would feel it. They both had to be calm today. This was it. The big race was here! Nothing could go wrong today. Henry expected the best from both of them. He was with Satan now, watching him, making sure everything was all right. Henry was afraid Boldt still might try something underhanded. They had made a fool of Boldt the day before at the stewards' meeting when they had produced the notarized bill of sale proving that Alec had sold Satan to his father. And after the meeting they had left Henry at the outside door, awaiting Boldt. Later in the afternoon Henry had shown up again, and when they had seen the bandages over his knuckles they had asked no questions.

As Alec pulled on his boots, Lenny Sansone entered the

room and hurried toward the lockers. Seeing Alec, he took the locker next to his.

Sansone's valet came up behind him, carrying his tack. As the stocky, broad-shouldered jockey pulled off his shirt, he turned to Alec and looked at him quizzically. "You feel all right?"

"Sure. A little nervous," Alec confessed.

"Yeah. I know. I was that way all my first year. But now," he went on, "it don't hit me until I get out there on the strip."

Alec said nothing.

"Guess all of us feel jittery one time or another in every race, no matter how long we ride," Lenny continued. "Even those guys." He nodded his head toward the other jockeys.

"You wouldn't know it to look at them," Alec said quietly.

Sansone sat down on the bench after pulling on his maroon silks. His valet helped him draw on his boots.

"They've all got their problems, just like me. We all know it and feel it. Might not show it, though." Lenny paused, jerking his head toward an old-faced, small-chinned man who was standing near them. "Take Ward there. He's up on Boldt's Comet," Lenny explained. "He knows he's got the favorite, an' that if he doesn't win old man Boldt will have his hide. I wouldn't want to be working for Peter Boldt . . . nope, not me. He pays well if you bring his horses home, but he's hard on you if you don't. Ward knows that. He's been riding for him for years. Ward's smart as they come . . . knows every trick of the game. You keep your eye on him, Alec. I've never seen him do anything dirty, but he has a way of coming mighty close to it, an' all within the rules. He's sorta like Boldt, y'know,'' Lenny said, as though that explained everything.

Alec's eyes were on Ward's wrinkled face when Boldt's jockey turned toward him. Their gazes met momentarily, and Alec didn't like what he saw there. Ward's eyes were sly, treacherous.

"But he's got guts,'' Lenny continued. "No doubt about that, and I've never seen him afraid of anything. No room for fear out there on that racing strip, especially in the thick of chargin' for the wire.''

"He's got heavy shoulders and long arms,'' Alec said, almost to himself.

"Yeah. Needs 'em with Boldt's gray,'' Lenny said. "The Comet is heavy-headed, wants to run wild all the time, I hear.'' Lenny stood up, knocking a wart of mud off the sole of his boot with his stick. Then he said, "Wish the Chief had a bit of that wildness to run in him. My horse is a strange one, Alec,'' he added confidingly. "It's no secret; everyone who's been around here knows it. The Chief lets the others come right up to him before he starts to run. He's lonesome when running alone, an' that's why I have to fan the stick at him plenty. There's no tellin' how fast he can go when he wants to, though. Maybe this is the day,'' he concluded hopefully.

Alec remembered Lenny's bay as Satan had borne down upon him during the workout; how the black-haired jockey had gone for his stick, and Satan, upon seeing it, had swerved into the fence. He was certain that it would be a different story today.

The jockeys had begun to file out of the room when Alec asked, "Who's riding Volence's Desert Storm, Len?"

Sansone pointed to a frail, sharp-boned boy with a gaunt, white face who was making his way out the door. "That's Eldridge. He's up on him," Lenny said. "He's only been riding for Volence a short while. Got plenty of stuff, though. He's a top rider. Did a whale of job with Desert Storm in copping the Grand Union Hotel Stakes last week."

"Yes, I heard," Alec said.

"He'll keep that blazin' chestnut back like he did last week, then start moving up coming down to the wire," Lenny confided. "You can bet your last penny on that."

Carrying their tack, the jockeys moved toward the scales. Alec's heart beat fast. Less than thirty minutes to go now. They'd be weighed out for the race, then go to their horses in the paddock.

The minutes marched on toward the running of the Hopeful.

As Alec walked down the stairs, he heard Lenny muttering to himself, "Maybe the Chief wants to run today. Maybe it's today."

Belmont Park was black with people. And still they came by bus, car and train, a wave of humanity surging at the gates, hoping to get inside the park before the running of the seventh race—the Hopeful! The roads were still packed with cars, their horns blowing incessantly, creating a raucous backdrop for the shouting multitude pouring through the gates and running toward the already overcrowded stands and rails.

And there they waited with throbbing expectancy for the great race that was to be run.

Two men jostled their way through the crowd, hoping to get a vantage point near the rail.

"We just made it, Harrity," one said. "They ain't out yet."

"Sure, Morgan, we did that," the taller man replied, wiping his brow. "If the old *Queen* had pulled into port an hour later, we woulda missed it."

They were reading their programs when suddenly Harrity exclaimed, "Bejabers, Morgan! Look who's riding that horse called Satan!"

Morgan read, "Ramsay." Then he turned to his friend. "I don't get you, Harrity."

"Remember Addis, that port in Arabia? Remember a couple of years ago?"

"Stop the quiz show, Harrity," Morgan said disgustedly. "Sure I know Addis. Hasn't the *Queen* put in there every trip? But how am I supposed to know what happened two years ago? You think I'm a mind reader or somethin'? . . ." Morgan stopped, the blank look in his eyes suddenly giving way to a new light. "Ramsay," he said slowly. Then he repeated, "Alec Ramsay . . . yeah, it's coming, Harrity."

"The black colt. We picked it up there. It was going to a guy by the name of Alec Ramsay."

"Might not be the same guy," Morgan said quickly.

"The colt would be a two-year-old now. Look at the program, Morgan. This Satan is a black one, too. A black colt sired by Shêtân, an' out of Jôhar. Arabian-sounding names if I ever heard 'em."

Morgan studied the program for a long time. Then, "Maybe you're right," he said slowly. He added eagerly, "I'll bet you're right, Harrity. Think of it! That black colt we lugged over here in the *Queen* running in this big race! Boy, Harrity, if that ain't a hunch, I never heard of one. C'mon!"

The two men hurriedly pushed their way through the crowd, running toward the ticket windows to place their wagers on the fiery, spindle-legged colt they had first seen in Addis, Arabia.

And far up in the grandstand, two other people sat quietly awaiting the appearance of the black colt. "Now, Belle," Mr. Ramsay said excitedly, "you must be calm. It'll only be a few minutes now. You wanted to come, you know."

"You don't sound very calm yourself, William," Mrs. Ramsay said, without taking her eyes from the gap in the fence through which the horses would come.

"Don't say I'm excited. I'm not excited." Mr. Ramsay kept shifting his field glasses from one hand to the other. "Perhaps you should have stayed at home."

"I had to come," Mrs. Ramsay said unsteadily. "I couldn't sit at home, waiting. . . ."

They were quiet for a long time, their gazes shifting

from the gap in the fence, now lined with eager spectators, to the excited, colorful crowd around them. Far below they saw a tall, angular man with a white beard walk toward his box. Mr. Ramsay raised his glasses for a better look at him. "There's something very familiar about that man," he said earnestly.

Mrs. Ramsay took the glasses and looked through them for several moments before putting them down and turning excitedly to her husband. "Why, it's Abu Ja' Kub ben Ishak!" she exclaimed. "He was at the house only once, when he claimed the Black," she reminded her husband. "But I'm sure it's he. . . . I could never forget that face."

Mr. Ramsay quickly took another look through the glasses. "Yes, you're right, Belle," he finally said. "It's he . . . I remember now." Pausing, he added, "I wonder what he's doing here?"

Mrs. Ramsay smiled. "What's everyone doing here?" she countered.

Exasperatedly, Mr. Ramsay turned to his wife. "I meant that Abu is supposed to be in Arabia. It's a long way to come for a horse race."

"But it's the Hopeful." Mrs. Ramsay reminded him, smiling. "And his Satan is running."

"You mean *our* Satan, Belle," Mr. Ramsay corrected. "But it isn't surprising after all that he's here."

They focused their attention again on the gap in the fence. The horses and their riders should be coming through any minute now.

In the paddock, Satan stood quietly waiting for Alec to come in to see him. His heavy ears came up alertly, and he shoved his small head toward the boy. Alec stroked him gently.

Henry said, "Take him up right from the start, go up front, an' stay there." The old trainer paused, smiled wanly, then added, "I'm talkin' just to hear myself talk, I guess. You know what to do as well as I do."

Alec nodded but said nothing. His heart was pounding heavily, and he was afraid that his nervousness would be felt by Satan. The colt was remarkably quiet, and Alec knew that the past few weeks of hard work with him had not been in vain. Picking up a stick, he rubbed it gently along Satan's neck. "Just so you don't forget, boy," he said quietly. "Don't be afraid. . . . No one will hit you with it. Easy, boy. No swerving today."

Henry watched them. They were both ready, no doubt about that. It would be a great race. Henry's lips tightened and he crossed his fingers.

The crowd in the paddock area surged forward, but the policemen kept the eager spectators away as the horses were saddled.

Henry tested the girth and smoothed the saddle cloth bearing the number three. "We didn't draw an outside position this time," he muttered. "Keep away from the rail. May be bumpy there."

Alec nodded, his hand upon Satan's black-hooded head. "Ward has number four post position," he said, without looking at Henry.

"Watch him. Watch his gray," Henry said. "Boldt still might be up to something."

Satan moved a little restlessly when they had him ready. The tension mounted as the time drew near. The roar of the crowd became louder.

Alec talked to his horse, soothing him. The black hood concealed the white diamond on his forehead, making him look more like the Black than ever before. He tossed his head, working himself up.

Henry bent down, feeling the colt's legs. Finally he stood up again. "Okay," he said. "Wanted to make sure. No rain in the past few weeks has made that racing strip hard as cement."

"And fast," Alec added.

"Hard strips are hard on a horse's legs," Henry said. "An' I'd hate to see him hurt that leg again."

The paddock judge came down the line stopping before each horse. Finally he reached Satan. "All set?" he asked Henry.

Henry looked at Alec, then nodded.

"Let's go then," the man said.

The Chief, number one, was led up to the parade circle a short distance from the saddling area. The crowd in the paddock pressed closer to the rail encircling the path over which the horses would be led until the bugle summoned them to the track.

A rangy roan followed the Chief, then Henry and Alec walked up the runway with Satan.

Alec took his eyes off his horse for a moment to glance

at the back of the large grandstand. A few more minutes, he thought, and they'd be out there. Just a few more minutes now. Satan crabstepped nervously at the shouts of the people on either side of the runway.

Seconds later they were in the parade circle, the horses walking, prancing around. Alec and Henry stayed with Satan, but many of the owners, trainers and jockeys were huddled together inside the ring. Last-minute instructions were being given.

Alec saw Boldt talking to Ward. The owner of the Comet had a large bandage over his beaked nose.

Some of the tension left Alec. "You did it, Henry. . . . I see by Boldt's nose," he said with a grin.

Henry, a trifle embarrassed, merely grunted.

A bell rang, and the old trainer said, "Ten minutes to post time."

The horses circled the ring a few more times, Satan's gaze shifting constantly from one horse to another. He moved uneasily, his eyes flashing. Alec concentrated upon his black colt, talking to him all the while.

Satan whistled his shrill challenge. The long-limbed roan in front bolted, but his groom held on to him. The Comet's ears lay back and his teeth were bared. Boldt's gray was a racer in build, splendid and proud; he showed fight. Across the ring Desert Storm raised his small head, looking in Satan's direction but seemingly unbothered by the black colt's challenge.

Alec watched Volence's squarish chestnut colt, who had also been sired by one of Abu's Arabians. Desert Storm walked with a short, choppy stride as though he had all he could do to stand on his four legs. Yet this was the horse which had set a track record in winning the Grand Union Hotel Stakes a few weeks ago. This was the horse, according to the experts, who would test the speed of Boldt's Comet.

Suddenly the ringing notes of the post bugle hung on the air, rolling over the multitude of people and finally coming to rest on the ten horses circling the ring.

"Go to your horses. Riders up!" the paddock judge ordered.

The sun shone brightly on their vari-colored silks as the jockeys were given a leg up.

"Good luck, Alec," Henry said, his hand still resting on the boy's knee. "Here's where I get off."

Alec nodded, but didn't say anything. He knew Henry would understand.

Satan pawed the ground when he felt Alec's weight upon his back. Then the horses filed toward the track and the thunderous ovation that awaited them.

The Hopeful

20

Satan shied as he stepped onto the track, and Alec felt the restlessness sweep through his great body.

"Easy, Satan," he kept repeating. "Easy, boy."

The black colt suddenly stopped in his tracks, his shifting eyes turning to the white rail now black with people. Then, tossing his head, he shied again. Alec let him move lightly away from the file of horses; then he brought him back behind the rangy roan who was following the Chief and the black-and-white-spotted lead pony bearing the red-coated rider who was escorting them past the stands and around the track to the starting stalls.

As they paraded past the stands, more than fifty thousand eyes were upon them. When the people saw Boldt's sleek, gray Comet their shrill yells rent the air.

272

Satan half reared. Alec brought him down, talking to him all the while. He knew the eyes of the crowd were upon Satan now, that the people were wondering about the giant colt who was burlier in stature than any other horse on the track. "A big horse," they were probably saying, "but he doesn't have the speed of the Comet or Desert Storm. His time in winning the Sanford was slower than what the other two have done."

Alec's hand slipped down upon Satan's neck. "We'll show them, boy," he said. "Easy now . . . but in a few minutes we'll show them."

He was glad when they had passed the stands and were making their way down the backstretch toward the starting gate. They were allowed to pull out of line now, and Alec let Satan go into a slow gallop. Still talking to his horse, he rose high in his stirrups, the reins held firmly in his hands, holding Satan back.

Ward rode the Comet alongside Satan as they neared the starting stalls. Alec was about to pull his colt away from the gray when Ward said, "Where's your stick, kid? You'll need a stick today."

Turning in his saddle, Alec looked at Ward's wizened face without answering.

"Aw, I forgot," Ward said sarcastically. "That big horse of yours is afraid of a stick, ain't he? That's tough, kid." Ward swung his stick alongside the Comet. "Mighty tough."

Satan's ears swept back as Ward's stick passed close by him. But he didn't swerve or pull away, and Alec stroked him gently while he kept his eyes on Ward.

"It's a pity the rest of us have to use 'em," Ward continued, his thin lips drawn back. "Make it lots easier for you if we didn't, wouldn't it?" Then he pulled the Comet away, moving his gray toward the starting stalls.

Alec brought Satan over to the far side of the track. The Comet had made his colt furious, and Alec tried desperately to quiet him down. As he sat there, waiting for his turn to go into the starting gate, he thought of Ward's remarks. It was obvious now that Boldt had instructed his jockey to make it as hard for Alec as he possibly could. And Alec knew that Ward would use his stick to every advantage.

The starter's crew called to him, and Alec moved forward. It would be only a matter of seconds now before they were off. Alec forgot everything but the race ahead.

Satan shook his fiery head as Alec rode him into his starting stall. The Comet, in the stall to Satan's right, bared his teeth, showing fight again. Ward said something, but Alec wasn't listening; his eyes were on the long straightaway before them. "Come out fast, boy . . . no swerving . . . no giving ground today," he whispered. Satan's ears lay back, then pricked forward; he rolled his blazing eyes in the Comet's direction, then looked at the track ahead.

From the corner of his eye, Alec could see the jockey on the rangy roan to his left. On the pole position was Lenny Sansone, up on the Chief. Lenny's face was set, his stick in hand. All the jockeys were ready with their whips. Alec hoped and prayed that Satan's fear of the whip had been cured once and for all during the past few weeks. But he knew that only the break would tell. The break . . . it would come any second now.

Suddenly the Comet broke out of his stall, drawing two horses on the outside with him. They ran a short distance down the track before their jockeys were able to pull them up. Then they turned and made their way slowly back to the starting stalls.

The tension was broken momentarily as the starter brought the horses back. They circled behind the starting stalls and came in once again.

As Alec waited he talked to his horse. Lenny called something to him, but he didn't hear. His eyes were staring at the dirt beside the rail. As Henry had said, it was bumpy there . . . better to keep away from it. He'd take Satan straight down . . . straight to the wire.

Ward had the Comet in his stall again. The other two horses were also in theirs. The starter's eyes swept down the line. . . . He wanted to get them away fast. It was coming. Alec felt it, and leaned forward, ready. All the months and years he had waited for this race were to be culminated in the next minute. Ahead, six and a half furlongs down the track, was the final answer. He felt Satan's muscles tighten. . . . His colt knew it as well as he did.

The barrier shot up! The roar from the packed stands swelled thunderously as it was carried across the infield, then died beneath rolling hoofbeats.

By a stride, Lenny Sansone had the Chief out first. Then came Satan and the Comet right together. Alec felt his colt's muscles hurtle them forward with the power of a mighty spring unleashed. The shouts of jockeys rang in his ears and sticks were brought down heavily upon sleek, straining bodies. Satan's head and eyes were set straight ahead in spite of the fanning sticks. "Go, Satan! Go!" Alec shouted to his horse.

For a few seconds Alec was conscious of nothing but the mighty surge of hard bodies and pounding hoofs. Then the Comet moved close beside Satan, and Alec felt Ward's knee against his own. He caught a glimpse of Ward's flaying whip, carried in his left hand, as he brought it down upon his gray's haunches. The stick had come close to Satan. Then it came again, and Alec felt Satan shudder as Ward's stick glanced off the black colt's shoulder.

In the close running, Ward's blow upon Satan could be looked upon by the judges as accidental, but Alec was furious. Then his fury gave way to despair as Satan pulled up and swerved hard toward the inside rail, just behind the Chief. The black colt stumbled as his hoofs hit the bumpy ground, then he recovered, with Alec urging him on. His body still trembled from Ward's blow, and for a few yards Satan's giant strides were pulled short.

Repeatedly Alec called to his horse. Gradually, but ever so slowly, Satan's strides lengthened and quickened until once again he was running like black flame before a strong wind.

"Satan!" Alec called, almost savagely. "It's come . . . the race . . . the race! Run them down!"

And the fury in the boy's body seemed to flood into the gleaming body beneath him. There was a shrill whistle from the running horse as he swept low, leveling out.

The Chief's hindquarters rose and fell in front of them; the bay was running as Lenny Sansone had hoped he would run today. Alongside the Chief, running stride for stride with him, was the Comet. The rest of the field was spread out to the right and a little behind the two hard-running horses in the lead.

As they swept by the half-mile post, Satan's nose neared the Chief's haunches. There was space between the Chief and the Comet to ride through, and Alec goaded his black colt on. Satan's strides quickened still more, and Alec knew his horse's speed was rising to its swiftest. If Satan could break through the gap in front, he would reach his limit with a clear track in front of him.

Less than a quarter of a mile to go! Sansone went for his stick, fanning it close beside his bay, and the Chief surged ahead. Ward too began using his stick and drove the Comet forward with the Chief.

Alec started to drive Satan on, then hesitated at the sight of the swinging sticks in front. There was just room for Satan to go through the gap between the Chief and the Comet, but dared he chance it with those flying whips? If Satan swerved now, so close to the finish, it would be all over for them.

As Satan neared the horses, Alec thought of pulling him around on the outside. And it was then that he saw Desert Storm. The flying chestnut was driving down on the outside and to the right of the Comet with amazing speed.

Alec knew he had no alternative now but to go through the gap. Desert Storm was the horse to beat! Alec had to drive Satan between the Chief and the Comet, or Volence's chestnut would beat them all to the wire!

Alec goaded his horse, and all of Satan's savagery and fury went into his tremendous strides as he extended himself. Alec's eyes stung and hurt; he was deafened by the sounds around him; and all he could feel was the mighty surge of Satan's muscles.

Foot by foot, Satan moved between the bay and the gray. Flaying sticks swept by on either side of him, but the giant colt was running wild now, and nothing could stop him. As he moved in front of the Chief and the Comet, Alec saw Desert Storm on the outside, running hard, a length ahead.

One hundred yards to go to the wire!

There was no need to ask Satan for greater speed. He was running down Desert Storm with the fury of a black, whirling tornado. He pricked his heavy ears forward as he swept by the driving chestnut, and then with a final burst of still greater speed, he swept under the wire!

The crowd surged from the stands, breaking the police lines and running toward the winner's circle where Satan stood.

Alec, his face flushed, sat quietly upon Satan's back and talked to him as the wreath of roses was placed about the colt's wet neck. "You did it, Satan," he whispered. "You did it."

The shouting crowd pressed heavily into the winner's circle, and the police formed a tight ring about Satan. Henry jostled his way through the crowd, spoke to a policeman, and then entered the ring. He came up to Alec, nodded his head vigorously, and took hold of Satan's bridle. The colt shied as Henry placed his hand on his head.

Alec held him, and as the colt quieted down, the boy saw the hurt look in Henry's eyes. Tossing his head, Satan pricked his ears forward and began nibbling at the flowers about his neck.

Henry said, "His pappy would be proud of him today, Alec."

The boy nodded as the news photographers took their pictures. "I know he would, Henry," he said.

Satan stopped nibbling the roses, and suddenly shoved his head against Henry, nuzzling the old trainer's shirt. Henry's eyes brightened; then he raised a gnarled hand and rubbed Satan's forehead. After a few seconds he looked up at Alec. "We're friends now," he said excitedly. "Satan and I are friends," he repeated, turning back to the black colt.

Alec dismounted and unsaddled Satan while Henry held him by the bridle. Then, carrying his tack, he walked to the scales, stepped on them, and weighed in. The clerk of the scales nodded and he got off. Officially, the race was over.

Walking away from the scales Alec passed Eldridge, who had brought Desert Storm in second. "Good going," the jockey said. "Y'got a horse."

Lenny Sansone, carrying his tack, was behind Eldridge. "The Chief ran for me today," he told Alec, "but he didn't have enough to beat your boy." He paused, smiling. "Got in ahead of Boldt's Comet, Alec. . . . We set him right back on his rump."

When Alec reached Satan again, he saw his mother and father standing beside Henry. Then toward them came a tall, slight man, and Alec gasped as he recognized him. Running forward, he grabbed Abu Ja' Kub ben Ishak by the shoulder.

The sheikh turned to him. "Alec," he said in his soft even voice, "it was a fine race. . . . He's the Black all over again."

They moved over beside Henry and Alec's parents, while newspaper men crowded around them.

"What do you think of Satan, Abu?" Henry asked after a few minutes.

The sheikh turned to him, smiling. "What do you mean, Henry?"

"How's he compare with the Black?" the old trainer asked.

"Racing horses is your business as well as mine," Abu replied, still smiling.

"We'll know better next year," Henry grunted. "Next year there'll be the Derby. Think of it, Alec. Satan in the Kentucky Derby!"

"I am thinking about it," Alec said, smiling.

Mrs. Ramsay moved forward and placed her hand upon Satan's neck. "He's hot, Alec," she said with great concern. "We should get him away from this crowd."

"Yes, let's take him home, Alec," his father said, ". . . where he belongs," he added hastily.

There was a frenzied commotion in the crowd, then a small man burst out from between two policemen, and Alec recognized Tony. The huckster, breathing heavily, came up to them.

"The big flatfoots would no let me come to heem," Tony said, sidling up beside Satan. Placing a hand on the colt, he looked at him with affectionate eyes. "Heesa my horse, too, you know, Aleec."

A newspaper man came up to Abu, and Alec recognized Jim Neville. "Mr. Ishak," he began, "I've heard that the Thoroughbred Racing Association has asked you to bring the Black to the United States next year. Is that correct?"

Alec turned quickly to Henry, and then he shifted his gaze to Abu, whose eyes were upon him. The sheikh was still looking at Alec when he replied to Jim Neville's question. "Yes," he said, "they would like the Black to run here next year."

"Will you bring him over?" Neville asked.

Abu's gray eyes still held Alec's as he said, "Yes, he'll run. I'm bringing him to the United States next spring."

Alec could feel his heart pounding. He turned from Abu to Henry and then to his black colt, standing beside him. He rubbed the long neck, and then pulled Satan's head down to him. Abu had said the Black would be in the States next spring! And next spring Satan would be a three-year-old, eligible to race for the biggest stakes! It could happen that Satan would race the Black!

Satan pushed his head against him, and Alec rubbed

the colt between the eyes. "Your pop is coming," he whispered. "And he'll be proud of you, boy. I know he will."

Then, as the police opened up a path for them through the crowd, Alec led Satan home, the wreath of roses still hanging loosely about his neck.

ABOUT THE AUTHOR

Walter Farley's love for horses began when he was a small boy living in Syracuse, New York, and continued as he grew up in New York City, where his family moved. Unlike most city children, he was able to fulfill this love through an uncle who was a professional horseman. Young Walter spent much of his time with this uncle, learning about the different kinds of horse training and the people associated with each.

Walter Farley began to write his first book, *The Black Stallion,* while he was a student at Brooklyn's Erasmus Hall High School and Mercersburg Academy in Pennsylvania. He finished it and had it published while he was still an undergraduate at Columbia University.

The appearance of *The Black Stallion* brought such an enthusiastic response from young readers that Mr. Farley went on to write more stories about the Black, and about other horses as well. He now has twenty-five books to his credit, including his first dog story, *The Great Dane Thor,* and his story of America's greatest thoroughbred, *Man O' War.* His books have been enormously successful in this country, and have also been published in fourteen foreign countries.

When not traveling, Walter Farley and his wife, Rosemary, divide their time between a farm in Pennsylvania and a beach house in Florida.